Icefire

Chris d'Lacey

ORCHARD BOOKS

for Val Chivers

with special thanks to Joseph Maude, Tom Gleeson

and Michelle

Wellaware Children's Publishing Ltd.
27-29 Old Cambridge Street
London

David Rain
42 Wayward Crescent
Scrubbley

Dear David Rain,

Thank you for sending us your novel

SNIGGER AND THE NUTBEAST

which we have now had time to consider. Unfortunately, although we think your writing shows promise, we do not feel that a story about talking squirrels is currently right for our list.

We are sorry to disappoint you on this occasion and wish you every success in the future.

yours sincerely,

Editorial Assistant

ORCHARD BOOKS
96 Leonard Street
London EC2A 4XD
Orchard Books Australia
32/45-51 Huntley Street, Alexandria, NSW 2015
First published in Great Britain in 2003
First paperback edition 2004
Text © Chris d'Lacey 2003
The right of Chris d'Lacey to be identified as the author of
this work has been asserted by him in accordance with
the Copyright, Designs and Patents Act, 1988.
A CIP catalogue record for this book is available from the
British Library.
ISBN 1 84362 373 0 (hardback)
ISBN 1 84362 134 7 (paperback)
1 3 5 7 9 10 8 6 4 2 (hardback)
1 3 5 7 9 10 8 6 4 2 (paperback)
Printed in Great Britain

Water is so intricately laced that it is almost a continuous structure...it is as though liquid water remembers the form of the ice from which it came...water is tremendously flexible.

Supernature by Lyall Watson (Hodder & Stoughton, 1973)

The Wishing Dragon

"David, if your face grows any longer your chin will be scraping the soles of your shoes." Elizabeth Pennykettle hung up her apron and half-scowled, half-smiled at her student lodger. "Whatever's the matter?"

"Give you one guess," the lodger muttered cheerlessly. He sloped into the kitchen, his mouth turned down in a curve of disappointment. In his hand, he was flapping a letter. As he approached the kitchen table he pushed the letter under the snout of a dragon, which was sitting by a pot of raspberry jam. "Here, torch that."

The little clay dragon remained unmoved.

On the far side of the table Mrs Pennykettle's daughter, Lucy, tutted. "You mustn't say that to the dragons. They're not allowed to burn things, are they, Mum?"

"No," said Mrs Pennykettle, glancing at the letter. "I take it that's another rejection?"

David nodded. "Complete with coffee stain. This makes fourteen now. And they all say the same. Dear Mr Rain. Thanks, but no thanks. No one wants to hear about Snigger the squirrel."

Lucy immediately put down her sticks. She had been busy modelling a brand new dragon, a handsome (if slightly bemused-looking) creature with wide, flared nostrils and enormous paws. She picked up the letter and frowned. "Well, *I* think it's the best story *ever*."

"You're biased," said David, peeling a banana. "I wrote it for you. You're bound to say that."

"It's not a bad rejection, though, is it?" said Liz, reading the letter over Lucy's shoulder. "They do say your writing shows some promise. Perhaps you should forget about Snigger for a while and start working on something new?"

"Yes!" exclaimed Lucy, spinning in her seat. *"The Adventures of Spikey the Hedgehog."*

Through a mouthful of banana, David said: "I'm not writing about blooming hedgehogs."

"But you said Gadzooks wrote 'Spikey' on his pad. And he underlined it. Twice. Gadzooks is your *special* dragon. You've got to do what he says."

David sighed and let his gaze drift across the kitchen. It settled on the top of the fridge, where a so-called 'listening' dragon sat: a studious-looking, bespectacled creature with ears like a couple of large rose petals. Dragons were everywhere in this house; Elizabeth Pennykettle made them for a living, in a room upstairs called the Dragons' Den. Gadzooks, the dragon that Lucy had spoken of, sat on the windowsill in David's room. Liz had made him as a welcoming gift when David had first moved into the house. In general appearance, Gadzooks was like most of the Pennykettle dragons: green and scaly with oval-shaped eyes and short, ridged wings. But in his left paw he carried a small white notepad and in the right he held a sawn-off pencil. He was 'special' in the sense that, now and again, when David had been writing his squirrel story, Gadzooks had seemed to help things along by scribbling a word or two on his pad. The last thing he had 'written' – some weeks ago now – was the word 'Spikey'. Lucy had immediately decided that this must be the name of a hedgehog she had once glimpsed in the garden. But David had refused to be so easily swayed. And as the autumn days had gradually lengthened, his mind had dulled to the possibility that there was any meaning to the word at all. Indeed, if the truth be told, he was slightly tired of the presence of dragons and embarrassed by the fact that he had once allowed himself to believe that they might, in some way, be real. So when he spoke again his manner was blunt. "Lucy, let it go. I love Gadzooks, you know I do. But he only 'writes' things because I imagine him doing it. He's no more 'special' than this one you're making."

Lucy sat back, looking incensed. "This is a wishing dragon. He can make things properly happen."

Across the room there came a slight hoot of derision. But this time the dissent was not from David; it had come from the pottery expert, Liz. She walked over and inspected the dragon, looping her red hair behind her ears so it wouldn't trail into the still-soft clay. "You'll be lucky, my girl. To make a true wishing dragon takes years of practice – and careful naming. Mind you, you've not done badly with him. His paws are very good. Excellent, in fact."

"They're out of proportion, surely?" said David. "He looks like he's wearing baseball gloves. Why are they so big?"

"Because," said Lucy, drawing out the word like a piece of gum, "you put your thumbs in his paws when you make a wish. Mum, can we kiln him? Please don't say I have to squdge him. I'll think up a special name, right now." And she closed her eyes and concentrated hard. "Gurrrr..." she said, meaning the name would begin with a 'G'. "Gurrrr—"

"Reth," said David, breaking in unexpectedly.

"Gareth?" Lucy turned up her nose.

"What made you say that?" asked Liz, flipping the

handle on the outside door to let the Pennykettle's tabby cat, Bonnington, in. Bonnington trotted straight to his bowl. He sniffed at his desiccated tuna-flavoured *Chunky Chunks*, turned and mewed to go out again.

Looking puzzled, David said, "Don't know. It just came to me."

"From Gadzooks?" asked Lucy, with a sparkle in her eye.

"Yes, but he wrote it in a funny sort of way."

"Show me," said Liz, pushing a scrap of paper in front of the lodger. "Jot it down, exactly how you saw it."

So David picked up a pen and wrote:

$$G'reth$$

"You missed the 'a' out," said Lucy.

Liz turned the paper round. "No, I don't think he did. That's an archaic spelling. I've seen dragon names written that way before." She drummed her fingers on the table top. "And you saw Gadzooks do this?"

David nodded and chomped his banana. Not only had he pictured Gadzooks doing the scribble, the dragon had stomped his feet several times and thrust his pad forward, as though keen to push the name right to the forefront of David's mind.

"How do you say it?" asked Lucy.

"Guh-reth," said Liz. "With a hard 'G'. Guh."

"Guh-reth," repeated Lucy. "You say it." She gave the lodger a nudge.

"Guh-reth," he said tiredly, just to please her. He looked at the dragon with its impish smile and sent it a silent, disparaging *hrrr*.

"Lucy, try making a wish," said her mum.

Lucy's mouth fell open in astonishment. "Is it allowed? It's David's dragon."

"What?" he coughed. "I don't want it."

"You named him," said Lucy. "You have to keep him."

David shook his head. "No," he said firmly. "One dragon's enough for me."

Lucy's face took on a hurt expression. "You can't stay in this house if you don't believe in dragons."

"Yeah, well," muttered David, tossing his banana skin into the bin. He traced the grouting in the floor tiles with his toe as if he had something more to add, something he didn't want to talk about now.

Liz noticed the movement but didn't comment. "The maker may have one wish," she said, turning the dragon face-on to Lucy. "That's a rule amongst dragon-makers. It must be something beneficial and completely unselfish. You can't just wish for a bar of chocolate. If you do, the wish will turn on you."

"OK," said Lucy, resting her thumbs in G'reth's dished paws. "I wish, I wish, I wish...it would snow."

"Snow?" hooted David. "How is that beneficial?"

"They like it," said Lucy. "Dragons like snow." As if to prove it, a gentle *hrring* sound echoed round the walls of the house.

David, who had heard this sound many times before (and had never quite got to the bottom of it) ignored the rumble and frowned in disbelief. "Why do dragons like snow? And don't tell me they're fond of skiing."

Lucy shook her head till her ponytail danced. "No one properly knows – do they, Mum?"

"No," said Liz, carefully shaping one of G'reth's wings.

"But when it does," Lucy went on excitedly, "they sit by the windows and watch it, don't they?"

"Yes," said Liz, turning G'reth back and forth on his stand. "This really is very good, Lucy. You're coming on in leaps and bounds."

"There," said Lucy, and stuck out a pimple of tongue at the lodger.

To take the wind from her sails, he gave a weather report. "Oh, bad luck. Sun's out and shining. Not a flake of snow in sight." He grinned at the Pennykettle women in turn. They stared back as if to say, 'Give it time'.

Time. David shot his watch hand up. "Oh, no!" he

exclaimed. "I should have been at college *ages* ago. I'm supposed to be having a tutorial with..." Leaving the end of his sentence hanging, he shot down the hall in search of his coat.

Liz patted Lucy's arm and told her to work on G'reth a little more. "Take him up to the den when you're finished. We'll kiln him when I get back." Grabbing her car keys, she went after David. "Come on," she said, overtaking him on the porch, "if it's that important, I'll give you a lift."

On the drive into Scrubbley, Liz said quietly, "You seemed a little uptight in the kitchen. Not just about G'reth. Is there something on your mind?"

David ran the zip of his bag back and forth. "I'm meeting Sophie for dinner tonight." A smile spread slowly across his face at the mention of his girlfriend's name. "She says she wants to tell me something important. I think she might want me to move in with her."

"I see. Do you think you will?"

David bit his lip and looked the other way.

"We'll miss you," said Liz, taking his silence as a 'yes'. "It's going to be hard telling Lucy, though."

"I'll come and see you. Regularly. I promise."

Liz smiled and touched his arm. "If you need to move on, that's all there is to it. You can't stay in our mad dragon house for ever. Don't worry. We'll cope." She brought the car to a halt at the gates of Scrubbley College. "Go on, we'll talk about this another time. I hope you're not too late. Who's this chap again? The one you're having the tutorial with?"

"Dr Bergstrom. He's a polar research scientist. He's only in the country for three or four weeks, doing a sort of lecture tour."

"Bergstrom," said Liz, running the word like a spell off her tongue. "Is that Swedish?"

"Norwegian; but he works in Canada – with polar bears."

Liz nodded and lifted her gaze. Her bright green eyes seemed suddenly very distant. "Well, he won't mind this weather, then."

David turned to the windscreen.

Impossible as it seemed, it was specked with snow.

"That's amazing," David gasped. "Where did that come from?"

Liz wound down her window and caught a few flakes. "Never underestimate a wishing dragon."

David gave her a withering look. "Liz, G'reth did *not* do this." He pulled up his collar and got out of the car. "I'll probably stay over at Sophie's tonight. Thanks for the ride. See you tomorrow." He blew a snowflake off his nose and looked at the sky. "Weird," he muttered, and hurried indoors.

The lift on the ground floor opened conveniently and he was up four flights to the geography department quicker than he might usually have expected. He swept through the map room, catching a globe with the corner of his bag and almost spinning it off its stand. By the time he'd reached the offices along the faculty corridor he was slightly out of breath and warm around the collar. He took a moment to steady himself, then knocked at a door labelled 'Seminar Room'.

"Come in," said a voice.

David eased himself inside. He'd been hoping to see at least three other students, but the padded orange chairs around the low coffee table were all abandoned. He grimaced and glanced at the clock. He was forty-five minutes late. The tutorial had happened without him. "Dr Bergstrom, I'm really sorry," he began. "I— gosh, it's freezing in here."

It was then that he realised the window was open. A chill breeze was rattling the vertical blinds, making them clatter against the glass. On an open wooden stand beside the large whiteboard, a row of journals were flapping their covers. Even in his greatcoat, David shuddered.

Dr Bergstrom was standing at the window, looking out, his hands pushed deep into the pockets of his slacks. He was wearing a plain white cotton shirt with the sleeves rolled loosely up to the elbows. Not a goose bump could be seen on his muscular forearms, just a gentle stream of honey-white hairs that matched the colour of those on his head. "You must be David," he said, without looking round. His voice was even, as soft as the snowflakes floating past the window. It carried just a hint of the country of his birth.

"Yes. Excuse me, aren't you cold?"

A smile touched the corner of Bergstrom's mouth. "Right now, off the shores of Hudson Bay, the temperature will have fallen low enough to turn the sea to an icy slush. That's cold, David. Glacial to you. Moderately chilly to the Inuit people. Still rather warm to a polar bear. It's all a question of acclimatisation. Do you want to tell me why you're late?" He gestured to the arc of empty chairs.

David unbuttoned his greatcoat and sat. "I, erm, got held up at home, sorry."

Bergstrom closed the window and joined him. He had a classic Scandinavian appearance: wavy, well-groomed, collar-length hair and a beard so fine it seemed taped to his face. "Yes, your colleagues had a theory on that. They thought you were probably talking to your dragon."

The tips of David's ears flared red. Many times in the past he'd regretted the day that he'd once let slip about keeping Gadzooks. The news had circled the geography department quicker than a virus infecting the internet.

Bergstrom, swift to see his student's discomfort, dismissed any awkwardness with a wave of his hand. "Please, don't be embarrassed. I'm really quite intrigued by dragons. And as we don't have time for a formal tutorial I thought we might spend a few minutes chatting about them."

"I thought I was here to talk about geography?"

"You are," said Bergstrom, opening a hand. "The

study of the Earth, its climate and inhabitants. That's geography, isn't it? We all have our place on this spinning rock. Why leave out dragons?"

"Because they're not real," David said bluntly. "They're mythical creatures. We made them up."

"And yet they've survived for centuries in our lives. I'm just curious to know how they came into yours?"

David glanced sideways, hiding a frown. Was he being teased here for being late? Where was Bergstrom going with this? Shouldn't they be talking about glacial activity or rock formations or sea levels or something? What was the point of yapping about dragons? "I'm a lodger with a woman who makes them," he said, answering the question as plainly as he could. "She's a potter. She sells them on the market, in Scrubbley. She has a room in her house called the Dragons' Den. She's the one you should ask about dragons."

Leaning forward, Bergstrom said, "I'm asking you. Come on, give me a folk legend. Anything. You have to have a story hidden away somewhere."

David shook his head. "You're not serious, surely?"

Bergstrom studied him carefully for a moment. "You forget, I live and work among the Inuit. Stories to them are like well-chewed bones: to be passed from mouth to mouth so their flavour might be shared and long-remembered. Much of the history of the Arctic regions has been told across the light of a seal oil lamp. Stories have a unique power, David. The Inuit believe they can capture souls." He reached into his trousers then and drew out a gold-rimmed pocket watch. He opened it on the table in front of them. "This saved my life on the ice one time. Would you like me to tell you how?"

David steered his gaze to the watch. The back of the casing was scratched and dented and the watch glass clouded by weather and age. A lot of history had passed between its hands. "OK," he ventured.

"Good. You first."

"What?"

"It's a trade. Your story for mine. Briefly, I'm afraid. We don't have long."

David snorted into his hands. A trade? A trick, more like. Only Lucy could have cornered him better. "OK, but it's not that much of a story. It's about a dragon whose name was Gawain. He was supposed to be the very last dragon in the world and when he died he shed something called a fire tear. That's like…his essence, wrapped up in teardrop."

Bergstrom nodded, a pale light twinkling in his eyes. He had strange eyes, David thought, deep-set and slightly close together. If he stared your way for any length of time the gaze became a bold, imperious squint. David thought he'd seen the look somewhere before, but for the moment he couldn't quite place it.

"A dragon's power in a teardrop," mused Bergstrom. "That sounds intriguingly precious. The sort of thing you wouldn't want falling into the wrong hands, I expect."

"A woman called Guinevere caught it," said David. "But I'm not really sure what happened after that. I fell asleep and never heard the end of the story. I dreamed she took the fire inside her, though. She was trying to preserve the spirit of dragons. That's why she went to Gwilanna, anyway."

"Gwilanna?" Bergstrom's blue eyes narrowed.

"A hermit; a sort of 'wise woman' type. She lived alone in a cave on a hill. She told Guinevere about the tear in exchange for one of Gawain's old scales."

Bergstrom folded his arms and nodded. "That seems a poor exchange. Why did Gwilanna settle for a scale when she might have had the fire of Gawain herself?"

"I don't know," said David, with a shake of his head. He'd thought about that many times himself and wondered, in passing, if Bergstrom had. Why did he get the niggling feeling that Bergstrom, far from listening to the tale, was interrogating him to find out what he knew? "Told you it wasn't a very good story."

"On the contrary, it's an excellent story. Merely incomplete. But it's given me a good idea for your essay."

"Essay?"

Bergstrom smiled again. "Your supervisor asked me to set you one. Not just you, all the students I've seen." He flipped open a satchel propped up against his chair and brought a small sheaf of papers to his lap. "So, I would like two thousand words, by a week on Friday, on the existence – or not – of dragons."

David felt the colour drain out of his face. "You're joking? That's impossible. How on earth am I supposed to write that?"

Bergstrom shuffled the papers and said, "Maybe 'where on earth' would be better than 'how'. That's the geographical challenge, David. What sort of terrain would a dragon inhabit? Find the terrain and you might find the dweller. I'm sure the library will have some interesting literature. Or perhaps your dragon-making landlady could help?"

"Liz? She's always dead secretive about the dragons."

"Well, here's an incentive to unlock her, then." Bergstrom pushed a leaflet across the table. "Details of an Arctic field trip. I've agreed to take a limited number of students up to my polar research base in Chamberlain, to work first hand with my team for a while."

David scanned the flyer with an envious gaze. "Chamberlain? Wow, I'd love to go. But...crikey, it costs *four hundred pounds*. I can't afford that! I'm a week behind with my rent as it is."

Bergstrom delved into the satchel once more, this time bringing out what looked to be a piece of polished bone. "It won't cost you a penny if you write a good paper. The essay I judge to be best of the bunch will receive a free passage. How's your coursework?"

David tilted a hand.

"Then maybe you could use some help. Tell me, do you believe in good luck charms?"

David glanced at the bone, which he'd guessed by now was an Inuit carving. It was creamy-white and about the same length as Bergstrom's hand. Its shaft was etched with a baffling variety of whirls and symbols, cut into the surface by something rough.

Bergstrom handed it over. "It was made from the tusk of a narwhal," he said, "and given to me many years ago by an Inuit shaman called Angatarqok – a man who claimed he could fly to the moon, commune with spirits and turn into a wolf. Be careful, David. What you're holding is a *tornaq*. A talisman of fortunes. If you shake it, tightly, in your left hand, the spirit of the narwhal will breach your consciousness and point you along the path of true destiny. That's the theory. Try."

A talisman of fortunes? David was tempted to throw it in the bin. It was politeness rather than fascination that made him switch the carving to his left hand. He closed his eyes and shook the tusk hard.

At once, Gadzooks popped into his mind. Great. That was all he needed. "Go away," David hissed. "What are you doing here?"

Gadzooks, as usual, ignored the slight and quickly scribbled a word on his pad.

Lorel

David's eyes blinked open in surprise.

"Any luck?" asked Bergstrom. He reached over and took the carving back.

David shook his head. "Erm, no. Sorry." Lorel? What was *that* supposed to mean? Before he could search his mind for an answer, the tring of an alarm broke into the silence.

With the tip of one finger, Bergstrom snapped the pocket watch shut. "I'm afraid that's all we have time for, David. Still, it's been a pleasure talking to you. You don't mind if I ask you to see yourself out?"

David said no and stood up, a little fuddled. He hitched up his bag and turned to go. He was almost at the door before remembering to ask, "Your watch; you never told me how it saved your life?"

Bergstrom slid the watch into his pocket. "Ask me again – when you hand in your essay."

"Right," said David, looking rather hard done by. He said goodbye and slipped out quietly.

For a moment after the student had gone, Bergstrom sat back, staring at the door. Behind him the snowflakes swirled and landed, making small drifts on the thin-lipped sills. He rolled the talisman through his fingers, rubbing his thumb along the length of the shaft as if he was shaping a lump of clay. And then, in a muted voice, he spoke. "Stay close to them. Follow their auma." And what had been amorphous, suddenly took shape. And the shape it made was that of a bear.

A *sticky encounter*

The snow fell steadily throughout the night. By morning it had covered Wayward Crescent with a generous icing, deep enough to bury a wellington boot. David discovered this fascinating fact as he lay in bed dozing about the Arctic. He'd been dreaming he was sitting on a drifting ice floe, looking across the cold, black ocean at an island shaped like a jagged tooth. As his sleepy mind pondered the significance of this, he became aware of movement behind him. Something large and heavy was scraping the ice, the sonorous thud of its swaggering steps sounding like the beat of a hollow drum. *Boom. Boom.* Closer. Closer. Until a humid snort of seal-stained breath was wetting the skin on the back of his neck. He shuddered, far too frightened to turn. The animal opened its mouth to speak...

"Mum! If I stand *here*, right outside David's window, I can't see the tops of my wellies *at all!*"

"Aw..." groaned David as the dream bubble popped and the Arctic disappeared north once more. That was the trouble with this house, he thought. You couldn't even have a decent dream without a loud eleven-year-old ruining it for you. With a sigh, he rolled over onto his side and promptly came nose-to-whiskers with Bonnington. Oh yes, and on top of the noisy child was the cat who usually slept under the duvet but had chosen to camp on the pillow that night. "Morning," David greeted him. Bonnington opened his mouth and yawned. The resulting stench was surprisingly close to what David imagined raw seal might be like. He grimaced and got out of bed.

Slipping on his sweatshirt and a fresh pair of jeans, he drew back the curtains and assessed the weather. The garden was truly covered. In the centre of the lawn, the long brown stem of the Pennykettles' bird table was the only spike of colour to have survived the fall. Icicles were hanging off the roof of the shed. The rockery looked like a small ski slope. David shivered and clicked his tongue. Winter had never been his favourite season.

"What do you reckon?" he said, rubbing out a small patch of condensation so Gadzooks had a clearer sight of things. The special dragon chewed his pencil in silence. David hurred against the glass, and in the canvas so created he wrote the word 'Lorel'. "What does it mean?" he muttered, watching a tiny rivulet of water dribble through the 'o' until it resembled the planet Saturn. He pressed a finger to its centre and at once a large belt of snow came sheeting past the window, landing with a whump on the dustbin outside. David jumped back with a frightened start, almost treading on Bonnington's tail. From the Dragons' Den above, he thought he heard the echo of a gentle hrrr. Snowballing dragons. Hilarious, not.

Dragging a comb through his mop of brown hair, he followed Bonnington into the kitchen – and almost tripped over Lucy in the process. "Oi, get out the way," he tutted. "What are you doing down there, anyway?" She was kneeling on the kitchen floor, scratting around in the bottom of the freezer.

"Nothing," she said, jumping up and slamming the freezer door shut. She leaned back against it, pushing her hands into her fawn-coloured duffel coat. Dirty little puddles of thawing snow were leeching from the soles of her bright red wellies. "Will you come into the garden and help me build a snowman?"

"I'm having breakfast," David muttered, brushing past. *What's she up to?* he wondered. *Is she hiding something? In the* freezer? There was only one way to find out. "Oh, I meant to tell you, Luce, if you look on the bookshelf in my room you'll find a little present from Sophie."

That did it. Lucy was gone in a flash.

In another flash, David was down on his knees and

pulling out the bottom drawer of the freezer. It was loosely packed with frozen veg. But in a space at the back behind the bags was a grey plastic box with a pale blue lid. On top of the box, there sat a dragon.

David frowned. He knew this creature. Its name was Gruffen and it usually sat on a shelf just inside the Dragons' Den where it was supposed to 'guard' the doorway. But what was a guard dragon doing in the freezer? What exactly did the Pennykettles have in that box? A remnant of dragonkind perhaps? A fragment of scale, or tooth, or claw? The thought both excited him and made him shiver. Wouldn't *that* be something to present to Dr Bergstrom: organic evidence of dragon life.

He picked Gruffen up to move him aside – and that was his first mistake. Immediately, his fingertips began to burn. It was a cold fire rather than a flame, of course, but the principal effect was identical: pain. As David let out an inflated whimper that seemed to stretch across several seconds, the stupidity of his actions dawned on him. Gruffen's surface temperature was the same as the freezer: minus eighteen degrees centigrade! That alone was enough to cause blistering and frostbite, but the secondary effect was even worse: he couldn't let Gruffen go. The difference in temperature between the dragon's cold scales and David's warm skin had caused his fingers to bond to the glaze.

Heat. He needed a source of heat. He had to get Gruffen off, and quickly. He reached for the hot tap over the sink and was just about to turn it when a voice screeched: "No!"

Liz swept in, casting a scowl at the open freezer. "Run *cold* water. Hot will crack him." And using a tea-towel to support Gruffen's body, she pushed them under a slow, cold stream.

"What's happening?" asked Lucy, running in. She had a glossy-backed wildlife book in one hand and a pretty little listening dragon in the other. She gasped in horror at the sight of Gruffen taking a shower.

David's face turned bright cherry-red. Caught dragon-handed. This was bad. "I was moving him to get to the, erm, broccoli, that's all."

"Broccoli? For breakfast? That's a new one, David."

"No, I was planning...a surprise meal."

"He wasn't," said Lucy. "He was looking at the—" She bit her tongue and went to the freezer. "It's all right, Mum. Gruffen guarded it properly."

"Good. Bring the box over here, would you."

"But—?"

"Lucy, do as I say. I want to show our inquisitive

lodger what's in it. If I don't, his curiosity will never be satisfied and he'll only cause more distress to my dragons." With a gentle tug she separated Gruffen from David's fingers and placed him safely on the table. Lucy fetched the box and gave it to her mum. "Thank you. Right, are you ready?"

David nodded.

"One quick peek, then it goes back."

"Mum, are you sure?"

"Quite sure," said Liz. And she lifted the lid. A fine wisp of icy vapour rose like a genie into the kitchen. From all around the house came a gentle *hrrr*.

David gulped and leaned his body forward.

Inside the box was a glistening snowball.

"A snowball?" he said, looking cheated. In actual fact it was more like a lump of off-white ice cream, frozen so hard it had grown a few extra icy ridges.

"Not just *any* old snowball," said Lucy. "Mum's kept it for ever, since she was little." She dug around in a batch of papers in a letter rack and pulled out a small, square photograph. "That's Mum. When she was eight."

"Crikey," David laughed. "Doesn't she look like you?" Liz was dressed in an anorak and wellingtons, with a matching red bobble hat, scarf and gloves. She was holding the snowball out at arm's length as if she had caught a falling star. "Sweet," he said, propping the picture up against the toaster. "So why have you kept it all this time?"

Liz marched across the kitchen and put the box away. "We all keep little reminders of our childhood. You have your teddy bear; I have my snowball."

"It's nothing to do with the dragons, then?"

Liz looped back her hair and looked at him hard.

"I only wondered, cos Lucy said they liked snow."

Lucy changed the subject. "Mum, Sophie's given me a book about hedgehogs."

"Very nice," said Liz, and cast her eye upon the dragon that Lucy had brought in. "What's Grace doing here?"

David's mood became suddenly glum. "As from last night, I'm her keeper."

Lucy looked up from the pages of her book. "Why has Sophie given her dragon to you?"

"Because Sophie has got a new job," he said tautly, "and where she's going, she can't take Grace."

"Oh?" said Liz, looking concerned. "Is this what she wanted to tell you last night?"

"Yes. She's leaving the Wildlife Hospital and going to work with elephants for a while."

"In a zoo?" piped Lucy. "Mum, can we go?"

"Lucy, shush a minute. Go on, David."

"No, not a zoo. A game reserve – in Africa."

"What?" Lucy closed the book in shock. "How's she going to come and see us from there?"

"She isn't," David told her bluntly, spilling cornflakes into a dish. "She'll be gone for eight months. She flew out early this morning. She had to make a snap decision about the job, which is why she didn't come and say goodbye. She wanted you to have the hedgehog book in case you – we – ever find 'Spikey'."

Lucy's bottom lip dropped a little. "Africa?" she mumbled as it finally sank in.

Meow, went Bonnington, springing onto a chair. His plaintive cry seemed to sum up the mood.

"Well, that's a bit of a blow," said Liz. "But if she's gone, she's gone. That's all there is to it."

David sighed and ate a cornflake (dry).

"Come on, eight months isn't all that long." Liz gave his arm a gentle squeeze. "The time will fly right by, you'll see. What you need is an occupation."

"I've got an occupation; I'm a geography student."

"I meant right now, to take your mind off things. After breakfast you can clear the patio."

"What?!"

"And you can cook tea, too – as you were planning a surprise meal. Just because your poor heart's broken, doesn't mean to say you're excused for Gruffen."

"Him? *Cook?*" Lucy looked on, horrified. "We'll all be poisoned."

Pride if nothing else forced David to say, "I make a very good lasagne, as it happens."

A-row? went Bonnington.

"Not from *Chunky Chunks*. Sorry, Bonners."

"Right, that's settled, then," Liz said briskly. "It'll make a nice change, someone else doing the tea." She patted David's arm. "The apron is yours. Something with broccoli would be nice…"

The snow on the patio was soft and unbroken and came up in huge, meringue-like blocks. David launched load after load onto the lawn. Lucy, trying hard to build her snowman, squealed every time a wedge came near her. But she complained only once, when David pretended that he'd seen a hedgehog and hit her with a chunk which exploded on her head and showered down into the hood of her coat. She packed a snowball and tried to retaliate. It missed and thudded into David's window.

"That reminds me," he said, as she blew Gadzooks an apologetic kiss. "What's happened to G'reth?"

"He's in the Dragons' Den, being kilned," she replied.

David glanced at the upstairs rooms. In the window of Liz's pottery studio, a dozen or so dragons were peering out. "Why *do* they like the snow?" he asked again. "You must have some idea?"

Lucy shook her head. "Will you help me now?"

David rested his shovel and joined her on the lawn. "You have to pack it tight, like this," he said, compressing the snow with several hard pats, "then roll it around and let the loose snow stick." And off he went, up and down the lawn, till the ball was so big it needed both of them to push it. Lucy made a head and plonked it on. She was about to set off to find twigs for the arms, and stones for the eyes and nose and mouth, when the sky grew dark and it started to rain.

"Oh dear, snowman abandoned," said David.

Lucy didn't argue. She was tired and complaining that her feet were wet. David sent her back to the house while he made a detour back to the shed, in order to put the shovel away.

As he was dropping the latch on the shed, he thought he heard something moving on the lawn. Just the faintest swish of snow, but enough to make him turn his head. The lawn was covered with the interlocking tracks of human footprints. But towards the top and centre were some larger marks, certainly not made by human feet. Picking up a rock, he walked nervously towards them, his heart beginning to beat a little faster. He was a metre or two from the first indent when he realised they were nothing more than a small arc of stepping stones peeping through the snow. He laughed at his stupidity and tossed the rock aside. For one ridiculous second he thought he'd seen the tracks of…what? Prints like that could only be produced by an animal of some considerable size, and as far as David knew, no one had ever yet reported polar bears roaming the gardens of Scrubbley…

The mystery of the Tear

The rain fell and continued to fall. By late afternoon, when David drifted into the kitchen to begin the preparation of his promised lasagne, the rooftops and trees had been rinsed of snow and the garden was beginning to look green once more. In the centre of the lawn, the snowman had sagged like an old used pillow, his head almost merging into his body. Bonnington was out there, sitting in front of it, looking like a damp, discarded rag. David frowned and tapped the window. Bonnington didn't budge. *Barmy*, thought David. *That cat is crackers.* He tweaked the blinds shut and got on with the dinner.

Within half an hour he had the pasta in the oven and broccoli and sweetcorn ready to heat. Liz and Lucy came in about forty minutes later, drawn by the aroma of garlic bread.

David was pleased. His 'occupations' had taken his mind off Sophie, and Liz was in a better mood now as well – though she did complain once when she tried to wash her hands and found the sink bunged up with carrot peel.

"Old habit, sorry," David said. "We always peel into

the sink at home." He dipped in his hand and scooped out the blockage.

Lucy set the places, dinner was served and soon everyone was sitting down to eat. Not surprisingly, Lucy ate all her lasagne and didn't die on the kitchen floor as she'd expected. But when seconds were offered she politely declined and suggested that Bonnington might finish off the dish.

"Where is Bonnington, by the way?" said Liz, glancing down at the half-full cat bowl.

"In the garden, last I saw," David said.

Liz leaned back and twiddled the blinds. "Oh, look at him, dippy animal. What's he doing in the middle of the lawn? He must be frozen from his whiskers to his tail."

"He's still there?" David craned to see. "He's been in that position for over an hour."

"Perhaps he likes our snowman," said Lucy.

"Your snowman's taken a bit of a battering," Liz muttered, standing up and knocking the window pane. "He looks more like a bear than a snowman, now. Bonny, come in!"

"Bear?" said David, thinking back to the prints that weren't. "How do you work that out?"

"They have a sort of hump in their backs, don't they? Maybe you need a potter's eye to see it. Talking of bears,

I meant to ask: how did you get on with your Arctic visitor? Lucy, go and fetch Bonny in, will you? Hand me your plate while you're at it."

Lucy rose from her seat and gathered up her plate and David's too. As she handed them over, David answered Liz's question: "Fine. You'd like Dr Bergstrom, I think. He's very...charismatic. He gave me a sort of talisman to hold and said a narwhal would show me my path of true destiny."

"What's a narwhal?" asked Lucy.

"A whale with a horn like a unicorn."

"Is it magic?"

"More importantly, did it show you your destiny?" asked Liz.

"I don't know, but I saw Gadzooks write something on his pad. I don't suppose you know what 'Lorel' means?"

Hardly had the words had time to leave his lips before they were met with a loud crash of cutlery. Lucy squealed and brought her fists to her mouth. All the knives and forks had clattered to the floor, spinning into every corner of the kitchen. They might have been followed by the crockery as well had David not jumped up and steadied Liz's hand. "Whoa! Are you all right? What's the matter?" The normal healthy pink of Liz's cheeks had drained to a shade on the white side of grey.

Her eyes were staring into nowhere. David guided her onto a chair.

"Must have stood up too fast," she mumbled. She took Lucy's hand. "I'm all right now. Come on, help me pick up these things."

"No way," said David. "You stay put."

"I'll pick everything up," said Lucy.

"And I'll wash the dishes," David offered.

"Goodness, now I do feel faint," said Liz. She rubbed David's arm. "Leave it, we haven't had our pudding yet. Apple pie. In the fridge. I'm all right. Really."

David found the pie and brought it to the table. As he served it into dishes, he glanced at Liz again. She looked anything but 'all right'. She seemed shocked and flustered and her hands were shaking. Did the word Lorel mean something to her?

It was Lucy who kept the intrigue going. "Is Lorel the name of someone?" she asked, plonking the cutlery into the sink.

"I thought it might be the name of a dragon," muttered David.

Lucy soon quashed that. "Dragon names begin with a 'guh', not a 'luh'. That's right, isn't it, Mum?"

"Yes," said Liz, offering no explanation. She picked up a carton of single cream and poured some over her portion of pie.

"Dr Bergstrom talked about dragons," said David, casually lobbing the remark at Lucy but all the while keeping an eye on Liz. "He set me an essay about them. I have to write two thousand words on whether dragons existed or not."

"That's *easy*," mocked Lucy. "Course they existed."

"Yes, it's all very well you telling me that, but in an essay I have to have some sort of proof. It would help if I knew where dragons lived."

"They liked mountains and snowy places," said Lucy. "Where they could cool off when they'd been flying."

"OK, then answer me this: why has no one ever found evidence of them? There isn't a single museum in the world that has a dragon's skull or a scale on show. If dragons had truly existed, someone, somewhere, would have dug up a bone."

Suddenly, out of the blue, Liz spoke: "Why has Dr Bergstrom set you this essay?"

David lifted his shoulders. "For the challenge, I suppose. If I do well with it, I might win a chance to visit the Arctic." He told them about the field trip to Chamberlain.

"Will you see polar bears?" Lucy asked brightly.

"Loads of them – if I manage to get there. Come on,

you're the experts, give me a clue: why has no one ever found the remains of a dragon?"

"Because they don't understand what they're looking for," said Liz. A sudden hush fell over the kitchen. Not a single *hrrr* echoed round the walls. Liz rose to her feet and turned towards the sink. "Dragons are spiritual creatures, David, far removed from the image most people have of them. They were born from the earth, they lived for the earth and when they died they returned to the earth. Their bones and scales became one with it."

"What, they just *dissolved*, you mean?"

"No, they changed. As all things must. Legend has it they formed a layer of soil – a layer we know today as clay."

David felt his heart hit a sudden bump. He looked at the listening dragon on the fridge and thought about Gruffen, G'reth, Gadzooks – all of them lovingly moulded from clay. "So your dragons *are* real – in a funny sort of way?"

Liz and Lucy exchanged a glance. "All things have their auma, David. You simply have to learn to sense it."

"Auma? What's that?"

"An ancient word for fire."

"Not crackly burny fire," said Lucy, keeping her voice to a reverential whisper.

"The fire that comes from within," said Liz.

David nodded as he thought this through. "What about a dragon's fire, then? That comes from within. That's crackly, isn't it?"

"It's specially crackly," Lucy said.

David laughed and threw up a hand. "Now you're making it sound like a breakfast cereal. Come on, stop talking in riddles. Dragons are spiritual, fair enough. But they're obviously flesh and blood as well. If their bodies eventually turn to clay, what happens to their fire, crackly or otherwise?"

"Can I tell him?" Lucy turned to her mum.

"Yes. Then go and bring Bonnington in."

David glanced through the window again. The Pennykettles' cat was still by the snowman. What *was* the matter with him?

"When dragons die, they cry their fire tear," said Lucy, "and each tear trickles into the ground, where the *proper* auma is."

David thought a moment before replying. "At the Earth's core, you mean?"

Lucy gave a vigorous nod. "Dragon fire helps the world to breathe."

"Don't be silly; the Earth doesn't *breathe*."

"It does," she insisted. "Doesn't it, Mum?"

"In a manner of speaking," Liz said quietly. "Go and fetch Bonnington now."

Lucy pushed back her chair.

"What about Gawain, then?" David said quickly. "His fire tear didn't go into the ground. When Guinevere caught it, what did she do with it?"

Lucy looked at her mum who said, "Go on. I asked you to go."

"But—?"

"Now, please."

With a sigh Lucy exited the kitchen.

David, now wary that he'd overstepped the mark, chose his next words carefully. "I'm sorry, I know this means a lot to you both. I'm not belittling the story, honestly. It's just…the legend of Gawain is a great angle for my essay, and I really want to win that prize. I'd appreciate any help you can give me."

Liz rested her hands in the washing-up suds. It was several seconds before she replied. "I'm sorry to disappoint you, David, but neither myself nor Lucy can answer your question. No one knows what became of the fire of Gawain. The legend is that Guinevere caught the tear – and hid it."

"*What?*" David sat up slowly, feeling a knot of tension in his stomach. "I thought she absorbed it into herself and became a sort of…human dragon?"

Liz laughed and looked back at him over her shoulder. "None of us could possibly endure such a force."

"But if she hid it? Then…where is it now?"

"David, if I knew the answer to that I'd—"

Before she could finish, Lucy hurried in, fighting to keep a hold of Bonnington. "Mum, he's hissing and clawing and – ow!"

Bonnington wriggled out of her arms, only to be scooped off the floor by David. "Hey, hey, what's the matter with you?"

"Do you think he's been bitten?" asked Liz.

David checked him over. "Doesn't look like it. But something's spooked him, that's for sure. Look at his eyes." They were wild and staring, as large as pennies. David loosened his grip and the cat jumped down and ran straight to the door. Lucy, wary of being scratched, backed up, covering Bonnington's cat flap. They watched him turn a frustrated circle, before he bounced onto a chair and then onto the drainer.

"Now what's he doing?" Liz said, astonished.

"Perhaps he's seen another cat," said Lucy.

David shook his head. "He's looking at the snowman."

"Snow *bear*," said Lucy. "I can tell the shape now. Do you think he's scared of it?"

"I'm not sure," said David, and he glanced at Liz.

She was staring at the snow bear and stroking Bonnington to calm him down. And then she said something quite unexpected. "I'd like to meet your Dr Bergstrom, David. He does sound very 'charismatic'. I feel as though I know him, in a strange sort of way. Thank you for cooking the tea tonight. Lucy, be an angel and do the drying up. I'm going to the den to finish G'reth." And she twiddled the blinds down again and left the kitchen, shutting the snow bear out of sight.

On-line with Zanna

With nothing better to do after tea (no football on the TV; no girlfriend to visit) David retreated to the quiet of his room and decided to make some notes for his essay. His mind was a jumble of polar bears and dragons and he needed the stark simplicity of a computer to separate those elements and keep things focused. But as he waited for his computer to boot, he couldn't resist another glance into the garden. The ice bear – or snow bear, as Lucy liked to call it – stood regally in the centre of the lawn, being steadily sculpted by the drizzling rain and looking ever more like its real life counterpart. Why was Bonnington so hooked by it? Could the cat see something that human eyes couldn't? And if he could, was he scared or awed by its presence? David closed his eyes and put the ice bear into darkness. But even as that visual shutter came down, a virtual world opened and there, at its bleak and frozen centre, was a genuine polar bear. David jerked in surprise but held tight to the image. The bear was sitting in a field of broken ice, its fur dragged leeward by a howling blizzard, spicules of snow whipping up around its paws. David reached out to it with his mind. "Who are you?" he asked, and felt his heart tremble as the great bear squinted through the ice wind at him. It trod its spectacular column-like paws and opened its black-lipped mouth to speak…

You have e-mail, it said.

Or rather, that was what the *computer* said. With a start, David opened his eyes. The polar bear disappeared back into the ether. Annoyed, David swivelled to face the monitor. He pointed the cursor at his e-mail inbox and immediately let out a mild groan. "Oh no, what do *you* want?"

The sender of the message was:

zanyzanna@worldmail.com

David clicked his tongue before thinking of doing the same with his mouse. Suzanna – Zanna – Martindale was a girl on his course. She was a 'Goth'. She had a face as white as a hard-boiled egg and she dressed from head to toe in black; black tiered skirts full of tassels and fringes that danced across the laces of her black kicker boots; black T-shirts, usually sporting some mystic picture of wolves or Indians or a heavy metal band; jet black hair (very long and very straight and usually festooned with beads or braids); black-rimmed eyes (people sometimes called her *Zan Zan,* like a panda); black nails (fingers and toes both painted) and, what really freaked David the most, her black pneumatic lips.

He had sometimes thought that kissing Zanna must be like smooching with a pair of black puddings. Not that he *wanted* to smooch with Zanna. She was one scary liquorice stick. She was friendly enough, in a jangly sort of way (she wore more bangles than a curtain pole), but not at all David's type. It made him shudder when she smiled at him, which she did, often, when they passed on the campus. People joked that Zanna had only come to Scrubbley because she'd missed the train to *Hogwart's.* What could she possibly want with David?

He opened her message. It was just two lines.

Heard you were lonesome. Fancy a drink?

A drink? With the panda? David's blood ran cold. He hit 'reply' and wrote something tactful. *Working on an essay. Another time perhaps.*

From the corner of his eye, he saw a dragon's face. It was Grace, Sophie's listening dragon. He'd never really looked at her properly before, but now that he did he thought he could detect a glint of disapproval in her oval green eyes. He put his nose close up to her snout. "Stop frowning. I turned her down. OK?"

The computer beeped again. *Bergstrom's essay? What'd ya get?*

David sighed and paddled his feet. An on-line conversation with the mad witch of Scrubbley was not supposed to be part of his evening's agenda, but there was one thing he was curious about... *Dragons,* he tapped, *the existence of. Someone tipped him off that I had one at home. I wonder who THAT could have been?* Zanna was in his tutorial group. She'd always taken a keen interest when he'd mentioned Gadzooks. It had to be her.

Yet to his surprise she wrote, *Not guilty. Hand on my cold, black heart.*

"Yeah, right," muttered David, not sure he believed her. But it amused him, the way she'd sent herself up. *Who, then?* he typed.

Don't remember anyone saying it, she wrote. *Maybe when I went to the loo, perhaps?*

Maybe, thought David, as a raindrop or two began to tickle the windows. He turned his head and watched a bullet of water ping the glass. If one of the students hadn't let on about the dragons, how could Bergstrom have made the connection? The computer beeped again.

I got the Loch Ness monster, by the way – just in case you were wondering. It's a sort of geo-biological thing as I'm on a joint course. I have to find out if a lake the size of Loch Ness could produce enough flora and fauna to support a 'monster' of Nessie's size. Been grabbing pix off the net all day. Great essay. He's cool, isn't he, Bergstrom?

He's weird, replied David. *Did you shake his talisman?
Pardon?!*

David tutted loudly and hammered a response. *He
gave me an Inuit carving to hold and said it would show me
my true destiny. He thought I might need some luck for his
competition.*

*Too right. Start saving, cos I'm gonna storm it. Didn't get
a talisman to hold, though. I'm piqued. What happened?
What'd ya see?*

This is dumb, thought David, sitting back. Why am I
telling *Zanna* this? *Nothing. Just a name. Gotta go now.
Bye.*

Rain, come on, she wrote back quickly. *Don't leave me
hanging. Spill. I'm agog.*

No, Zanna. You'll take the mick.

*Rain, play nice boy or I'll turn you into a squelchy toad.
The cauldron is a-bubbling, beware…*

To his horror, David found himself laughing at that.
But before he could type a response, Zanna came back
with another incentive. *OK, handsome, I'll make you a
deal. You tell me about your mystic experience and I'll lend
you a really smart book on dragons.*

That made David sit up and think. Handsome? He
smiled at Grace. No doubt about it, that dragon was

frowning. "Sorry, you're going in the wardrobe," he told her. And he picked her up and put her on the shelf above his shirt rail. A reproachful dragon he could do without. He went back to the keyboard and tapped out a message. *Why do you want to give me a book? Could help me win the comp.*

Well, I guess under this chimney sweep's outfit I'm just a plain old-fashioned girlie at heart. Could pop it over tonight if you like? Have car. Will travel. Not busy. Hint.

Didn't know you had wheels?

More convenient than a broomstick.

Very funny, thought David. But she was; *very* funny. Despite his reservations, he was warming to her. What's more, she was just the type to know about dragons. But bring her to the house? That was risky. A Goth: what would Liz and Lucy think? And Bonnington? She'd probably terrify him. *Tonight's not good*, he typed. *How about Sunday afternoon?* (when Liz and Lucy would be out selling dragons at a local craft fayre).

It's a date, she tapped back.

No, it isn't. You're bringing me a book.

Relax. I don't bite – except when I'm draining necks. Come on, let's hear this name.

David paused over the keyboard. It felt odd, giving the name away, as if he might be betraying some special kind of confidence. He looked at Gadzooks who was staring through the window, his gently-curving smile reflected in the glass. David took that as a sign of approval. He typed out *Lorel*.

The reply almost scorched the screen. *NO WAY?! YOU'RE KIDDING ME???*

David frowned and felt a shudder run down his spine. *You know what it means?*

That's spooky, she wrote. *You got THAT in Bergstrom's presence? Wow. Swear you're not pulling my braids?*

Got out of the playground years ago, Zanna. Just tell me what it means, OK?

I read it in a book about the Inuit once. Lorel is the Teller of Ways. He has all the legends of the Arctic in his head.

David gulped. *An Eskimo?* he typed.

It seemed an age before the answer came back. When it did, David almost wished he'd never asked the question. A cold breeze circled his neck and shoulders as Zanna's explanation flickered up in blue. *No, dummy. Where's your sense of romance? Lorel's not a man. He's a polar bear.*

Bonnington's treasure

Within minutes of Zanna's strange revelation, David broke the e-mail connection and said he would talk to her some more on Sunday. He closed the computer down and flopped out on his bed, staring at the ceiling with his hands behind his head. He needed a time-out. Space to think. There was definitely something strange going on. First Lucy, with her wishing dragon, bringing the snow; then Bergstrom wanting to talk about dragons; then Bonnington being upset by the snow bear; and last but not least, Liz being spooked by the name Lorel. What was it about the bear that had rippled her nerves and made her drop the cutlery? He was absolutely certain she knew the name and that that was why she would like to meet Bergstrom. And that, in turn, could only mean one thing: there had to be a primeval connection between dragons and bears. But what? Was it something to do with Gawain and his fire tear? The mysterious hidden fire? Hidden where? In the Arctic? A teardrop, lost in a thousand miles of ice?

The ceiling creaked like an ice floe groaning – Liz, moving around in the Dragons' Den above. If she knew the answer, she would never let it out. But maybe he could hear it from another source? Twice he had dreamed that a polar bear was trying to speak to him. Could that have been Lorel, the Teller of Ways, come to give up the ancient legend? David closed his eyes and threw down a challenge. *If you are him*, he whispered, *show yourself. Tell me, now, about the fire…*

But the harder he tried, the more obstinate the gateway to the dream state seemed. To make matters worse, after half an hour or so, the door wafted open and Bonnington nudged his way into the room. He yattered something catty then leapt up and sat on David's chest. He was showing no further signs of anxiety, just the usual inclination to tread his paws against a human ribcage before he settled down for the night. As the cat nodded off, so did David – on the bed, fully dressed. He slept fitfully, and dreamed about Sophie's dragon, Grace. She seemed to be whispering in Sophie's ear. The next thing David knew he was being chased by elephants, a whole herd of them trumpeting, *Zanna? Who's Zanna?*

He jerked awake, panting, but thankfully untrampled. It was morning. Dawn had broken, grey and wet. The ice bear had disappeared from the garden. What had been a double helping of snow was now no more than a shallow island, isolated in the middle of the lawn.

Even so, Bonnington was still watching over it. He

was sitting on the windowsill, paws tucked under him, suspended in some kind of sentinel's catnap. David frowned and touched the cat's whiskers, concerned that Bonnington had still not escaped whatever spectre (Lorel or otherwise) was haunting him. Bonnington burbled and shook himself awake. He ducked the lodger's hand and peered anxiously through the window. "It's gone," David told him, "all washed away. Come on, I'll show you." And gathering Bonnington into his arms he cradled him, chest-high, into the garden.

Crossing the lawn was not a good idea. After only four paces, David's feet were coated with a soggy band of mud. But once sludged there was no going back. He took Bonnington up to the ice. They circled it. They studied it. They did not try to cross it. When David put him down, the cat put his nose to the lip of the island, pulled back suddenly, then trotted away to the bottom of the garden.

"Now what?" David tutted, squidging after him. "Bonnington, the polar bear isn't in there." The cat was heading for a patch of wild ground, covered over with weeds and a criss-crossing den of rotting branches. "Come out," David commanded, as Bonnington wriggled into a hole. "You'll get mucky, and I'll get into trouble." With a sigh, David dug his hand into the mound – and touched something prickly that wasn't a cat. Carefully, he lifted the branches. There, amid the bracken, was an old hair brush.

And a shoe lace. And a keyring. And half a picture postcard (of the seafront at Skegness). And a golf ball. And a coaster. And what looked like chicken bones. Two lollipop sticks. A clothes peg. A potato peeler. And a Scrubbley Wildlife Hospital badge. There was even a felt-tipped pen that David remembered had once rolled under his bed.

"Bonnington," he muttered, crouching down, "how long has this been going on?"

Brr-up went the cat, a picture of innocence.

"You're a robber," David told him. "A furry footpad. And what's more, I'm having this back." He picked up the pen and tapped the cat playfully on the nose. "I ought to tell Lucy you've got her hairbrush, too, but…" He stopped and a wicked grin lit up his face. "But, why don't we play a little trick on her instead?"

A-row? went Bonnington.

"Watch," David whispered, and he drew a little face on the end of the brush then wrote, 'My name is Spikey' along the handle. He put the brush back and pulled the branches over it. Bonnington gave him a short, sharp stare. "You started it," said David. And he dusted down his trousers and squelched back to the house.

He was met on the kitchen threshold by Liz. "And what exactly have *you* been doing?" Her gaze dropped straight to his mud-clogged feet.

"Erm, I was helping Bonnington..."

"Don't you go indicting my cat, young man. I'm sure he didn't willingly drag you round the garden, buttering your shoes with half a ton of dirt."

"He's a kleptomaniac."

"I beg your pardon?"

"He nicks things and stores them down the garden. He's got a hidey hole near the tree."

Liz pursed her lips. Leaning sideways into the kitchen, she grabbed an old toothbrush from a jar of utensils and slapped it into David's hand. "Clean those shoes at the outside tap. Don't come in till they're spotless, or else. Honestly, calling my Bonnington a thief." She tutted and pushed the door to.

"He's a villain!" David shouted. "A tabby desperado!" *You'll find out,* he muttered in his thoughts, *when I send Lucy on her hedgehog hunt.*

But the moment wasn't right for that. So David scrubbed his shoes clean and left them just inside the kitchen door to dry, then kindly gifted Bonnington the toothbrush for his haul.

He was heading to his room when he found two letters propped up against the microwave. Both were addressed to him. He ripped the first open and groaned.

"If that's the bank telling you you're overdrawn, I advise you to keep it quiet," said Liz, sweeping in from the hall just then. "You owe me nearly a fortnight's rent."

David winced. It was indeed a letter from the bank reminding him he owed *them* quite a bit more than a fortnight's rent. He tore the second letter open. "Oh."

"Oh?" said Liz. "'Oh, good'? Or 'oh, not so good'?"

"Not sure," said David, slipping into a chair. "It's a letter from a publisher."

"It's from a woman at Apple Tree Publishing," he said, "the last people I sent *Snigger* to."

"Well, don't keep me in suspense," said Liz. "What does she have to say?"

David folded back the letter and read: "'Dear Mr Rain, thank you for sending us *Snigger and the Nutbeast*. While I do not feel this story is currently right for our list, I nevertheless enjoyed its freshness and charm and think, with a little work, that your style might be developed for today's children's market.' Is she telling me I'm old-fashioned or what?"

"Don't be so negative. What else did she put?"

"Not much. 'I wondered if you would like to drop into my office sometime and have an informal chat over coffee? Please call and make an appointment blah blah. Yours sincerely, Dilys Whutton.'"

"Gosh, how exciting. Coffee with a publisher. That's a step forward."

"Dilys Whutton? She sounds older than my gran."

"Which means she'll have a lot of experience, doesn't it? You get on your phone and call her. If Lucy finds out you passed up this chance, your name will be mud. Speaking of which."

"I did them." David pointed to the mud-free zone that were his shoes.

"No, I meant…" Liz nodded at the door, just as Lucy breezed in crying, "Mum, the bear's gone flat! Can I wish for more snow?"

"No. Now G'reth is kilned, he belongs to David."

Lucy tutted and turned to the lodger. "Wish for more snow for me. Please?"

David shook his head. "I think Lorel's gone into hibernation, don't you?"

Lucy's eyes lit up at once. "Was Lorel the *bear*?"

"Hmm, that's the name I gave him," said David, smiling and flicking a glance at Liz. No cutlery crashes this time. She merely reached for a tea-towel and bunched it in her fist. "When you said he wasn't a dragon, I thought he might as well be the bear. Grrr."

"Grrr," laughed Lucy. "Are you going to do a story about him?"

David closed up the letter from Apple Tree Publishing. He didn't want Lucy to see it and start building up false hopes about *Snigger*. "Maybe. Lorel did look the sort of bear who might be involved in lots of stories. I was even wondering if he hadn't bumped into a dragon or two on his Arctic travels – as they both like snow and ice?"

Lucy turned to her mum. "Is that right?"

Liz folded the tea towel and left it on the worktop. "Dragons lived a long time ago," she murmured. "I don't think the dynasties overlapped. Anyway, come on. It's time for school."

Lucy hovered by David's shoulder. "Wish for more snow. Please. For Lorel."

"Nah, we've had enough snow," he said. "What if I wished to find Spikey instead?"

"Hhh!"

"Upstairs. Hair done. Now," said Liz, turning Lucy before she could speak. "We've no time for hedgehogs – or any other creatures." And casting David a penetrating glance, she bustled Lucy out of the kitchen.

OK, thought David, smiling to himself. *That round to me, I think. Now that we both know who Lorel is, let's see where we go from here...*

'Here' turned out to be nowhere, really. The next few days went by without incident. And as the weekend loomed and Sunday came around, David found his thoughts turning once again to Zanna.

Liz and Lucy were leaving for the craft fayre at eleven,

which meant there would be plenty of time between their departure and Zanna's arrival. In other words, no embarrassing encounters. That suited David fine.

Until eleven, everything went pretty smoothly. The Pennykettle women spent their morning parcelling dragons in thick bubble wrap and packing them neatly into cardboard boxes, ready to be taken out to the car. This had meant a few quiet hours for David, who had stayed in his room catching up on college work and making further notes for his essay. He had still not played his trick on Lucy; the ground had been far too wet underfoot. He didn't dare send her out on a 'wild hedgehog chase' in filthy conditions; Liz would not see the funny side of that. But by late morning a drying wind had blown over Scrubbley, raking the water out of the ground. And when Lucy cornered David on the stairs and asked, "Did you make a wish about Spikey, yet?" David couldn't help but reply to her, "How can I? Your mum's not given me G'reth. But funnily enough, I thought I saw something small and pointy shuffling about in those brambles near..." And Lucy was gone before he had finished.

Two minutes later, she was back. David steeled himself for a sharp tirade. Strangely, it didn't come. Instead, she flashed past him and dived into a cupboard.

She pulled out a torch, then shot out again.

Half an hour went by. David began to panic. Lucy had been 'hunting' all that time. What's more, the clock was approaching noon and that meant Zanna could arrive at any minute. It didn't help when Liz threw the kitchen door open and asked him, "Do you know much about cars?"

"Cars?"

"Engines. It's coughing. Won't start."

"*What?* It's got to start. I'll come and have a look."

"What's Lucy doing?"

"Hedgehog patrol."

Liz frowned and knocked the window. "Lucy, come on! We're going to the fayre – if we can start the car, that is…"

She joined David on the front drive a few moments later. The bonnet of the car was raised and David was looking distinctly puzzled.

"Well?"

"Erm, not quite sure. It's, erm, probably a jizzle on your sproggleclonk or something."

Liz tapped her foot. "I'll ring the garage."

Just then the gate swung open in the house next door and Mr Bacon, the Pennykettles' neighbour, stepped out. He was dressed in a baggy old shirt and trousers held up by a pair of splendid yellow braces. David immediately started to tense. He didn't get along with Henry Bacon, who had a habit of sticking his nose into things. That morning was no exception. Henry saw the raised bonnet and immediately asked, "Problem, Mrs P?"

"Car won't start. Sproggle on the jizzlewots, according to David."

"Jizzlewot? There's no such thing." Mr Bacon brushed David aside, leaned across the engine and started to fiddle. "Sit in, Mrs P. We'll soon have her running. Turn her over, if you would."

Liz seemed a little uncertain, but she got in anyway and fired the ignition. The car spluttered but failed to start.

"Stop!" cried Henry, and tweaked another screw. "Once more, please."

Liz turned the key again.

To David's relief, the engine shook and the car exploded into life. Liz left it running and came to offer thanks. "Henry, you're a marvel. I'm indebted to you."

"My pleasure, Mrs P. Learned a trick or two in my army days. Needs a good service. Plugs and points. Happy to oblige. Anytime at all."

"Thank you," she said, and would have added more had she not been nearly bowled over by an on-rushing Lucy.

"Mum," she panted, her fine hair plastered all over her face. "You've got to come and look. He's here. I've found him!"

"Who?" said Liz and David together.

Frowning, Lucy turned to the lodger. "Spikey, silly. Why didn't you tell me he was *special*?"

"Special?" A hairbrush with a funny face was special?

"Yes," said Lucy, eyes almost popping. "Mum, he's the most brilliant hedgehog ever!"

"And why might that be?"

Lucy danced and knocked her fists together. "Because he's *white*!"

"White?" Liz repeated, raising an eyebrow.

"White?" said Henry Bacon, wiping his nose and leaving an oil stain on his moustache.

"*White?*" spluttered David.

"With pink eyes," Lucy added, looking at all three adults in turn.

"That means...well, I'll be blowed," said Liz.

"Think you mean 'albino', strictly, Mrs P."

"Where?" rasped David. "Where did you find it?"

"In the brambles," said Lucy. "Where you said. Mum, can we please get the rabbit hutch out of the attic and make a proper den for Spikey?"

"Not now, we'll be late for the fayre," she said, aiming Lucy towards the car. "Say goodbye to Mr Bacon and David."

"Look after Spikey," Lucy shouted to David.

"Yeah, right," he muttered, totally confused. How could Lucy have missed the hairbrush and found a proper hedgehog instead? Sighing, he waved the car goodbye. It chugged unconvincingly up the crescent, giving another little cough along the way. "Are you sure that car's all right, Henry?"

"Sound as a pound," Mr Bacon sniffed. "Mind you, if you want a decent vehicle, that's the thing to be in, boy." He pointed down the drive. A sleek black car had just pulled up.

David grunted in agreement. "Bet it costs a bit to look after, though – flipping heck!" Suddenly, his mouth was wide enough to take an apple, whole. The driver of the car had just stepped out. It was none other than Zanna.

"Good Lord!" Mr Bacon exclaimed, as Zanna came clip-clopping down the path. She looked the image of a tall dark mermaid, with her lower half enclosed in a tight-fitting skirt that flared at the ankles like a large tailfin. To David's relief she hadn't ghosted her face, and looked quite stunning in a shocking sort of way, with her eyes shadowed purple and a plum-red rinse washed into her hair. But with a silver-studded dog collar round her neck and at least two rings for every finger, she stood out like a runaway scarecrow in the sleepy leafiness of Wayward Crescent. Fearing Mr Bacon would either faint or, worse, set about her with a stick, David moved forward to explain that Zanna was merely a friend from college, come to drop off a book en route to a fancy dress party, when, to his astonishment, she veered towards the Pennykettles' neighbour and said, "Hi, Mr Bacon. Gosh, didn't know you lived around here?"

Mr Bacon flicked a crusty glance at David. "Have you come to see *him*, Suzanna?"

"Sure have," she beamed. And before David could stop her, she'd leaned over and plopped a kiss on his cheek. "Hi, David."

"Hi," he said, ripening. "How do you two know each other?"

Zanna swished round, tassles flying. "The library, of course. Mr Bacon is the best librarian in the world. He finds loads of interesting books for me, don't you?"

"Why are you wasting your time on him?" said Henry.

Zanna smiled and said, "I'm educating him – in the ways of dragons." She plonked a book into David's hands, a large format hardback with a cover picture of a sleeping dragon.

"Thanks," he said. "Do you, erm, want to come in?"

"Tch, first mistake," she said, slipping past him, "inviting a vampire over your threshold." She giggled, showing a set of perfect white teeth, said goodbye to Henry, then stepped into the house.

"Right," said David, banging the door shut as he followed her in. "Liz, my landlady, isn't at home. So promise me you won't do anything—"

"Shush," she interrupted, flapping a hand. She stooped sideways and peered wide-mouthed up the stairs, then rolled her eyes to every corner of the hall. "Wow, this house is really buzzing."

"Yeah, it's the fridge. The thermostat's wonky."

Zanna turned a circle. "Rain, don't be dumb. This place is singing. Can't you feel the energy? These walls must have a fantastic aura."

"Yeah, right," he said. "Cup of tea? This way." He bundled her towards the kitchen.

"Honestly, you really can't feel it?"

"No. Sit down – and don't scare Bonnington."

"Oh, you've got a cat!" With a squeal of excitement, Zanna scuttled across the kitchen to where a dazed-looking Bonnington was hanging over his food bowl. Zanna crouched down and tickled his ears. "Hello, Bonnington. I'm David's friend, Zanna. He thinks I'm very strange because I dress in dark clothes and talk about things he doesn't understand. But we don't care about *him*, do we? You're lovely, aren't you? Would you like to be my familiar?"

"Leave him alone," David tutted. "He's very sensitive. Don't lead him astray."

Zanna stood up and flicked back her hair. "I hope you're not going to be horrible all day. I did bring you a book, after all."

David flicked through it, then put it on the table.

"Looks good. I'll check it out later. Thanks. Is that really your car out front?"

Zanna nodded and looked around the kitchen. "Rich dental daddy. Spoils me rotten. Is this one of your landlady's dragons?" She touched a finger to the dragon on top of the fridge.

"Yes," said David. "One of many."

"It's cute. Why are its ears so frail?"

"It's a listening dragon. And before you ask, I don't know what that means. It's probably spying on us. If its eyes turn purple, run for it – quick."

"Purple's my favourite colour," said Zanna, closing her eyes so that David could see her painted lids. "Is that how the dragons come alive, then – like this?" She spread her fingers and flashed her eyes open.

David gave her a withering look.

"Just a joke. Chill out. Is this Lucy?" She pointed to the photograph of Liz with the snowball.

"No, it's Liz – when she was a kid. She keeps that snowball in the freezer."

"Really? Can I see it?"

"No. Behave."

"Spoilsport. Where was it taken – the photo, I mean? Doesn't look like England, with all those firs in the background."

"I don't know," said David. "I've never asked. Look, I'm going out into the garden for a minute. Stay here and fuss Bonnington. I won't be long."

"I like gardens," chirped Zanna, following him.

"Zanna, I'm only going to look at a hedgehog."

"I like hedgehogs," she added. "Come on, Bonnington." And she was out of the door before David could stop her, with Bonnington trotting along at her ankles.

As they approached the chunk of ice, Bonnington gave it a good wide berth.

"There was a snowman there," David explained. "It spooked him a bit. He hasn't got over it."

Zanna slowed to a halt. She looked at Bonnington, then at the ice. "No, he senses something. Animals are far more perceptive than humans. They can touch other planes of existence. You know the first thing I thought of when I looked at that?"

"Ice?" said David, facetiously.

"The Arctic ice cap, to be exact."

David groaned and rolled his eyes. "Hang on, I'll get a lollipop stick and we can mark the north pole."

"I mean it, Rain. I get impressions. Things come to me. I'm never wrong. Think about it. What's it doing here when all the rest of the snow has gone?"

David stared at the ice with his hands in his

pockets. "Melting – very slowly?"

Zanna shook her head. "It's Lorel," she muttered. "It's definitely a sign."

A-*row*, went Bonnington, padding away.

"See, he knows."

"No, he *doesn't*. All he cares about are *Chunky Chunks* and *Truffgood* biscuits." David shook his head at her and headed up the garden. He'd had all the weirdness he could take right now. Zanna, Lorel, Bonnington, white hedgehogs. He snatched the brambles aside. No Spikey, and no catty treasure trove either. Frowning suspiciously, he turned to the cat. "Where's your swag?"

Bonnington looked at the empty space as if it was a total mystery to him.

"Don't give me that. You've *moved* it all, haven't you?"

Brr-up, went Bonnington and sat down to give his paws a wash.

"What's happening?" asked Zanna, catching up.

"That cat is a thief and a smuggler," said David. He explained about the hairbrush and how Bonnington and Lucy (and Spikey, it seemed) had all turned the tables on him.

"Serves you right," Zanna said, laughing. "Cats are far

73

smarter than you think. White hedgehog? That's interesting. According to ancient folklore, white hedgehogs were a symbol of—"

"Don't," said David, holding up his hands. "I don't want any more mystical babble."

For the first time, Zanna appeared quite hurt. "I don't understand you," she said. "You tell me stuff about Inuit talismans and how the name Lorel pops up out of nowhere, and when I come to your garden it's obvious that something strange is going on, so obvious that even your cat knows about it, and all you do is try to deny it. I know you want to make sense of it, Rain, but you won't let me help you because of all this." She flicked her hands down the front of her dress, folded her arms and brushed her way past him. "I'm sorry I came. You can keep the dragon book until you hand in your essay. See you in college. Bye."

She was halfway to the house before David turned and came running after her. "Zanna, stop. I didn't mean to be rude. I'm sorry. I'm just…confused, I s'pose. I keep having dreams about him."

Zanna paused and dropped her shoulders. "Lorel?"

"Mmm. I think so. A bear, anyway. He keeps trying to speak, but when he opens his mouth something always wakes me."

Zanna turned slowly. As she did, she caught sight of the dragons in the window of the den. "That's because you're scared of what you might hear."

"Pardon?"

"Your logical mind is shutting off your subconscious because you won't allow yourself to believe what's happening. It's like Tinker Bell in Peter Pan. Tink dies unless you convince yourself that fairies truly exist."

"Fairies?" David gave his nose a sceptical twist.

"Forget it," said Zanna, and turned away again.

"OK," he said quickly, hauling her back. "Let's say I believe it. Why would a polar bear want to talk to me?"

Zanna glanced back at the ice. "Don't know, but it won't be through chance. Lorel is a legendary guardian of the Arctic. If he's here, that means he's come to help you. Or protect you, perhaps. Or he wants something from you. You've been singled out."

"Oh, cheers," said David as the hairs on his neck began to tingle. "Singled out? By a dream bear? For what?"

"Don't know," said Zanna, with a gentle shrug. "But I'd bet my last bangle it's tied up with them." She nodded at the window of the Dragons' Den.

David drew a shallow breath. That was one thing he *could* agree upon. In this house, everything centred around the dragons. "Liz knows the name 'Lorel'," he said. "It means something to her, but she won't say what. Tell you something else, she wants to meet Bergstrom. That's pretty weird, don't you think?"

Zanna parted her lips with a gentle smack. She stretched back her neck and let her hair shower down to the level of her waist. For once, David saw her as a girl, not a Goth. In profile, she was really quite beautiful, he thought.

"Think I'll have that cup of tea now," she said, boldly looping her arm through his. "And break out the biccies; we need to talk."

"About Lorel?"

"Lorel, the dragons, your landlady, everything. It's time to unlock a few secrets, David."

"Secrets?"

"Of forty-two, Wayward Crescent..."

David makes a wish

"This is Gadzooks," David said, putting the dragon on the kitchen table.

Zanna rested two fingers on his wide flat feet and turned him carefully left and right. "He's sweet. Does he like biscuits?" She waved one hopefully in front of his snout. Gadzooks, as always, remained perfectly composed and flawlessly polite. Zanna gave up and ate the biscuit herself. "So, what's he do? Write your shopping list or something?"

David pulled out a chair and sat. "Not far off. He's kind of…inspirational. I wrote this story for Lucy once and—"

"Story?" A crumb or two of oatmeal landed on the table as Zanna's mouth struggled to contain her surprise. "Rain, I'm impressed. You're heaving with talent. What was it about?"

"An injured squirrel we found in the garden."

"Wow. How glam. I'm mates with a writer. Are you going to have it published?"

"I don't know. Maybe. I've got to go and talk to an editor woman. Which reminds me, I need to ring her, actually."

"Cool, do it now."

"Later, I'm telling you about Gadzooks. When I was doing the squirrel story, I'd get stuck sometimes and he'd sort of…help me. If I picture him in my mind I sometimes see him write things on his pad. It was him who wrote 'Lorel' when I was talking to Bergstrom."

"Really?"

"Mmm. He got very excited."

"Bergstrom?"

"No! Zookie, you woodentop. I thought you were smart? When Gadzooks showed me the name, he stomped and blew smoke rings. He doesn't normally do that."

Zanna munched on her biscuit and frowned in thought. "Did you tell Bergstrom this?"

"Are you kidding? He'd think I was nuts. Listen, can I ask you something?"

"I'm all ears," she said (though mostly they were occupied by silver skulls and rings).

David traced the grain of the table a moment. "When you came in, you said the house had an aura."

"Hmm. It's like a thumping heart."

"Liz used a word called 'auma' once. Is that different? She said it meant 'fire'."

Nodding gently, Zanna replied, "The auma is supposed to be an animating force, just like dragons are the animating spirit of the natural world. All things bright and beautiful and creative: that's the auma at work. As for dragons, all that stuff about them capturing maidens is a pile of tosh. That's a picture people have painted because they're scared of things they don't understand. The dragons' true role was much more dignified. They were the defenders of the Earth and the servants of Gaia."

"Of who?"

"Gaia – the Earth goddess. You've never heard of the Gaia principle?" She took another biscuit and dunked it in her tea. "Tch, Rain, you're such a dunce. The Gaia principle posits the idea that the Earth is a living organism."

"It breathes..." David muttered, remembering now what Lucy had said about the dragon fire at the centre of the Earth.

"Yes. One good housepoint. It regulates its environment and weather patterns according to its changing needs. No matter what nastiness we get up to, zap ourselves to dust with nuclear weapons, poison the oceans with toxic pollutants, Gaia – the Earth – will always adjust and survive, in time. This is not to say that we, the nauseating dots of life that corrupt every corner of this beautiful planet, can afford to be totally irresponsible and do what we like. Far from it. Our role is to live in harmony with Gaia. The more we nurture the planet, the better and more natural a life we'll have. Hey, I'm good at this soap box stuff, aren't I?"

"Wonderful," said David, with his tongue in his cheek. "So where does he fit in?" He nodded at Gadzooks.

"Well, the more auma something has, the more animated or lively or creative it is, and therefore the closer to Gaia it becomes. When you picture Gadzooks in your mind, you're basically admitting you believe in him. That raises his auma – to a pretty high level by the sound of things. I reckon Bergstrom was thinking about Lorel when you took that talisman, and Gadzooks picked up on it. When you're in that enlightened state, you can access other planes of being. A bit like Bonnington being aware of Lorel in the garden."

"But that still doesn't explain why Lorel's come. How am I supposed to find that out?"

"Keep dreaming. Let him talk or show you things. Just be open to it, that's all."

David sat back, frowning heavily. He thought about the dream he'd had – of the island which looked like a jagged tooth. Was Lorel trying to show him something then? Where did that fit in with dragons? He rocked forward and stroked Gadzooks. "This auma thing. Is it possible for someone else to raise it, to make it seem like...?" He tipped his head towards the dragon and flapped his fingers to indicate flight.

"He flies?" Zanna whispered, letting her mouth drop open.

David stood up, with a finger to his lips. He took the listening dragon off the top of the fridge, opened the bread bin and shut it inside. "Precaution," he said, and took his seat again. "Liz told me this story once about a dragon called Gawain, the last dragon in the world. Liz has a funny way of telling stories. She sings you a sort of growly lullaby that makes you dream you're living the plot. And that means you see things you wouldn't...normally see."

"Cool," went Zanna. "Sing me the lullaby."

"I can't. She kind of trills it from the back of her throat."

"Dragonsong, yes. I've read about it somewhere. Wow, this is great. Tell me the story."

So David repeated what he'd told to Dr Bergstrom, and Zanna, like Bergstrom, was intrigued by two things: Gwilanna, and what had become of Gawain's fire tear.

"Don't know about Gwilanna," David said, "but Liz told me the fire tear is hidden somewhere. I reckon it's—"

"In the Arctic," Zanna guessed, shortening her gaze.

"That's the connection to Lorel. It must be."

"Fine. I get that. But what does he want?"

"Don't know," she muttered, thinking hard. "Show me this den, the place where Liz works. There's gotta be a clue there, somewhere."

"I'm not sure," said David, leaning back. "There are dragons up there that are very special to Liz and Lucy."

Zanna tilted her head. A sparkle danced in her large dark eyes.

David squirmed and knew he was powerless to resist. "All right," he caved in, "but just a quick peek."

As he led the way upstairs, every creak sounded like a cannon shot. He felt sure that Gruffen would appear at any moment, life-sized, wings spread, forks of fire pouring out of his throat. But the door of the Dragons' Den was ajar, and no guard dragon barred the way to it. David took a deep breath and pushed it open. "In you go; lady Goths first."

Zanna walked in, gasping with a mixture of joy and astonishment much as David had done when he'd first seen the room. Shelf upon shelf of green-eyed dragons, all frozen in their various scaly poses. To David's relief, Gruffen wasn't on his usual perch. G'reth stood there instead, glazed and beautiful in his newness and looking terribly eager to be of assistance.

Zanna homed in on him straight away. "Oh, you gorgeous, gorgeous creature."

"He's mine, actually," David said, with a modest streak of affiliated vanity. "I named him G'reth."

"He's fabulous," said Zanna. "Very photogenic."

"He's a wishing dragon. You put your thumbs in his paws and make a wish."

Zanna immediately had a try. "I wish some tall, mop-haired geography student would shower me with roses and whisk me into his open arms."

A second went by. Zanna removed her thumbs. She smiled bashfully at David, whose face was like stone. "Hasn't worked, has it?"

"Only the maker – that's Lucy, who's already had a go – and the owner are allowed a wish. And it has to be something beneficial."

"Oh," said Zanna, suitably chastened. "What did Lucy wish for, then?"

"Snow, as it happens."

"It worked?" Zanna's pupils blossomed like flowers.

"*Zan-na?*"

"You try."

David screwed up his face. "I'm not playing wishing games."

"It's not a game, dummy. You're raising his auma. *Believe*. Wish for something – about Gawain."

"Such as?"

"Such as finding out where his *fire tear* is hidden?"

David stepped back, shaking his head. "No. That's not a good idea." *Not here*, he thought, *with all these dragons looking on*.

Zanna grabbed him by the sleeve and tugged him forward. "The fact that you're afraid of this only confirms you think it could happen. Do you want to know the truth or not?"

David sighed and looked away. This is ridiculous, he told himself. It won't work. It can't work. A wishing dragon? It was the stuff of fairy tales. But knowing he'd get no peace until he tried, he touched his thumbs to G'reth's smooth paws.

"Careful," whispered Zanna, "you're making him wobble."

David steadied his hands and tried again. "I wish," he drawled, "that I knew the secret of Gawain's fire tear."

He drew away, into the silence. Not a *hrrr* could be heard. Not a scale was rattled. He peered about the room. Not a purple eye in sight. Phew.

"Hey ho," shrugged Zanna. "It was worth a try."

"Um," David grunted, and closed his eyes briefly,

trying to picture Gadzooks. And that was when he knew that all was not well. The dragon had lowered his pencil and pad and was rolling his eyes in search of something, as if some force was about to descend. Something was coming.

Something bad.

"Zanna—" David turned to tell her, but she had moved across the room to another long shelf.

"These are sweet," she said, bending forward to examine a row of baby dragons, all breaking out of their eggs.

"Bestsellers, for broody mums. Listen, I—"

"Here's one that hasn't hatched." Zanna picked up a fully-formed egg, nestling in a stand of intertwining sticks. It was bronze in colour and had a slightly pitted surface.

"Zanna, put it down. Liz'll go spare if you break anything."

"I won't drop it," she said, cupping the egg very close to her breast. "It's very relaxing, holding this. It makes me feel...I don't know. Warm."

"Well, cool off quick and put it back. We should leave. I've got a feeling that something's not right."

But Zanna held tighter than ever to the egg, caressing it and speaking softly to it as she moved towards the window and Liz's workbench. "Who's this?" she asked, coming face to face with an elegant dragon at the back of the bench.

"Definitely, one hundred percent, do *not* touch that. That's Guinevere, Liz's special dragon. If you knock that over, we're cinders, I'm telling you."

Zanna tilted her head. "She wants it," she whispered.

"Eh?" said David. "What are you talking about?"

"Can't have it," said Zanna, almost spitting like a cat. "My baby. My egg. It's Zanna's b—"

"Zanna, what's the matter?" David grappled her arm.

"No!" she squealed, trying to fight him off. In the struggle, the egg fell out of her arms. It dropped onto the workbench, spinning. Whole.

"Zanna!" David shook her till her eyes began to clear.

"What – what happened?" she whispered, flattening herself against his chest.

"I don't know. You went weird. You were talking about babies. You wanted that bronze-coloured egg."

"Egg…" she blinked and reached to touch it.

"No," said David, knocking against the bench as he pulled her away. The egg jostled and twitched like a compass needle, then rolled to a rest at Guinevere's feet. At the moment of contact, David thought he saw the surface of the egg begin to ripple. But as he squinted and focused, the clunk of a car door sounded nearby and he jerked his head sharply to the front of the house. "What was that?"

Zanna touched his hand and gulped.

"Oh no," said David, turning white. "They shouldn't be home for ages yet." He yanked Zanna's arm and dragged her to the landing. "Quick. Downstairs. Let me do the talking. You've been here two minutes, dropping off a book. Got it?"

"Yes. No! What about the tea mugs?"

"All right…ten minutes. Make yourself presentable."

"David!"

"Zanna, don't argue. Come *on-nn*." They clattered downstairs and bumped to a halt beside the front door. David pulled her to his opposite side. "You never went upstairs. And I'm just showing you out, OK?"

"Such charm," she muttered, parting her hair.

"Ready?" David was panting now. He bit his lip as a figure appeared behind the wafers of stippled glass in the door. He said a quick prayer and whooshed it open. "Liz!" he exclaimed in a cheery voice.

But it wasn't Liz. It was a stern-looking woman with pinned, white hair and black brogue shoes, dressed in a smart-fitting slate-grey suit. By her side was a suitcase. Perched on top of the suitcase was a dragon. A

Pennykettle dragon. It had a sort of quiver over its shoulder and a posy of flowers between its paws.

David looked at the woman. The woman looked at him. Then she looked at Zanna. Then at him once more. When she smiled, it seemed to David that a whirling vortex flickered in her eyes. When she spoke, her voice carried with it all the chilling austerity of a Victorian governess.

"Well, well," she said. "What have we here? Good afternoon, children. Trick or treat...?"

Aunty Gwyneth calls

"If you've come to see Liz, she's out," muttered David, flicking his gaze between the woman and the dragon, and wondering what the suitcase was for.

"How very inconvenient," the woman said. She slid one fine hand over the other as though she was about to draw a rabbit from a hat. "Let me guess: you must be Elizabeth's lodger?"

"Yes. How did you know that?"

"Are you her mother?" asked Zanna.

The woman gave out a derogatory laugh. "We are related," she said, in a lofty tone. "But that's really none of your business. Now, let me in. It's beginning to rain."

"No, it isn't," said David. "It's—" But to his astonishment, the space behind the woman, which a moment ago had been occupied by sunshine, had suddenly filled up with a transparent drizzle. The woman produced an umbrella from somewhere and snapped it open above her head.

Before David could respond, Zanna gave him a nudge and nodded down the drive. Liz's car had just pulled onto it.

With a curious mixture of dread and relief, David said

tartly, "Mrs Pennykettle's home," just as Lucy jumped out of the car and said, "Mum, who's that?"

She doesn't know one of her own relatives? thought David. He glanced at Liz. Her expression was not far short of his own: surprise, with a hefty element of shock.

Lucy raced up. She jerked, wide-eyed, at the sight of Zanna, stared boldly at the woman and then at her dragon. "You've got a dragon," she said, which, despite being a rather elementary observation, was nonetheless one that David would have liked to have voiced himself.

"Yes," said the woman, her voice as clear as a glacial raindrop. "Her name is Gretel, and you may carry her indoors if you wish."

Lucy picked up the dragon and caressed it like a doll. Her gaze fell on Zanna. "Who's she?" she asked David.

Liz was on the premises before he could answer. "Well, this is very…unexpected," she breezed. She plumped her hair and forced a smile onto her lips. She glanced briefly at Zanna, then turned to the woman. "Have you…introduced yourself?"

"My feet are beginning to ache," said the woman. She put her nose in the air and folded her umbrella. The rain stopped as if she'd brought the clouds to a close.

"What kind of dragon is Gretel?" asked Lucy.

90

"Lucy, never mind that for now," said her mum. "Say hello to…Aunty Gwyneth."

The white-haired woman cast her eyes down. "The last time I saw *you*, my dear, you were no bigger than a seaside pebble."

"Pebble?" queried David, thinking that was a strange comparison.

"Why don't we all go inside," said Liz with her customary habit of bustling things along. "Lucy, run and put the kettle on, please. David, could you bring Aunty Gwyneth's case."

"Take it directly to my room," said Aunty Gwyneth. She stepped inside, parting David and Zanna like a couple of skittles. She was halfway down the hall when she paused and hooked a spider's web off the stairwell. For one dreadful moment, David thought she was going to eat it. But Aunty Gwyneth merely squashed it between her fingers and let her gaze roll slowly up the stairs. For a second or two, the whole house seemed to be holding its breath, as if the aura that Zanna had spoken of was suddenly as taut as the skin of a balloon. David was convinced he heard dragon scales rattling, but before he could really tune his ears to the sound Aunty Gwyneth snapped her fingers and everyone jumped. "Come, child," she barked, and with a twist of her heels she took a sharp left turn and disappeared into the lounge, Lucy bearing Gretel like a standard in her wake.

"Is she staying?" David said immediately to Liz.

Liz blew a deep sigh and gave a slightly woolly answer. "I'm just as surprised as you to see her here."

"What did she mean 'take the case to her room'? What room? Where's she going to sleep?"

"Leave the case in the hall for now. I'll sort something out, once I've had a chance to assess the situation."

"She's not having *my* room," David said bluntly. "I'm not moving. I'm a lodger. I pay."

"David." And now there was a nip in Liz's voice. "I said, we'll talk about this later. Just live with it for now, OK?"

"I'd better be off," Zanna said meekly. David and Liz both turned to her then and started to make apologetic noises.

It was David who eventually simplified things. "Liz, this is Zanna from college. She's a friend. She's on my course."

Liz held out a hand. Zanna shook it. "Pleased to meet you, Mrs Pennykettle. I really like your dragons."

"Yes," said Liz, looking deep into her eyes. "Yes, I expect you do." She dropped Zanna's hand and backed away slowly. "Excuse me. Lucy seems to have disappeared, so I'd better go and put the kettle on myself." With that, she drifted into the kitchen.

"What was all that about?" Zanna whispered. "Did you see the way she looked at me? What's going on?"

David realised he was shaking slightly and couldn't for the life of him understand why. "I don't know. Liz doesn't miss much, though. Maybe she knew you'd been in the den?"

"So? I didn't *do* anything, did I?"

David shook his head, but privately he was wondering about that egg. And Gadzooks. The dragon had not been happy. Had he sensed that Aunty Gwyneth was coming? And if so, why had he looked so worried?

"Here," said Zanna. She unzipped a purse that looked no bigger than a pirate's eye patch. From it, she pulled out a business card. "My address and mobile number. Call if you need me. Anytime, OK?"

"Erm, fine. Thanks. But why would I need you?"

Zanna clicked her tongue and steadied herself. Then sliding her hand round the back of David's neck, she pulled him forward and kissed him on the mouth. "There. That's just in case you never do. But somehow, I think you will. I don't know who that woman is, but I'll tell you who she's not."

"Uh?" muttered David, still shocked by the kiss.

Zanna found her car keys and stepped outside. "She's not Liz's aunty, and her name's not Gwyneth. Take care, Rain. Use the number."

Flower power

David watched Zanna disappear up the path and continued waving till her car was out of sight. He tried more than once to utter 'goodbye' but his mouth was still recovering from the strength of her kiss. It was like being numbed by a dental injection, though much more enjoyable and not as long-lasting. He thought about Sophie then, and his lips, though deadened, soon managed to straighten to a guilty line. Sophie might be in Africa, but they were still going out. Did that mean he'd two-timed her? Did a single kiss count? Sighing, he turned and looked at the suitcase. So, he was a bell-boy now. But who for exactly? Who *was* the mysterious white-haired visitor who might not be an aunty or a Gwyneth? He searched for a name tag, but none was present. Neither could he see a zip or a buckle anywhere on the case at all. Puzzled, he carried it into the hall. It felt weightless and airy, as if all it contained was a box of tissues. He was about to turn it over and examine it further when Liz's voice called him into the kitchen.

The moment he walked in, he knew he was in trouble. Her gaze rolled away from him towards the bread bin. She had taken off the lid, but not removed the contents. The listening dragon! He'd forgotten to put it back on the fridge.

"You know, this has got to stop," she said.

"I'm sorry," he muttered, trying to look anywhere but into her face. He stepped forward and returned the listener straight away.

"And that?" Her gaze flickered over the book. It was still on the table where David had left it.

"Zanna brought it. Research – for my essay."

"Research," Liz repeated, folding her arms. Not a good sign, and David knew it. He braced himself for what he knew was coming next. "Did you take Zanna into the den?"

"Yes," he answered quietly. There was no point lying.

"Did she touch anything?"

"No, not really."

"What do you mean, 'not really'?"

"She picked up an egg."

"The bronze one?"

"Yes."

Liz closed her eyes. When she opened them again, her gaze settled into the middle distance. "I see. You'd better go to your room."

David looked up, annoyed. "I'm not a little boy."

"This is my house," Liz said curtly, stabbing a finger

onto the dragon book. "I don't object to you bringing friends home, but I do expect you to respect my privacy. You should not have taken Zanna into the den, not without my permission, anyway."

"But—?"

"David, please. Disappear for a while. I need to make arrangements…for my aunt."

Knowing protests would be futile, he turned to leave, but found his way immediately blocked by Lucy. "Mum, Aunty Gwyneth says don't forget to put a slice of lemon in her tea and, Mum, Gretel is a *potions* dragon."

"What?" said David. "What's a potions dragon?"

"I'm not talking to you," said Lucy.

"Oh, thanks. And what have I done to *you?*"

Lucy, contradictory as ever, replied, "*She* had a dog collar round her neck—"

"Lucy, do the lemon," Liz said tartly.

"—and a tattoo."

"Lucy."

"And tassles."

"So?" said David. "What's wrong with tassles?"

Lucy pinned him with an unforgiving glare. "Are you going to tell Sophie you snogged a *witch?*"

"Lucy!" said her mum. "That's very naughty."

And David, for once, had right on his side. "What I

do is my business," he said to Lucy, almost coming nose to nose. "Zanna is a *friend*, not a girlfriend, or a witch. And I've told you before not to spy on me." He shoved her aside and stomped to his room, closing his ears to any more jibes.

His first impulse was to pack. Get out of this madhouse. Live a life of jolly squalor with other students. But as he paced back and forth, weighing his outrage against his guilt, he decided that quitting was the weaker option. He should stand firm, assert himself, protect his rights. No cantankerous old woman was going to oust him! Or any nosy little girl for that matter. And as for Liz. Well, she often showed people round the Dragons' Den, didn't she? And putting a dragon in a bread bin was hardly a crime! He sat at the computer and switched it on. A short, sharp letter would suffice for this. A list of his grievances and expectations. He would apologise, of course, for causing any upset, but remind Liz, in no uncertain terms, that he had a verbal contract to rent this room and would not, in any circumstances, think about resigning it.

"Come on, come on," he moaned at the computer. As usual, it was taking a lifetime to boot. Impatient, he dashed upstairs to the loo. By the time he'd returned, the desktop was loaded. He reached for the mouse – and leapt back in shock. Aunty Gwyneth's dragon was sitting on his mouse mat.

"Lucy!" David shouted. "This isn't funny!" Now who was invading whose privacy, exactly?

He waited half a minute, but Lucy didn't come. Frowning, he studied Gretel hard. She was a pretty little dragon with short, neat wings but a slightly larger pattern of scales than the others. Her glaze was a darker shade of green as well, which gave the impression that despite her sweet, charismatic appearance, she was really rather old, even from another age. What fascinated David most were her eyes. They were specked with a myriad of tiny pits, which caught the light from all directions and spiralled it around like a swirling pool.

David rolled his chair a fraction closer. Was it his imagination, or was the dragon inviting him to smell her flowers? She had three in her posy: pink, yellow, white. David leaned in to sniff them. Away to his right, he thought he heard a gentle rattling sound, like the noise the scales of a dragon might make if the dragon was gently quaking with fear. It didn't stop David inhaling. A light scent of honey and cinnamon sticks pricked the capillaries in his nostrils. He blinked cross-eyed and pulled away again. "Hmm, very refreshing," he muttered. "Now, where was I...?" And he reached out and switched his computer off. Then he dropped to his knees and fished out a sports bag from under his bed. Ten minutes later, he'd filled it with clothes and some of his smaller personal effects. He put on his jacket and hoisted the sports bag onto his shoulder. He waved at Gretel. Her eyes had turned a very bright violet. Then he left the room.

Reaching the lounge he knocked politely and popped his head around the door. Aunty Gwyneth and Lucy were watching television and having a debate about dinosaurs. A taut-looking Liz was sitting in her chair.

"Right, I'm away," David announced. "Thanks for having me. I'll be back for the bigger stuff in a few days."

He smiled and pulled the door to.

He was halfway up the drive when Liz came haring after him. She put herself in front of him and held his arms. "David? What are you doing?"

"Leaving," he said, with a smile and a shrug. "I thought it was all arranged?"

"Arranged? Who with?"

"Aunty Gwyneth of course."

"David, nothing's arranged. What's she done to you?"

David chuckled softly. "Liz, I know we had a bit of a spat, but when it's time to go, it's time to go. Come on, give me a hug. Then I'll be off."

"David, you're not going anywhere," she said, crossly throwing back her thick red hair. "Turn round and walk back into the house."

"Liz-zz, I'm going to miss my bus."

"David, look at me. Straight in the eyes."

David looked. "That's funny, they've gone all purple," he muttered, then immediately fell into a heap at her feet.

"Oh, David, what am I going to do with you?" she sighed.

Strangely, her answer was close at hand. A door clicked open and Mr Bacon stepped out onto his porch. He raised himself on tiptoes and peered across the drive. "Problem, Mrs P?" he asked.

The quickened egg

The next morning began with an argument.

"Henry's?! You want me to move in with *Henry?*"

"Just for a day or two," said Liz.

Lucy, stomping past in her coat and boots, said, "Serves him right, for bringing *her* here. I'm going in the garden to look for Spikey."

The back door banged. Liz winced and shut it to.

"I am not living with Henry," said David. "I'd rather sleep in Bonnington's basket!"

"That's a point. Have you seen Bonnington this morning?"

"No. Can we get back to the important subject, please?"

Liz moved forward and held his forearms. "Look, I really need this from you. Lucy's room is too small for Aunty Gwyneth – she likes to have space…to spread out her things."

"What things? That case was as light as a feather."

Liz counted a moment then tried again. "Please, you'll be doing me a huge favour. You can still eat here. None of that changes. I just need your room, that's all."

"Liz, I'm not going to Henry's, full stop. You know we're like chalk and peas."

"Cheese," she corrected. "The expression is cheese."

"Peas, cheese…whatever. We're *different*. We don't get on. I can't believe you even thought of it!"

"David, it was *his* idea. He offered – to help me out of a scrape. Say yes, and I'll forget about the rent you owe. A whole two weeks? That's got to be worth considering, hasn't it?"

David chewed it over. Rent debt removed? That *was* tempting. But living with *Henry?* He took a deep breath. "Make it three and it's a deal."

"Good boy." Liz smiled and pinched his cheek. "Best of all, Henry says you can stay for free – as long as you keep to his rules, that is."

"Rules? What rules?"

"He has rules, David, all landlords do: thou shalt not put the dragon in the bread bin, hmm?"

David glanced at the bread bin and grimaced. "You know that dragon of Aunty Gwyneth's?"

"Yes," said Liz, looking slightly piqued.

"I dreamt last night that it asked me to leave."

"Really?" said Liz, whipping up a false smile. "Well, that'll be your writer's imagination at work, won't it? Which reminds me, have you rung Dilys thingy?" She tapped the letter from Apple Tree Publishing, which was still on the worktop, in front of the microwave.

"Left a message on her voice mail," David replied, just as the outside door swung open and Lucy raised her shoulders in a bit of a huff. "Mum, I can't find Spikey."

Liz groaned with motherly frustration. "Well, that's hardly surprising, is it? Hedgehogs are nocturnal. They only come out at night."

"And he won't have like being disturbed," added David. "You've probably scared him off."

"Or your *witch* has."

"Oh, pack it in, you two," Liz scolded. "Things are difficult enough without the pair of you bickering like a couple of sparrows. Lucy, stop calling…Zanna, is it? a witch. I'm sure under all that make-up and metal she's a very nice girl. You certainly know how to pick them, David. She's got a gorgeous figure."

"Eh?"

"Don't pretend you haven't *looked*," said Lucy. She turned again to her mum. "What shall I do?"

"What about?"

"*Spikey.*"

Liz batted a hand. "I agree with David. If Spikey's got any sense he'll have gone next door for some peace and quiet."

Lucy dropped her shoulders and sighed.

"Anyway, have you seen Bonnington this morning?"

"No." Lucy switched her gaze to the lodger. "If I say I'll properly talk to you again, will you look for Spikey when you go next door?"

"No, I'm busy."

"But you promised *ages* ago that you'd help me look after any animal that came to our garden."

David opened the door to the hall. "I'm *busy*," he repeated. "I'll go and make some space in my room," he said to Liz, "then I'll pop next door and see what's what." He shot Lucy a withering glance. "Oh, all right. When I get a chance I'll have a root round Henry's garden, OK?"

"Yes," she beamed, balling her fists. "Spikey's important. You ask Gadzooks."

"Yeah, yeah," David yawned, and he drifted away.

It took about fifteen sweaty minutes to rearrange half his room into a corner and pack some loose things away into his wardrobe. He even dragged his desk into the opposite alcove to give Aunty Gywneth as much 'space' as possible. The last thing he did was move Gadzooks. "You don't want to go to Henry's, do you?" he asked. Gadzooks offered no opinion either way. David tickled his snout and took him to the wardrobe. "Brought you a friend," he said to Grace, and slid Gadzooks into place beside her.

Grace stared frostily back.

"Try and look a bit more grateful," said David, and hurriedly closed the wardrobe door.

In the hall, on his way out, he bumped into Aunty Gwyneth. She was dressed in a watery, lilac-coloured suit that looked to be a replica of the one she'd arrived in. "Leaving?" she enquired with a faint air of triumph. "You appear to have forgotten your bag."

"I'm coming back to pack, when I've spoken to Henry."

"Make it a short," she said, and sailed into the kitchen.

Cheek, thought David, sticking out his tongue. He went to the front door and opened it. But on the step, he teetered and changed his mind. Maybe the weird old biddy was right. Pack now. Get it over with. Grab some things. Go.

He banged the door shut and returned to his room.

He was reaching underneath his bed for his sports bag (and having a strange bout of *déjà-vu*) when a pair of eyes glittered like sequins in the darkness and he realised Bonnington was under there too. "I wouldn't stay there if I were you, Bonners. Aunty Gwyneth is moving in. I don't think you'll be allowed to share the duvet with her."

Bonnington didn't budge. "Come out," David whispered, scratching the mattress. Still Bonnington wouldn't move. Frowning, David stretched out a hand and grabbed the loose skin at the back of the cat's neck, dragging him forcefully into the open. Bonnington gave out a pitiful meow, jumped into the sports bag and huddled in the bottom. "What's the matter?" David tutted and hauled him out, spreading the cat longways against his shoulder. Bonnington flattened his big brown ears and dug his claws into the lodger's chest. Mystified, David bounced him like a baby till the faint swell of purring was rippling the air. "Come on, let's get you some *Truffgood*," he said, and carried the cat into the hall. He was about to shoulder his way into the kitchen when Aunty Gwyneth's gritty voice floated out.

"I understand my accommodation is settled at last?"

"Yes," said Liz, moving round the kitchen doing clattering little tasks that seemed to reflect a shortness of temper. "So no more repeats of last night's incident."

A brittle laugh escaped Aunty Gwyneth's throat. "You disappoint me, Elizabeth. I thought free-spirited dragons were your speciality. Gretel was made by your hand, after all."

The fridge rattled open. In a tone that could have been cooled by it, Liz said, "When Gretel left this house her auma was untainted. Whatever 'tricks' she performs are down to you."

"Ah, yes, the auma," her aunt said dryly, as if she had swallowed a piece of sacking. "You've been rather busy in that department, haven't you? A special dragon here; a special dragon there. All with the very special Pennykettle spark. Why is it that you have so much 'spark' at your disposal? I never have managed to work that out."

"I've told you before, I don't know," said Liz, and the bitterness in her voice was almost feudal. It was clear that her feelings about her 'aunt' ran deeper than mere annoyance at the imposition of having to house an uninvited relative. "Is that why you're here? To audit me?"

"I was called," said Aunty Gwyneth, "by a wishing dragon."

"*What?*" There was shock in Liz's voice now. In the hall David's heart began to beat so hard it was almost throwing Bonnington into the air. He switched the cat to his opposite shoulder and put his eye to the crack of the door.

Liz was frowning in disbelief. "Called? By G'reth? That's impossible. Lucy can't be advanced enough to make a true wisher. Besides, David wouldn't know what to say."

Aunty Gwyneth put her fingertips on Liz's shoulders and pressed her gently into a chair. "Be calm, my dear. Perhaps you underestimate your daughter's talent? She has clearly inherited something of your...gift. As for your dreary lodger, he was curious – about the tear of Gawain."

"Oh, and that would bring you running," seared Liz.

"Do not mock me," Aunty Gwyneth hit back. "We need each other; it's always been the way." She picked up an apple and turned it in her fingers. David blinked and looked at it twice. He could have sworn it had just changed colour: from a pale pinky-red to a soft yellow-green.

"I am intrigued," said Aunty Gwyneth, her voice floating again, "to find myself drawn by this dragon's call. It remains to be seen, of course, what part I have to play in attempting to grant your lodger's wish."

"No." Liz shook her head fast and hard. "This is nonsense. There's been a mistake. If we were meant to know where the tear is hidden, you would have found out long before now. Go back. There's nothing for you here, Gw—"

Aunty Gwyneth stopped her with a finger to her lips. "Oh, but my dear, you must not be so hasty. The universe has strange ways, does it not?" She let her hand drift sideways, catching the curls of Liz's red hair. "So beautiful. So like Guinevere herself." She dropped her hand and stared Liz in the eye. "The boy has done you a surprising service. You will be thankful of my presence before the full moon rises."

From the doorway, David saw Liz start. "What's that supposed to mean?"

Aunty Gwyneth's voice came circling like a hawk, low and steady, cold and bewitching. "I sent Gretel into your den last night. And before you think of it, she quickly subdued the foolish little dragon you employ to stand guard. Amongst your trinkets, she found an egg."

"It's just a bronze," said Liz.

"It's been quickened," said her aunt, "and claimed by your dragon."

"Don't be ridiculous. That can't happen."

"It can," said Aunty Gwyneth with a whip of her tongue. "The girl your lodger brought into this house has the quickening gift. You must have sensed it."

"She...?" Liz faltered and lowered her head. "I thought I felt something in her aura. But it's been so long. I wasn't sure—"

"Then let me remind you," Aunty Gwyneth cut in. Slowly, she opened her hands. In the cup of her palms was the bronze-coloured egg that Zanna had jealously protected in the den. David eased his position to get a better look, all the while keeping a tight hold of Bonnington. The egg appeared to be gently glowing, but its shell, or something just below the shell, was in constant movement, like clouds circling the surface of a planet.

"The change has begun," Aunty Gwyneth said. "In four days time the egg will be kindled. You must be readied for the transfer of auma."

Liz shook her head. "This can't be possible. I wasn't trying for a child. I—"

"Trying is meaningless," Aunty Gwyneth snapped. "You know as well as I do the child does the choosing, not the parent." She lowered the egg into Liz's hands. "You should count my coming as providence, my dear. Gretel has reported a high proliferation of egg-like sculptures in your den. This would indicate broodiness, would it not?"

Liz looked away, troubled. "But this is so sudden. What am I going to say to Lucy?"

"You will tell her the truth. The girl will be charmed."

"And David? Don't tell me to send him away. Lucy adores him. He's like one of the family. I can't just throw him out."

Aunty Gwyneth stood back, drumming her fingers.

"The boy does present slightly more of a problem. But I will find a way to deal with him. Look into the egg, now, tell me what you see."

Liz breathed deeply and held it to the light. "Oh, Gawain…" she gasped.

In the hall, David's eye almost leapt from its socket. In the centre of the egg, where one would expect the yolk to be, was a small dark form.

"A boy," Liz breathed.

"The first for nine hundred years," said Aunty Gwyneth.

Liz sighed in wonder and held the egg close. "A boy," she whispered, and shed a light tear.

Aunty Gwyneth caught it at once and smeared it over the surface of the egg. A ray of soft purple light enveloped it. Aunty Gwyneth stood back, pleased. "Now you are joined to him in water," she said. "During the kindling, the fire will follow. The boy has chosen you as his kin. You cannot refuse; he has touched your auma."

David closed his eyes and fell back against the wall. This couldn't be happening. Liz, having a *baby*? From an egg made of clay? He risked another look. From this cramped position, he was only able to make out the crudest of shapes in the egg. He didn't doubt Liz's word:

it was a boy, for sure. But what kind of boy? What creature were they hatching? For the shape as he saw it had legs and hands and a well-pronounced forehead.

And at the base of its spine, a dragon's tail.

Flight

With clinical bluntness, Aunty Gwyneth took the egg back and somehow secreted it out of sight. "Of course, the tail will recede," she said.

"And the eyes?" asked Liz, sounding anxious.

"Oval in the early years. Oval and amber. He will be feared. You must do what you can to avoid attention. There must be no interference – from the lodger, his girl…or the bear, of course."

The mention of bears took David by surprise. The shock wave continued on to Bonnington who dug in a claw and faintly spat. David put him down and raised a finger to his lips. As the cat scuttled quietly up the stairs, David turned and listened in again. Aunty Gwyneth was talking about Lorel.

"You are aware, of course, of the Teller's presence? I could taste his stinking, seal-stained breath in every foul draught of wind along the crescent."

"Lorel is no enemy of mine," said Liz.

Aunty Gwyneth let out a scathing hiss. "Romantic poppycock! The ice bears are charlatans, not to be trusted. The time has long since passed when they might have been considered to be guardians of the tear."

Guardians? thought David. *Bears? How?* He saw Liz shaking her head.

"Why do you insist on peddling that? The bears have always kept the secret of the tear. You distrust them because they won't give it up."

"Their kingdom is in total disarray," said Aunty Gwyneth. "Their dynasties were finished millennia ago. All that exists of their *Nanukapiks* now are scraps of legend, fed to them by their storytelling phantom. How can they guard the tear? They can barely protect their precious ice. Every year more of it ebbs away. How long can it be before their stupid, lumbering kind is at an end? You and I should be the true custodians of the fire. You know it every time you roll the clay. Every time you put a spark into one of your dragons you wish for more of the essence of Gawain. You are a daughter of Guinevere. How can you deny what is yours by right? Now, speak to me about the Teller. What does the narrow-eyed snow-slinger want?"

"I don't know."

"You expect me to believe he has made no contact?"

"Not with me, no."

"With the dragons?"

"With David. He knew of Lorel's presence before I did."

"Impossible," Aunty Gwyneth snapped. "Where was your listening dragon? Asleep?"

David squinted at the dragon on the top of the fridge. It may have been the wonky thermostat, but he could swear that the little creature was trembling.

"David's...sensitive," Liz replied edgily. "He has a special dragon he named Gadzooks. A writing dragon. Their auma is high. It was Gadzooks who found the name Lorel."

"A *writing* dragon?" Aunty Gwyneth's tone became deeply nasal. She picked up the dragon book and leafed through its pages, dropping it again with a disapproving snort. "A writing dragon and a storytelling bear? Are you saying that your lodger *drew* the Teller here?"

"I don't know," said Liz, sounding flustered. "It's hard to know what David's capable of. He's inquisitive; that leads him into bother sometimes. But he's confused about the dragons, and that includes Gadzooks. He doesn't know what he has."

"He knows about Gawain," Aunty Gwyneth said coldly.

"I told him the legend; it's a fairy story to him."

"Then why is the boy in pursuit of the tear?"

"He's not," Liz insisted, touching a tired hand to her forehead, "at least, not in the way you think. He's doing

116

an essay, for college. He wants to write about the fire so he can win a competition."

"And the prize?"

Liz paused and her breath became a sigh. "A field trip – to the Arctic."

"*North?*" Aunty Gwyneth wheeled around. "He wants to travel to the land of the bears and the Teller of Ways is on his doorstep?"

"I agree, it's odd," Liz said, becoming gritty. "But I'm telling you, all David has are half-truths and fantasies. He's a geography student, working on a project. It's nothing more sinister than that. Neither he nor Gadzooks could have brought Lorel here."

"But something did," Aunty Gwyneth said, in a voice fortified with dark suspicions. "This must be addressed. The boy must be watched and the dragon tested. Removed if necessary. Returned to the clay."

Tested? thought David, jerking back. *Zookie? Returned to the clay?*

"No," said Liz. "I won't let that happen."

"You have no choice, I— wait, what was that?"

In the hall, Bonnington had suddenly come thundering down the stairs. He had skidded round the newel post, careered into a plant stand (spilling the pot, which had broken on the floor) and continued his breakneck flight into the lounge. He was either having one of his 'mad half hours' or he was trying to escape from something. David didn't hang around to find out what. The thought of being caught eavesdropping by Aunty Gwyneth filled his heart with a sinister dread. At the moment the kitchen door whooshed open he was carefully dropping the latch on his. Heart thumping, he dashed to the wardrobe, opened it quickly and grabbed Gadzooks. "I'll come back for you," he promised Grace. Then snatching his greatcoat off the bed, he rolled Gadzooks up in it and raced across the room. Within seconds he was out of the window. Lucy, hunkering by the brambles at the top of the garden, was too preoccupied to hear him touching down. Crouching low, David hurried across the slippery grey patio. With the mildest of creaks, he was through the gate and running – to the only immediate sanctuary he could think of. The house at forty-one Wayward Crescent. The home of Henry Bacon.

A surprise at Henry's

Henry was in his small conservatory, stripping dead leaves off his yucca plant, when David arrived. He almost jumped into the branches in shock when David knuckled the window and mouthed, "It's me. Let me in."

Henry stormed to the back door and threw it open. "What are you playing at, boy? Can't you use the front door, like everyone else?"

David glanced back the way he'd come, anxious that his flight had not been discovered. "I was, erm, in the garden, with Lucy. Took a short cut. Didn't think you'd mind. Can I come in? I'm sort of in a hurry."

Henry raised a hand. From his trousers, he pulled out a folded sheet of paper. *Two* sheets of paper, stapled together. It was a list of house rules. He handed them over. "Read, inwardly digest, and observe."

David glanced at the 'rules' and winced. There were thirty on the first sheet alone. He refolded them and pushed them into his pocket. "Anything you say. Now, can I please come in?"

Henry stood aside at last. With a sigh of relief, David swept past him into a kitchen that was a mirror image of number forty-two. Unlike Liz's, which bore the trademark clutter of the presence of a child, this kitchen was fastidiously clean and tidy. The tiles around the worktop glinted like stars. There wasn't a single dragon in sight.

Henry closed the door and put his hands on his hips. "Where's your luggage, boy?"

"This is all there is for now," said David, carefully unwrapping Gadzooks. "He's precious. Is there somewhere safe I can hide— I mean, put him?"

"This is a house, not a bank," Henry barked. "Put it on your bedside table if you must. And don't scratch the polish. Rule number twenty-four: lodger will be financially liable for breakages, scratches, stains—"

"Stains?"

"—and blemishes of any kind," Henry finished darkly. "Suppose you'd like to inspect your quarters?"

"Pardon?"

"Your berth, boy. Place of rest."

"Oh...yeah. Love to. Do you mind if I make a phone call first? I need to ring Zanna. It's really urgent."

Henry stiffened his shoulders.

"What now?" groaned David.

"Rule number three, boy."

David checked the list. "No *canoodling*?"

"On sofa or elsewhere," Henry said sharply. "Far too good for you, anyway, that girl. Can't see what the attraction is."

"Henry, Zanna and I are not an item."

Henry threw him a quizzical glance.

"We're not going out – not 'courting', OK? And we certainly don't 'canoodle' – not if I can help it." David frowned and dug her card from the pocket of his jeans. "Where's the phone?"

Henry nodded at the lounge. "Table, by my chair. Twenty pence, minimum charge. In the tin."

"That's robbery! You're worse than Bonnington."

"What?"

"Oh, never mind," David grumbled. He fished a twenty pence coin from his pocket and went.

Like the kitchen, Mr Bacon's living area was light, airy and extremely well-furnished. The wall that would have separated David's room from the lounge in Liz's house had been knocked out to create one large, long space. Not a cushion was out of place. A wide-screen television and an expensive-looking music system dominated one corner. A lengthy aquarium, dotted with a selection of brightly-coloured fish, also caught David's eye. He put Gadzooks on a coffee table inlaid at its centre with frosted glass, then twisted down into a leather recliner.

He lifted the phone and rang Zanna's number.

Hi, this is Zanna, her answerphone crackled. *Probably in the shower or journeying in the astral or listening to something very loud right now. Leave a message. You know you want to. Mwah!*

David switched the phone to his opposite ear. "Zanna, get out of the shower, now. It's me, David. I'm at Henry's. Gotta talk. Ring me, pronto: Scrubbley... four, double five, treble seven. It's major."

He put the phone down and flopped back, sighing.

Immediately, Mr Bacon's face appeared – upside-down over the top of the chair. "Comfortable, boy?"

"Very," said David, swinging gently from side to side.

Mr Bacon stared at him, hard. It was the sort of upside-down look that said, *The next time I catch you lounging in my chair you'll be sleeping outside in the gutter. Got it?*

David leapt up (and brushed the seat clean). "You haven't got a computer, have you?"

Mr Bacon bristled with indignance. "I'm a librarian. Of course I've got a computer."

"With internet access?"

Henry jiggled his moustache.

"Can I use it? Please?"

"Certainly not."

"But Zanna might be online in the college library."

The word 'library' seemed to soften Henry's heart. "Oh, very well," he said in a bluster. "It's in the upstairs study. Come on."

Grabbing Gadzooks, David followed Mr Bacon up the lushly-carpeted stairs. They paused on the landing by a door marked 'Study' where Henry laid down yet another of his rules. "Entrance prohibited without permission, understood?"

David nodded.

"And don't touch the models."

"Models? What models?"

Henry swung the door open.

It was like walking into a maritime museum. On the walls were a number of small glass cases; each containing a model of a sailing ship. Charts and maps were everywhere, some rolled up on an antique desk, on which sat a globe and an ancient-looking compass; others were pinned to the walls below the ships. There were books, of course – hundreds of them – in rows of maroon and burnished blue on solid wooden shelves showing no signs of bowing. And photographs, lots of photographs, mostly in sepia or black and white – in frames on the desk, on a pin board on the wall, propped up here and there against the spines of the books. One image stood out above all others; a striking monochrome poster that took up half of the chimney wall. It was a close-up of a polar bear, photographed head-on. The bear was poised by a lead of water. It had its head bent low as though about to take a drink, but its darkly rounded eyes were raised in full and lordly awareness. One glance made David feel strangely humble.

"Lorel," he whispered, and for a moment the room seemed to whisper back, as if every book had rustled its pages and every sailing ship had creaked its beams.

"What's that, boy? Did you utter something?"

"No, nothing," David said, turning and looking more closely at things. It occurred to him now that this room was set in a certain age, somewhere at the start of the twentieth century. The ships were old-fashioned sailing vessels, the maps all charted the polar regions, and the photographs... He popped Gadzooks down beside the computer (which looked a little incongruous amongst so much memorabilia) and picked up a small framed photo of a group of men dressed in heavy sweaters and crumpled, baggy pants. They had the look of wartime aviators. They were standing on an ice field, resting on spades. Behind them rose the bow of a three-masted ship.

"My grandfather; polar explorer," explained Henry.

"That's him there, boy, second on the right. Just lost an ear and two toes to frostbite. Didn't stop him doing his share of digging. Took sixteen men to free that ship from pack ice in the South Weddell sea. If they hadn't, Bacon grandson, H, wouldn't have been here to tell the tale."

"I can see the likeness," David said, nodding. He put the snap down. "Who photographed the bear?"

"Ah," said Henry, turning away. "Interesting tale behind that one, boy. Man who took that disappeared in unusual circumstances in 1913. Lost, presumed dead, on an exploration to the Hella glacier."

"Hella? I've heard of that. Isn't it one of the oldest and largest glaciers in the Arctic? What happened?"

Henry picked a reference book off the shelves. He used a handkerchief to flag some dust off the spine, then flipped the pages, talking as he searched, "No one knows. Bit of a mystery. People say he wandered off to find his watch."

"*What?*"

"Had a dodgy incident a few months before. Found himself stranded near a native settlement with a large male polar bear for company. No rifle, and too far away from camp to summon help. All he had about him was a pocket watch. Played a tune when you opened the casing. Our chap set it down in front of the bear. Story

125

goes, the beast swaggered up to the watch, sat down, watch betwixt paws, and listened. Our chappie backed off and escaped to camp. Went back with his comrades twenty minutes later, but the watch and the bear had both disappeared."

"Who was this man?" David asked nervously.

Henry turned the book around. He pointed to a plate at the bottom of a page. "Third from the left. Fair-haired. Scandinavian."

David cast his eyes down.

It was Dr Bergstrom.

To the library gardens

As David's mind wrestled with the impossible conundrum of how a man in his forties, who lectured at Scrubbley College, could look exactly like a polar explorer reported missing in 1913, the house came alive with the trill of telephones. David thought he detected four at least. Henry snapped the book shut and returned it to the shelf. "Something amiss, boy? You look a bit pasty."

"I'm fine," said David, "just...thinking, that's all." He cupped his hand around Gadzooks and looked through the slatted window blinds. There was a good view of the Pennykettles' garden from here. He picked out Lucy right away, still by the brambles, pottering about with her hedgehog book. A slightly moody-looking Bonnington was sitting near the rockery, paws tucked under his tummy, watching. And in the centre of the lawn, as if a cloud had dripped and left a great white blot, lay the hunk of ice that had once been a snowbear, still surviving despite the rain. As Henry lifted a phone and the house became silent, David thought about Lorel and turned to look at the bear print again. For a fleeting moment he became the bear, looking back into the lens of Bergstrom's camera. And from somewhere between the bear and the man, from the bright cold wilderness of frozen ages, from the leaves of books, from the creaking timbers of ice-bound vessels, came a voice like a wind from another world saying, *There was a time when the ice was ruled by nine bears…*

"Nine…" David whispered – then nearly hit the ceiling as he took a sharp prod in the ribs from Henry.

"Suzanna. For you." Henry handed him a phone. "I'll be downstairs. Don't touch anything."

David waited for his pulse to return to normal then said a clipped hello.

"Rain!" she breezed back. "You called. I'm dazed. You sound kinda toasted. What're you doing at Henry's?"

"Liz needed my room for Aunty Gwyneth. I'm staying with Henry till she goes."

"Cripes. Have a medal. What's happening in dragon land?"

"Lots. We need to meet."

"Sure. Come to college. Remember college? Big stone building. Holds things called lectures, which you frequently miss on Monday mornings."

"Too public. I need to see you somewhere quiet."

"Steady, you're making my tassles dance."

"Zanna, get serious. Listen to this: Mr Bacon's just

shown me a picture of Bergstrom."

"Bergstrom?"

"Yeah. It's over ninety years old."

"Erm, right. I *think* you need to be a little less generous next time you put the clocks back, David. I've just seen the fair-haired doctor in the car park. I know he's kind of old but he's not a pickled wreck, which he'd have to be if—"

"Zanna, this isn't a joke. There's something weird going on here, believe me. We *need* to talk. Do you know the library gardens in the middle of town?"

"Course."

"Meet me there in twenty minutes."

"Rain, I've got a lecture. So have you, come to that. And it's miserable outside – Zannas don't like wet."

"Fine. Bring a brolly."

"Rain!"

"This is urgent. Liz is sort of … pregnant. She's going to have a dragon child!"

There was a gulp at Zanna's end.

"Twenty minutes," said David. And he put down the phone.

They sat in David's favourite location: a small wooden bench along the narrow tarmac path where David, Lucy,

129

Liz and Sophie had once fed a host of grey squirrels by hand. No squirrels were there to greet them today, just the rain, misting through the leafless trees, casting a grey sheet over the gardens. Zanna, dressed in her usual black with only a fishnet cardigan around her shoulders, shuddered and couldn't stop her teeth from chattering.

"We need help," she said.

David nodded. A droplet of rain ran down his fringe and splashed off the middle button of his greatcoat. "Sure you don't want to wear this?"

Zanna bunched up close. "A cuddle will do."

David swung out a hesitant arm and Zanna shuffled up closer again. She felt surprisingly frail in the wrap of his shoulder. He squeezed her unintentionally as she nestled.

"Thank you," she whispered, pushing her hand inside his coat. "How's Zookie doing?"

David, who'd been holding Gadzooks in his lap, brought him up to chest height. "Better than us." He ran a thumb down the dragon's snout, smearing water off the smooth green glaze.

"Aunty Gwyneth scares me," Zanna said, shivering. "We shouldn't mess with her. She's...I don't what she is; more than a dragon midwife, that's for sure."

David lowered Gadzooks again and blew a cloud of

breath into the air. "I want to know why she's really here. She didn't come to the crescent because of the egg; finding it quickened surprised her, I think."

"If you ask me, it's obvious why she's here," said Zanna, her warm breath flowing over his neck. "You've drawn everyone into this space because you made a wish to know about the tear. Somehow, you're going to get an answer – and when you do, Aunty Spooky will be right on the scene."

"But no one knows where the fire tear's hidden."

Zanna flexed her fingers. "Lorel does."

"A ghost bear? He's hardly going to tell me his closely-guarded secrets."

"He told you that nine bears ruled the ice."

"Yeah, and what's that s'posed to mean?"

"Exactly what it says. Once, nine bears ruled the Arctic."

"Yeah, I know that," David said impatiently. "But what's it got to do with the tear?"

Zanna lifted a shoulder. "I don't know – yet. But Lorel wouldn't say it without good reason. Don't look now, but there's a squirrel on the fence."

David turned his head. A pepper-grey squirrel was balancing neatly on the flat bar between two railing hoops. "Oh, wow. It's Snigger – I think."

Chuk! went the squirrel, flagging its tail. It lifted one paw and appeared to smile.

"Cute," said Zanna. "Hello, Snigger." She dibbled her fingers and smiled right back. "He's probably come to ask you for ten percent of whatever you earn when you publish his story. Did you ring that editor yet?"

"She was in a meeting; I left a message."

Zanna raised herself to a sitting position, looked at Snigger and shook out her hair. "I'll see that he pays you – in nuts," she told him.

Snigger, who was either terribly excited at the prospect of nuts or somewhat put off by his Gothic agent, jerked back slightly then scrabbled down the fence. Within seconds he had hopped away through the trees.

"Oh, well done," David tutted.

"He'll get used to me," Zanna said, standing. "Everyone does in time; even you." She pirouetted round. "How's my bum? Is it wet?"

David glanced a bit sheepishly at it. Liz was certainly right about one thing: Zanna did have a very good figure. "No, not really."

"Good. Come on." She pulled him to his feet. In the background, the library clock (which was always wrong) bonged three times. "Eleven," said Zanna. "Lecture's over. Let's go."

"Where?"

"Walkies – to Rutherford House."

"What for?" David asked, as she looped his arm. Rutherford House was an academic residence.

"The only person who can help us happens to be staying there."

"Bergstrom?"

"Yep. He's the key to all this. He's interested in dragons and he works in the icy land of Lorel. I vote we go and ask him what he knows about the tear, and what happened on that glacier in 1913."

A meeting with Dr Bergstrom

Rutherford House was a large, grey-walled Victorian building. It was set in the grounds of Scrubbley College, close to the London railway line along the border of Scrubbley Common. It was hard to believe that a hundred years ago it had served as the local lunatic asylum, but as he crunched up the shale path with Zanna at his side, David couldn't help but think that what they were about to do could qualify as madness and see them both committed at the very first breath.

"Are you sure this is a good idea?" he asked, as they marched through a small, ivy-covered portico and Zanna ran her eye down the ladder of address tags beside the main entrance.

"Room four. Let's hope he's in."

David tried again. "There are underground cells here where they used to lock mad people up, you know. We might never get out alive."

"Then we'll end our days together, won't we?" She kissed a fingertip and dinked it to his nose. "Come on."

Through a maze of corridors, they found the room – an unimposing blue door with a small brass number. Zanna raised her fist to knock, then quickly lowered it again. "Who's doing the talking?"

David threw her an incredulous look. "Oh, good time to be asking that!"

"It's you; you're making me nervous. We'll both talk – but you start, OK?"

"Zanna?"

"That's fair. How's my hair?"

"Hair? What's your hair got to do with—?"

Suddenly, the door curled open. Both students jumped to attention. Dr Bergstrom, looking as composed as ever, scanned them with his air of unruffled poise. "Miss Martindale and Mr Rain...and dragon."

David winced and swung Gadzooks out of sight. This was a bad, bad, bad idea.

"Am I expecting you?"

"Not exactly," gulped Zanna.

"We can go if you're busy," David added.

"You look as if you've had a long walk," said Bergstrom. He smiled and waved them in. "Take a seat. The sofa's very comfortable. Swedish design. Coffee anyone?"

Both students shook their heads. They settled together on the edge of the sofa, a stylish two-seater with high curved wings and dark blue corduroy covers and cushions. Bergstrom, arms folded, perched against a writing desk strewn with academic journals and papers. He was dressed much like the last time David had met him, in a pair of grey slacks and a loose cotton shirt. He was wearing no shoes.

"Is this visit to do with your essays?" he asked.

"Done mine," said Zanna, sitting up brightly with her hands in her lap.

David made a clucking sound and looked away.

"He's still researching his," she said.

Bergstrom smiled again. "And is this a part of your research effort, David?" He stretched out a hand towards Gadzooks. "Please, may I?"

David glanced at Zanna. She gave a hesitant nod.

"That's David's writing dragon," she said, as David put him into Bergstrom's hands. "It helps him do stories. It writes things – on its pad. In his imagination, of course."

"Of course," said Bergstrom, running a hand down the dragon's spine the way David had often seen Lucy do.

There was a pause, then David felt a nudge on his ankle. "We want to know about Lorel," he said.

Bergstrom touched Gadzooks on the snout and set him down beneath the shade of a table lamp. "The only Lorel I know of is a polar bear, David. A mythical creature reputedly with ancient knowledge of the Arctic. He's well documented. You can find his name in any number of books."

"He got it when he held your talisman," said Zanna.

Bergstrom's reply was measured, but blunt. "As I recall, he didn't get anything at all."

"I keep dreaming about him," David said.

Bergstrom fixed him with a steady blue gaze. "I dream about bears all the time, David. What is it you're trying to say?"

"Lorel's here," whispered Zanna. "In David's garden."

A puff of laughter escaped the Norwegian's lips. "Then he's a very long way from home. Forgive me, this may seem rather rude, but I don't understand what you want from me."

"The truth," said Zanna, gathering courage. "About what happened on the Hella glacier."

Once again, Bergstrom paused before replying. "The Hella glacier is a dangerous place. I would advise you both to steer well clear of it."

This David took to be a warning shot, a chance for he and Zanna to back off with dignity. But he also suspected that Bergstrom was testing them, pushing them to see how much they knew and how far they were truly prepared to reach. So he took a bold chance and in a hurried voice said, "I saw your picture – in a reference book. On an expedition, in 1913."

"A fatal expedition," Zanna added quietly.

There the conversation teetered for a moment. The pause grew so intense that David almost volunteered to leave the room. It was cold in here. Colder than the gardens. His skin began to prickle as Bergstrom moved towards them. "Please. Both of you. Touch my hands. Satisfy yourselves that I am not a ghost. Perhaps you might be interested to know that several generations of my family have worked in the Arctic, in some capacity or other."

"It was you," said David, surprised at the brashness and speed of his response. "I know it was. I know about the watch. How it saved your life. You put it down on the ice to distract the bear."

"Was it Lorel?" pressed Zanna. "Was it Lorel that you met?"

"How did you get the watch back?" asked David.

Bergstrom looked at them both very carefully. "The watch was in the keeping of an Inuit shaman, who brought it to me in exchange for...the bones of a polar-bear cub."

Zanna immediately caught her breath. "Shamans have magical powers," she said. "They can—"

"What?" said David. "What can they do?"

"Become bears," she said, in a voice so frighteningly low that it seemed to soak into David's skin and pull every hair down into its root. He slowly lifted his gaze. Bergstrom was staring unwaveringly at him with that peculiar, narrow-eyed, imperious squint. Now David knew where he'd seen the look before: in the face of every polar bear he'd ever stared at – in particular, the print on Henry Bacon's study wall.

"You're Lorel?" he whispered.

Bergstrom parted his lips. "My name is Anders Bergstrom," he said. "I'm a polar research scientist, based in the town of Chamberlain, Canada. You have a vivid imagination, David. Maybe we should put it to a further test. The Inuit say that if Lorel has visited your *inua,* your soul, he will have told you something of lasting value to aid you on your journey through this life – if, and only if, you are worthy of receiving it."

"Tell him," said Zanna. "Tell him what you heard in Henry's study."

With a catch in his throat, David said quietly, "There was a time when the ice was ruled by nine bears."

Bergstrom pushed himself away from the desk. He took a key from the pocket of his slacks and unlocked one of the three desk drawers. "They had names, David, these ruling bears. Lorel was one of them. Give me one more. Then we'll talk."

"I don't know. I don't know any more."

"Try," hissed Zanna. "Use Gadzooks."

"Gadzooks cannot help him with this," said Bergstrom. He opened the drawer and took out the hand-carved, narwhal talisman. "Take the charm – right hand this time. Think about Lorel. You may experience some odd sensations."

David looked at the section of tusk. Perhaps it was a trick of the afternoon light, but he thought he could see the etchings moving. "Who are you? Really?"

"Your destiny," said Bergstrom. "Now, take the charm. Tell me what you see."

The Tooth of Ragnar

It was like entering a waking dream. As David closed his right hand around the tusk, an iris-like darkness quickly enveloped him and he was sucked back into a distant singularity, as though he had travelled through aeons of time. He found himself in an Arctic wasteland, breathless, down on his hands and knees, fists sunk hard into a seam of snow just deep enough to chill his aching wrists. Somewhere, he sensed the rhythm of water, but superficially all he could see was ice, stretching out in every direction. It was cold. Very cold. Hypothermic. The pores of his face were crusted and dry. His eyebrows, heavily frilled with rime, felt like small weights crushing the sockets. Icicles were forming in his tear ducts.

As he lifted his head and rocked back on his haunches, the wind threw a voile of white into the air. Out of it stepped a figure, a girl. Though his lips were almost rigid with cold, David managed to utter her name. "*Lucy?*"

She came forward, holding G'reth. She was humming in dragonsong, but did not speak. She set the wishing dragon on the ice, then stood back to watch him play. G'reth, bent forward, breathed on the surface to soften it a little then scooped a layer of slush into his paws. He fashioned it into a lop-sided ball, patting and smoothing until it was roughly the shape of an egg. But this was not an egg. As G'reth stood back and opened his paws (as though to utter a magic word: *hrrr!*), the thin end of the snow developed a snout. Then spikes appeared on the flanks and rear. And before David knew it, he was staring at a hedgehog. A white hedgehog, with pink, blind eyes. He leaned forward for a closer look. Tiny as the eyes of the hedgehog were, he could see in them an image of a black-lipped bear. It was old and there were fighting scars on its snout. Half of one ear had been clawed or bitten off. Bloodstains marked its neck and paws.

Suddenly, the ice bear opened its jaws. It put back its head and roared in pain. Not a pain that had come from a blow to its body, but a pain that ran deep, from a blow to its heart. It roared so hard that a tooth worked loose from its upper palate and fell, spiralling, onto the ice. As it hit, David found himself removed into the scene, watching the events from a weak ridge of ice that shook with every swipe of the bear's giant paws. Then, in a desperate fit of rage, the bear brought its left paw crashing down, pounding the lost tooth deep beneath the surface. The ice split with a plangent creak and out of its mourning rose a rock. The bear struck again and the ocean gushed. Ice lifted. More rock burst through its crust. The quake sent David tumbling off the ridge. The world shook. The Arctic ocean roiled. The cold air chimed with ice-wrecked crystals. Only when the dots had ceased to fall did David look back to see what damage had been wrought. A whole island had grown up out of nowhere. The same island he had dreamt about a few nights earlier.

And then a voice like a wind from another world spoke: *This is the tooth of Ragnar,* it said.

David fell backwards against the ridge. Now, for an instant, he saw another bear. It was younger than the first and its fur was spotless. It was treading its front paws like a cat.

"Lorel?" he muttered.

The bear shimmered in a moment of sunlit haze, then disappeared in a show of white fire.

At this point, David woke with a jerk. He was on the floor in Bergstrom's room.

"David!" cried Zanna. She dropped to her knees and draped her arms around him.

"W-what happened?" he gasped.

Bergstrom stooped to retrieve the tusk. "You released the talisman; it broke your encounter."

"You were writhing and shouting," Zanna said. "What did you do to him?" she snapped at Bergstrom.

"I'm all right," said David, getting to his knees. "I saw things. A bear. A really big male. I think his name was Ragnar."

"Yes," said Bergstrom. "A fighting bear; one of the original nine."

"Sit up," said Zanna, helping David to the sofa.

Bergstrom handed him a glass of water. "Drink, slowly. What else did you see?"

David rubbed his fingers across his forehead. "Spikey. I saw it through Spikey's eyes."

Bergstrom looked inquisitively at Zanna.

"A hedgehog," she explained. "A white albino. It's in David's garden. Lucy, the daughter of David's landlady, has been trying to protect it."

Bergstrom gave a thoughtful nod. He looked at Gadzooks, still sitting impassively on the table, and closed his fist tightly around the talisman.

"Ragnar was bloodstained. He'd been in a fight." David was finding his breath again now. "He punched a hole in the ice and an *island* grew out of it. A whole *island*. Is it real or what?"

Bergstrom rolled the talisman quickly through his fingers and holstered it smoothly in his pocket. "It lies to the west of the Alaskan mainland. There are many legends attached to this rock. The Inuit call it a place of souls. They fear it, yet revere it in the same breath. It is thought by some to be a sacred grave, the resting place of the last true dragon to inhabit this Earth."

David looked up suddenly. A droplet of water spilled from his glass. "Gawain? He *died* there? Have you been? Has anyone checked it out?"

Bergstrom smiled and clapped a hand to his arm. "That would make your essay very simple, would it not – an archaeological dig on the snow-capped ridges? Yes, I have been to the Tooth of Ragnar. Female polar bears den there occasionally. To the human eye, there is nothing to suggest that a dragon is set in stone on its peak."

"Tell us about the fire tear," said Zanna.

Bergstrom lifted a golden eyebrow.

"We *know*, Dr Bergstrom. Gawain shed a fire tear when he died. It's hidden in the Arctic. You know where, don't you? Is it on the island? Deep within the core?"

Bergstrom raised a silencing hand. He paced across the room and rattled two ice cubes into another long-stemmed glass. "Let's suppose that I did know the whereabouts of the tear. What would you do with this precious information – assuming I was willing to give it out?"

Zanna sat up, straight and challenged, regally indignant in her body of black. "Dragons are the servants of Gaia!" she declared. "I would…protect the fire for the good of the Earth!"

David groaned quietly under his breath.

"Very commendable," Bergstrom said, pouring water from a tall decanter. "But what makes you think you could guard such a treasure better than a mighty *Nanukapik?*"

"What is a *Nanukapik?*" David asked. He remembered Aunty Gwyneth using this word and had been trying to work out what it meant ever since.

"It means 'greatest bear'," Bergstrom translated. "A leader. The highest. A bear to whom Ragnar, for all his strength, would lower his head and gladly die for." He turned again to Zanna. "The location of the dragon's fire has been guarded by ice bears for longer than you could possibly imagine. There may come a time when one of you, or possibly both of you, will know the secret and defend it wisely, but I cannot run the risk of speaking out when there are forces around you that would seize that knowledge and use it in a way that might damage the very fabric of the planet you love."

"Forces?" asked David, suddenly growing anxious. He looked at Gadzooks, still under the lamp.

The scientist levelled his gaze. "There is a woman staying with you who is not what she seems."

"Aunty Gwyneth? How do you know about her?"

"Trust me, David. I know about her. Aunty Gwyneth and I are old acquaintances. She has been seeking the tear of Gawain ever since the dragon closed his eye and shed it. She will stop at nothing to have it. She is a sibyl, sometimes called a crone or a seer. She hails from a time that man has forgotten. She goes by the name...Gwilanna."

An open and shut case

At the exact same moment that Anders Bergstrom was revealing the true identity of the mysterious visitor to Wayward Crescent, Aunty Gwyneth was in David's room with Lucy. They were packing a bag for the absent lodger and Lucy was finding it quite a strain.

"Aunty Gwyneth, do I *have* to do this?" she was saying, as she rummaged around in David's socks, pinching her nose with a finger and thumb and trying to find a pair that didn't have a hole.

"Be quiet," said her aunt, "my ears are burning."

"Pardon?"

"Ssssh! I hear whispers, child." She swung round like a weathervane until she was facing the open window. "Someone – or some *thing* – spoke my name."

"It was me."

"It was not. You must learn to be aware of distant impressions, particularly when they are tainted by *bears*."

"Bears! Was it Lorel?" Lucy ran to the window.

Aunty Gwyneth looked at her with piercing contempt. "For a daughter of Guinevere you can be very foolish."

Lucy lowered her chin into her chest.

"Bears are pathetic creatures, girl. Were it not for bears, we would have the fire of Gawain in our possession."

"But we do," returned Lucy. "That's why we're special."

Aunty Gwyneth sighed as if this was such a trial. "What you and your mother possess is a spark, a mere cinder of the dragon's true essence. With every new generation that spark becomes weaker, which is why I find it particularly odd that your mother is so talented with the clay." She smiled and sidled up closer to Lucy. "It is an intriguing fact that your mother appears to have inherited far more of the dragon's auma than most other female descendants of Guinevere. Do you know anything about this, child?"

Lucy shook her head and looked a bit puzzled.

Aunty Gwyneth turned away with a disappointed humph. "No, I don't suppose she would tell even you. Still, we mustn't mind that. One day I – or rather *we* – will have the true fire, and then…"

"Then what?" asked Lucy, sounding a little frightened. Aunty Gwyneth was wringing her hands together and a hint of wickedness was present in her eyes.

"Nothing," she snapped. "Continue packing."

Lucy sighed and tugged on the wardrobe door. She frowned at the sight of the dragon, Grace, tucked away alone in the darkness and the dust, but she did not report this to Aunty Gwyneth. Instead, she blew Grace a lingering kiss, dragged a couple of likely-looking shirts off the hangers, stuffed them in the bag and closed the wardrobe again. "Aunty Gwyneth?"

"Yes, what is it now? Do hurry up, child. I don't want that irritating lodger in here any longer than is absolutely necessary."

"It *is* his room."

At this, Aunty Gwyneth brought forth a glare that made Lucy close up like an overnight flower. She tucked the loose arm of a shirt into the bag, zipped it up quickly and dropped it by the door. "I was just going to say that no one knows where the tear is, do they?"

Aunty Gwyneth made a snorting sound in her nose. "Bears do," she hissed, stepping forward and crooking a finger under Lucy's chin. "Bears are keeping that knowledge from us."

Lucy, on her tiptoes now, asked, "W-why?"

"Why?!" Aunty Gwyneth's sneering bark almost ruptured the ceiling plaster. She whisked away, throwing a hand into the air. Lucy thought she saw sparks jumping out of the nails, but it could have just been a glint of anger in Aunty Gwyneth's coal black eyes. "Has your mother never told you the story of the tear?"

"I know about Guinevere catching it."

"After that, child. After that. Don't you know that Guinevere betrayed Gawain and sided with bears to keep the fire from us?"

Lucy sank on to the bed. "She wouldn't do that."

"Hah!" Aunty Gwyneth spun away again, the heels of her shoes nearly grinding through the carpet. "It is time you were properly educated, child. You know that the stubborn red-haired girl went to the dragon and caught his tear?"

"Yes," said Lucy. She wanted to say 'I just told you that', but she didn't dare risk another hard stare.

"And having caught the fire, supposedly hid it?"

"Yes, Aunty Gwyneth."

"It is a fable, child. Tittle-tattle. There is more to the legend than you know. When Guinevere caught the tear of Gawain it consumed her body with a cleansing fire that even she, for all her righteous devotion, could not hope to restrain or endure."

"You mean it was like having dragon pox – but worse?"

Aunty Gwyneth laid a tired hand on her hip.

"Compared to this, dragon pox would be an ant-sized snuffle. She was overtaken, child. Seized by a fire that boiled her blood. It was all she could do to release the tear into the body of a hollowed-out bone, which she used as a vessel to carry the fire back to the only one wise enough to know how to manage it."

"Gwilanna?"

"At last, we seem to be getting somewhere."

Lucy smiled, glad that she wasn't being barked at for once. Then she made another poor error of judgement. "I don't like Gwilanna."

"I beg your pardon?"

Lucy shrugged her shoulders. "When Mum tells stories about Gawain, she always says Gwilanna was horrid and sneaky."

"*Sneaky?!*" Aunty Gwyneth screeched so hoarsely that a pin shook loose from her bun. She looked quite comical with a curl of hair bouncing out above her ear. But Lucy knew better than to risk a laugh.

"I taught your mother everything she knows! And this is how she repays me? By calling me a *sneak?*"

"Not you," defended Lucy. "I said…" But here she stopped, afraid to use the words queuing up on her tongue. She lifted an ear to the Dragons' Den and thought she could hear a few younger scales rattling.

Aunty Gwyneth snapped her fingers and the pin leapt sweetly into her hand. She fixed her hair and in a low voice said, "I meant, of course, Gwilanna and her *kind* – the sibyls, the ancients – of which I consider myself one. Now, apologise at once."

"But—?"

"Apologise, child."

Lucy skimmed the floor again. "Sorry. May I go now?"

"No, you may not. You are being taught. No school could provide you with the knowledge I dispense."

"No," Lucy mumbled, wishing for once she could *be* at school, or that half-term had come a little later that year. She was desperate to obey her mother's wishes and do everything to please her new-found aunt, but the woman was as welcome as a stinging nettle. Lucy pulled up a sock and waited.

"Now, where were we?"

"In Gwilanna's cave."

"Ah yes, with the witless girl and her even more witless love for the dragon."

Witless? Lucy frowned again. That didn't match up with her picture of Guinevere. She opened her mouth to query the meaning, only to receive another rebuke.

"Oh, do stop interrupting, child. Listen and learn. If Guinevere had listened to Gwilanna's advice, things would not have happened the way they did. The girl would not release the fire. All Gwilanna wanted was to harness its power for...well, never mind what for. There was supposed to be an understanding, a *trade*. The girl would be given a child to foster; a child born of clay and hair and scale; and Gwilanna, in turn, would be the keeper of the tear. But at the final moment the girl refused to give the tear up, and when Gwilanna did her best to reason with her, the foolish creature...ran into the hills, where she was aided by a meddlesome bear."

"Was it Lorel?" Lucy couldn't help herself.

"It was not," said her aunt. "It was a brown bear, the worst and most stupid kind. She had befriended it once before. It protected her while she...escaped...to the mountain."

"Mountain? What mountain?"

"Oh! The resting place of Gawain. She was trying to return the fire to his deathbed – to release it to the earth near to where the dragon lay."

"So...she didn't *hide* it, not properly?"

Aunty Gwyneth humphed and turned away. "There were...disturbances. Great winds. A plague of dust. The earth quaked. The old land broke in two. The island where Gawain lay collapsed into the ocean. The abyss was covered by flooding waters, then by a layer of freezing ice."

"But what happened to Guinevere – and the bear?"

"Drowned." A tiny measure of self-satisfaction creased the line of Aunty Gwyneth's lips.

Lucy gripped her arms, a little lost for words. "But what about the fire? Did it go out in the flood?"

At this, Aunty Gwyneth wrung her hands so tightly that Lucy could hear the small bones cracking. "That is a mystery, child. Soon after this…catastrophe, call it what you will, the white bears came, claiming that the fire was under their protection."

"They found it? The ice bears found the fire?"

"Ice bears," Aunty Gwyneth sneered. "Their word is as slippery as their seal-smeared paws. They speak in riddles about the fire. The only true link to Gawain was the girl."

"Guinevere?"

"Oh, bones and spittle! Are your ears made of blubber? Guinevere was lost! I am speaking of the daughter she left behind, Gwendolen."

"And I'm speaking as one of her descendants," said a voice. Liz entered the room with a look of disapproval on her face. "I trust you've given Lucy *all* the facts, Aunty Gwyneth? I wouldn't want my daughter growing up with any misconceptions about her ancestors."

"I am tired," said Aunty Gwyneth, fluting a hand.

"You may leave now, both of you. And take the boy's bag."

Liz frowned at the bag but made no comment.

Lucy, unhappy in the midst of this hostility, smiled and attempted to relieve the tension. "Aunty Gwyneth, would you like me to help you unpack?" She hurried across the room and put her hand on the suitcase.

"Leave it," said her aunt, almost spitting out the words. "Never meddle with my possessions. You could not open the case anyway. It requires a password, in dragontongue."

"Hhh! Will you show me?!"

"I most certainly will not."

Lucy gaped at her mum, who beckoned her away. "Come on. You heard Aunty Gwyneth; she's tired."

With a tut of disappointment, Lucy mooched into the hall. Liz picked up David's bag. "You should have spoken to me before talking of Guinevere."

"The child needs to learn."

"I agree. And she will. She'll hear the truth – when I'm ready to tell her." And with that, she went out and closed the door behind her.

Seconds later, there was a fluttering sound at the open window. Gretel landed with a scratching of claws on the sill.

"Well?" snapped her mistress.

Gretel, loaded up with a strange variety of seed heads and petals and small feathers and fur, bundled her collection to the end of the sill and let out a negative-sounding *hrrr*.

Aunty Gywneth narrowed her gaze. "Then he must have the dragon with him," she muttered, as Gretel flew across and landed on her shoulder. "The boy knows something. He has gone to the bears. I can feel it in my bones."

Hrrr, went Gretel, blowing a puff of smoke.

"Will you stop doing that in my *ear*," said Aunty Gwyneth, tutting and wafting the smoke away. "Tonight you will prepare a special potion. Rosehip with spider web, poppy seed and dill. We need to bring this lodger under our…guidance. He is dangerous, unruly. He may be a threat." And with that strange and faintly chilling instruction, she cast her gaze down at her feather-light case. "Open," she hissed and let out a guttural *hrr-raar-r-aar*.

There was a click and the lid of the case rose up. Spiralling wisps of yellowish mist began to tumble over the front and sides. A cloud of what looked like cotton-wool padding floated gently into the air. Blue sparks fizzed and glittered all around it. Gretel, still on

157

her mistress's shoulder, paddled her feet in great excitement and was sent to the bedhead and told to stay there.

Aunty Gwyneth snapped her fingers. At once, the cloud began to dissolve and the object inside it fell into her hands. It was about the same size and thickness as a roof slate, but curved and tapering at one end. "Yes, we have waited so long," she breathed, caressing the green, uneven surface. "This time there will be no mistakes. Once we know the truth about Elizabeth's auma, you will be ready to rise again, under my tutelage and my will. Then the tear will be ours for the taking."

And with a smile so smug that even Gretel had to wince, the sibyl, Gwilanna, resealed the case, completely unaware that in the darkness of the wardrobe a pair of sail-like ears were doing what they'd been made to do best.

Listening.

David makes plans

In the grounds of Rutherford House meanwhile, David and Zanna were about to part company.

"Are you sure you'll be OK?" she was asking, turning up part of his greatcoat collar.

David, who was looking anywhere but at her, cradled Gadzooks against his midriff and sighed. "I just don't get this," he grumbled.

"Why? What's eating you now?"

"Bergstrom. He shows me all this stuff about the Tooth of Ragnar and says it's my 'destiny' to know about 'the Nine', but he hasn't uttered any kind of explanation. Then he casually lets slip that Gwilanna, the zillion-year-old crone of dragon legend, is sleeping in my bed – and all I'm s'posed to do is go home and treat her like a normal relative!"

"And watch over Lucy. Don't forget that."

"Oh, yeah. Top of the 'must do' list. Stay close to Lucy. What's that all about? While Gwilanna is destroying 'the fabric of the planet', I'm supposed to go merrily looking for *hedgehogs*? No chance. Not while she's threatening to harm Gadzooks."

Zanna turned her stark white face to the sky. It was

darkening early and a rumble of thunder was not far off. "David, it's for your own safety, you goop. You can't take on someone who hatches dragon eggs and changes apple colours and has outlived everyone else on the planet. How's she done it? That's what I want to know. It's spooky. How's she survived this long?"

"The suitcase," David muttered, gritting his teeth.

"Pardon?"

"Her suitcase. I know what's in it. So does Bergstrom, I bet. He asked me about it the first time I met him. I think he's using us to get to it."

"David, you're talking in riddles. Get what?"

"The scale," he breathed, drawing close to her now, near enough to see the drifting storm clouds reflected in her wide, dark eyes. "Remember the legend? Gwilanna took Gawain's scale. She's got a little piece of the last true dragon. A piece that didn't go back to the clay. She must have found a way of using it to keep herself alive."

Zanna cast her gaze to the ground for a moment. "Maybe she's developed some sort of elixir? There's no real agreement on the lifespan of dragons, but they were always thought to live for several hundred years. She might have tapped into their longevity somehow. Who knows what she can do? I'll tell you this, too. I think what I said in the gardens was right. She *is* a midwife –

of sorts. I reckon she's been present at the births of all of Guinevere's descendants. That would explain how Liz knows her so well. What's in it for her, though, I wonder – keeping the line of Guinevere going?"

"I don't know," said David, "but I'm sure that scale is the key to her power. It's in that case. And I'm gonna get it."

"Wait," cried Zanna, hauling him back. "You go for that scale and you'll be hopping on lily pads before you know it. Gwilanna's not going to be fazed by the threat of some cavalier geography student. That case is probably protected – by something very nasty indeed. Besides, if you do get hold of the scale, what are you going to do with it? Fold it up and make a nice hat for Gadzooks?"

"Very funny. I'm going to give it to Liz. She's the only one of the three of them I trust."

Again, Zanna dragged him back. "David, you don't know what you're messing with here. If push comes to shove, how do you know Liz won't side with Gwilanna? You're just her lodger, remember; Gwilanna probably helped bring Lucy into being."

"Then I'll keep the scale myself," said David. "Either way, they're not going to harm Gadzooks."

For a third time, he made to turn away. But as he did a bolt of lightning knifed through the clouds making

Zanna squeal and throw her arms around his neck. For a second, they remained in an awkward clinch until Zanna freed her mouth from his shoulder and whispered, "Any chance you could move Gadzooks? His wings are digging right into me."

David opened his arms, allowing Zanna to close the space between them. He repositioned his arms in the small of her back.

"Thank you. Lightning frightens me," she said.

David raised an unseen eyebrow. For a Goth, that seemed an incongruous admission. "I'll walk you to the college. Come on, it's not far."

"David?"

"Hmm?"

"I know you care about Gadzooks and stuff, but promise me you won't do anything silly?"

A drop of rain blotted David's greatcoat. "I'll call you," he said, stroking Gadzooks with the flat of his thumb. "Come on. We're gonna get drenched."

"No, wait. There's something else." She placed one hand against his chest. "Not sure how to say this, really. It's been bothering me since I came to your house."

David sucked in sharply. Thinking he knew what was coming, he said, "Look, Zanna, I like you a lot. I'm sorry if I've treated you like an alien in the past. I was ignorant and stupid; a bit scared of you, I s'pose. You're a lovely, funny, caring person. But you know I've got a girlfriend. I can't go out with you, and I shouldn't really kiss you every time we say goodbye. It's not fair to Sophie, is it?"

The wind ripped at Zanna's skirt, making it swirl around her ankles. "Nice sentiment," she muttered, "but it's got nothing to do with what I was going to say."

"Oh," said David, blushing fit to burst. "What, then?"

"The egg."

"The egg? What about it?"

"Watch over it. Please."

"But—?"

"Please." Her nails raked into his chest.

"Zanna, you're drawing blood," he said. "Yes, I'll watch over it, but what's the big deal?"

She shivered then and David instinctively held her. "I quickened it, didn't I? Gwilanna said so, didn't she?"

"Yes, but—?"

"Quickened means fertilised, don't you think?"

David stepped back so he could look into her eyes.

"I want to know," she said, clearing hair from her face. A trickle of water ran down her cheek. She brushed it with a knuckle. It wasn't rain. "I want to know whose child it truly is, Liz's – or mine."

163

Welcome to the family

It was nearly eight o'clock before David arrived back in Wayward Crescent. By then, the seemingly unstoppable rain – that had delayed his return and kept him at the college playing endless games of pinball; and eating a tray of half-cooked chips in the corner of a dismal, sweltering cafe; and sheltering in the upstairs half of the library, staring out over the library gardens, beautiful under their phosphorescent lamps – had slowed to light but fickle outbursts, and he was able to dodge the worst of the showers and walk home with only his feet getting soaked.

On the way, he thought about Zanna and the egg, but mostly he thought about the ice bear, Ragnar. Among the many questions he had not set Bergstrom was why was Ragnar so upset? What kind of tragedy could drive a bear to pound the ice with such tremendous force that the earth had literally broken and moved? And if Gawain *was* set in stone on that place, did that mean he had risen again, waiting, perhaps, to be called or awakened? A dragon, alive and flying in the Arctic. The thought made a hollow in David's chest. But was it excitement he was feeling – or fear?

With a shake of his shoulders he erased those thoughts and turned his mind to his mission at home. There were lights in every window at number forty-two, but he stopped off first at Mr Bacon's, where he left Gadzooks on the bedside table of the neat guest room, then steadied his nerves for the trip next door.

As he slipped discreetly into the house, he became aware of Liz's voice. She was upstairs, somewhere, reading from his squirrel story, *Snigger and the Nutbeast*. Lucy had gone to bed early by the sound of it. This was not uncommon on stormy nights. Lucy, like Zanna, was not fond of lightning. Bonnington was also up the stairs, sitting rather glumly at the point where the steps fanned round to the landing. He opened his mouth and made a gentle meow. "Shush," David whispered, having a peek at the door to his room. A sliver of yellow light told him it was open. He took two fairy-footed steps towards it, but retreated sharply when he heard the light clicking off in the kitchen. Silent as a ghost he was up the stairs again, just in time to avoid being seen by Aunty Gwyneth. *Aunty Gwyneth*. He must keep calling her that. One slip of the tongue and—

"Mum, what does witless mean?"

Lucy's voice broke into his thoughts, and also into Liz's reading of the story.

"It means foolish or ridiculous," Liz replied quietly. "Why? What made you ask?"

"Aunty Gwyneth said that Guinevere was witless to love Gawain."

In a voice that suggested she was stroking Lucy's brow, Liz replied, "Then she's wrong. I think what Aunty Gwyneth fails to understand is that Guinevere admired Gawain for his majesty, but loved him for what he truly stood for. Dragons were defenders of the natural world – just like someone not a million miles from here."

"Me, you mean?"

"Mmm. Every squirrel you save or hedgehog you protect shows how close you are to Gawain. No matter what Aunty Gwyneth says, you keep on believing that. Now, where were we?"

"Snigger was in the watering can. Mum, did Guinevere *really* drown?"

Drown? thought David, sitting down next to Bonnington. He'd never heard this before.

"It's a long, long story," Liz replied. "Aunty Gwyneth has only given you the scraps."

"But why haven't *you* ever told it to me?"

Liz paused, then said in a hesitant voice, "I've been waiting – for a special time."

"Christmas?"

"No, more special than Christmas. For...the right time of the moon."

She's going to tell her about the baby, thought David. He rested his hand between Bonnington's ears and the cat gave out an appreciative purr.

"You remember, the moon goes in phases?" said Liz. "Well, in four days time, when it's bright and full, I'll tell you about Guinevere...and Gwendolen."

"And the bear as well?"

Bear? David raised his head. What had made Lucy mention bears? This reminded him of something he'd meant to ask Bergstrom: how had bears become guardians of the tear in the first place? In all the drama at Rutherford House, it was one of those questions that had somehow escaped.

"Everything," said Liz. "It's the best story ever."

"Better than *Snigger?*"

"Yes – but don't tell David I said that."

Lucy laughed – and in the same breath, sighed. "I wish David would write *another* story."

"So do I," muttered Liz. "This must be the fifth time I've read this to you. Are we done for the night?"

"No! The watering can is a good bit."

Suddenly, David heard a noise in the hall. Peering

carefully over the banister, he spied Aunty Gwyneth coming out of his room. She paused a moment and cocked her head, then carried on quietly into the lounge.

David seized his chance. Telling Bonnington to stay well put, he trod the stairs softly and hurried along the hall and into his room. The suitcase was on the bed, on the mattress to be precise. Someone had removed the sheets and blankets and dumped them into a vacant corner. That in itself was weird enough, but it wasn't the only odd sight to see. The light shade was missing, it lay crumpled on a chair. The resulting glare from the clear, bare bulb was stark and blinding and frighteningly cold. The carpet had been rucked and the curtains torn down. They lay ripped and scattered across the desk. There was dirt on the floorboards, too, and what looked at first to be a few small stones. David knelt down and rubbbed them in his fingers. They crumbled to powder. Building plaster. Where had that come from? He looked around. On the bedside wall, a long strip of wallpaper had been half-peeled away and left lolling like a dog's tongue over the bed head. The plaster underneath had been gouged right out to reveal the rough red brickwork below. David's senses shuddered and crawled. There was something primal going on here. Something cave-like.

He snatched up the case.

His first thought was to run with it. Get out of there. Skedaddle. But there was little point in handing the case to Liz. She knew about the case; it was the contents that mattered. So David tried again to find the right means to open it. He turned it, banged it with the heel of his fist, twisted the handle, pressed the seams. Nothing. "Got to be a way in," he muttered, and closed his eyes as he often did to concentrate. Straight away, an image of Gadzooks appeared. And, as usual, he had a message,

Grace

David glanced at the wardrobe. "Not now," he hissed. "I'll fetch her tomorrow."

Gadzooks tried again, this time scratching a zigzagged line beneath the word. He even drew a pair of makeshift ears.

"I know she's a listening dragon," said David. "What's your point?"

Gadzooks snorted in frustration and tore the page away, ready to try a different approach. He was just about to write another quick note when something floated over his shoulder and skated to a rest by the tip of his pencil.

A flower petal.

David whipped around.

"Well, well," said Aunty Gwyneth, "the lodger returns."

She was standing in the doorway with her arms loosely folded.

David dropped the suitcase and stumbled back. "I just came in for some things," he gabbled. He pulled the desk drawer open. "Floppy disk. Bye."

"You will stay," said Aunty Gwyneth, and her cold eyes froze him into position. Yet somewhere in his mind, as if his brain had split in two, he could still form a picture of Gadzooks. He too had turned around, to stare into the eyes of the dragon, Gretel.

"You and I need to talk," said Aunty Gwyneth, as if she was inside David's head, having a walk round, blowing out the cobwebs. "Elizabeth is due to have a baby."

There it was, right up front. David somehow managed to feign surprise. "Baby? Good grief. I— who's the father?"

"A dragon called Gawain. I think you may have heard of him."

"Nmph," went David, still unable to move and grimacing wildly as he struggled to concentrate on Gadzooks. Gretel was wafting her posy of flowers

170

seductively under his twitching snout.

"In four days time, the process will be done. The egg your girl so charitably quickened will hatch, and from it will come…a child. You will not speak of this to anyone. You will keep the secret as the family always have."

Through tightly-gritted teeth David managed to say, "I'm not one of the family, *Gwilanna*."

Gwilanna smiled and looked at herself in the mirror. A corner cracked. It seemed to amuse her. "You will call me Aunty Gwyneth," she said. "I like it. It has a quaint ring, don't you think?" She let out a short, but guttural *hrrr*.

In that portion of his mind where Gadzooks held sway, David watched Gretel put her posy to her snout. With a waxing of her nostrils, she snorted on the petals. A cloud of what looked like pollen dust wafted through the air towards Gadzooks.

"Don't sniff!" David managed to shout.

Too late. The dragon took a gulp of air and the dust cloud disappeared up his snout. His oval-shaped eyes took a dreadful spin. David, likewise, saw half a dozen lightbulbs swinging for an instant. He shuddered and blinked, then found he was free to move again.

"Wh-what happened?" he gasped, stepping sideways to steady himself.

"You came in for something called a disk," said Aunty Gwyneth.

David looked at the floppy as if it had landed from another planet.

"Your bag is in the hall. Now you may leave."

Fuddled, David headed for the door.

"You will return when I call you," Aunty Gwyneth said, speaking again as he moved behind her. "There will be work to be done around the house."

David nodded. "Yes, of course. If there's anything I can do for Liz, I will."

"Good. Welcome to the family, David."

"Thank you," he muttered and stepped into the hall.

Straight away, a dragon flew past. It zipped up the hall and landed on the rim of a Swiss-cheese plant pot. David watched it dig the tip of its tail into the soil, then examine it to see if the plant needed watering. Smiling, he turned away, into the kitchen. "Evening," he said, to the listening dragon on top of the fridge. The dragon nearly keeled over in shock. The lodger, speaking in broken dragontongue? It took off its spectacles and polished them hard. "I've been meaning to ask you," David said, "can you hear the football results on those?" He pinched his earlobes and pulled them out, mimicking the shape of the listener's ears. The dragon narrowed its violet eyes. It did not appear to welcome this silly remark. "Just wondered," David said. He picked up an apple and bobbed it in the air. "I'll be round at Henry's if anyone wants me."

The listening dragon blew a short sharp smoke ring.

David grinned and blew it a kiss. Dragons. No sense of humour whatsoever. Sometimes, they were worse than kids.

Crossed words with Henry

David spent the next few days mostly in the company of Henry Bacon, managing to break nearly all of Henry's rules. These included using the butter knife in the marmalade, leaving unwashed cups on the drainer, sitting on the sofa in his outdoor coat, tapping the glass of Henry's aquarium (causing his guppies to hide inside their wreck), spraying globs of toothpaste on the bathroom mirror…the list went on and on.

On Thursday morning, David came downstairs and discovered he had broken yet another regulation. As he flopped onto the sofa (definitely not in his outdoor coat) Henry gathered his newspaper across to one side and said, "Have you *shaved* this morning?"

"Uh?" David grunted.

Mr Bacon clucked like a farmyard hen. "The shadow, boy. Rule number one: *lodger will be smart and presentable at all times*. You look like something out of the Stone Age."

David ran a hand across his stubble. "It's Wednesday, day of rest – for chins."

Mr Bacon folded his paper and supported the crossword page on his thigh. "It's Thursday, you dolt."

He tapped the date. "Been in bed so long you've missed the best part of it."

David checked his watch. Ten-forty. Early by student standards. He looked around for Gadzooks and spotted the dragon on the occasional table just behind Mr Bacon's chair. He was pacing about, looking restless again. He'd been doing this ever since they'd moved out of Liz's: huffing and puffing and pacing a lot. David waved a hand and wished him good morning.

Henry immediately slapped his paper. "Will you please stop doing that?"

"What?" David looked to Gadzooks for guidance. The dragon blew a smoke ring and shrugged.

"Clearing your throat," Mr Bacon complained. "You've been glugging like a drain ever since you got here. Suck a lozenge if your clacker's gummed. Pack in the bathroom. Cabinet. Top shelf."

"I haven't got a sore throat."

"Then stop going *uh-hrrr!*"

David was, frankly, peeved about this. He knew his grasp of dragontongue wasn't that good – even Gadzooks still preferred to communicate via his pad – but to compare him with a drain was a bit unfair. "'*Uh-hrrr*' doesn't sound like a blocked drain, Henry, more like a car on a frosty morning."

Mr Bacon drilled his pen into the arm of his chair. "This is my day off, boy. I trust you're not going to spend it lounging about my sitting room? You must have assignments? Or a *college* to visit? Go and save a squirrel; I'm trying to do the crossword."

David yawned and stretched out a leg. "Want any help?"

Henry gave a contemptuous snort and tapped his pen against his teeth. "Oh, very well. You might try this. Eight down. Rather tricky. Two word answer. First word nine letters, second word three. GEG."

"What?"

"GEG. That's the clue."

"Sounds like a mis-print."

"This is *The Times*, you twerp. Of course it's not a mis-print. It's a cryptic puzzle to test your faculties. If you possess any faculties, that is – other than a primitive instinct for grunting."

David turned to Gadzooks. "Eight down; what do you reckon?"

Mildly annoyed to have his pondering interrupted, Gadzooks pottered to the end of the table and studied the clue over Henry's shoulder. With a huff, he produced his pencil and pad and quickly scribbled something down. He showed the result to David.

"Scrambled egg," said David.

Gadzooks allowed himself a hurr on his claws, crumpled the page and threw it away (it twinkled briefly and dissolved to dust). He went back to his pacing.

"Egg?" said Henry, looking confused. "No, boy. You eat next door. That's the arrangement. Meals confined to the making of drinks and the occasional round of toast, at breakfast."

"No, it's the answer to your clue, Mr Bacon. GEG. The letters of egg, scrambled up."

Mr Bacon squinted at the puzzle. "Good Lord," he exclaimed. "You're right. It fits. Have a congratulatory cough for your trouble."

David winked at Gadzooks instead. As he did, the dragon grew very excited. He clapped his paws to keep David's attention, then whipped out his trusty notepad again. When he turned it, there was a drawing of an egg.

"Yes, egg. We've just 'cracked' that," David joked.

Gadzooks shook his head, then began rushing back and forth at speed with his drawing. He skidded to a halt and showed the egg again.

"Fast food?" David guessed, a little confused. Why was Zookie doing this? Over the past few days he'd shown a marked indulgence for 'dragon charades'. Each time it had ended as this was doing now, with David shrugging and Gadzooks slapping a paw to his scaly forehead.

David let it be. He felt a sneeze coming on and pulled a tissue from his pocket, dislodging a small card on to the carpet. Gadzooks caught the movement and hooded his eyes. He glanced at Henry, who was filling in his puzzle, then fluttered down under the sofa to investigate. A second later he was up in David's lap, tapping the card and making telephoning gestures.

"Ring Zanna?"

Gadzooks nodded and paddled his feet.

"That's the third time you've asked me to do that. Why?"

"Oh, for goodness' sake!" Mr Bacon removed his glasses and swung his chair to point at David. In a flash, Gadzooks assumed solid form. "If you don't cough up that blasted phlegm I shall call out the fire brigade and have them pump it off your chest! What are you cradling that thing for?"

"Zookie? He's my special dragon, Mr Bacon."

The door bell rang. Muttering something about the 'barminess of youth', Henry threw down his paper and went into the hall.

Gadzooks resumed his animated form and flagged Zanna's card under David's nose.

"For the last time, no," David told him firmly.

Gadzooks discharged a frustrated grizzle and ripped the card into confetti-sized pieces. He flew to the coffee table and kicked a loose grape into a bowl of fruit.

Meanwhile, in the hall, Henry was talking to Lucy Pennykettle. "Yes, child, what is it?"

"Can David come out to play?"

"Gladly. You've got a visitor, boy."

David jumped up. "Are you coming or staying?"

Gadzooks emitted a grumbling *hrrr* and turned away, tapping a petulant foot.

"Please yourself," said David and exited the room.

Gadzooks blew a smoke ring and spiked it with his tail. He was about to adopt his solid pose again when he spotted something wedged between the cushions of the sofa.

David's mobile phone.

He twiddled his toes and rolled his eyes to the hall. David had just gone out to meet Lucy, and Henry Bacon was climbing the stairs.

Gadzooks the dragon saw his chance. He fluttered to the floor, gathered up the bits of Zanna's card and flew them over to the mobile phone. He turned each one till the writing was uppermost, then carefully started to piece them together.

A *dash of* Honesty

Lucy had arrived in her outdoor clothes. "Come and see Spikey's house," she begged, dragging David across the drive. "Mum got the rabbit hutch down for me. I've put it in the garden with some leaves for a bed and a ramp for Spikey to properly climb up."

"OK," said David. "But I can't stay long. I really ought to be working on my essay."

"The dragon one?"

"Yes."

"How much have you done?"

"Erm, nothing. I always leave them till the last minute."

Lucy reached up and opened the door. "Is it true what Mum says, you can see the dragons now?"

David looked at her as if she was being silly. "I've always been able to see the dragons."

"I mean *properly* see."

"Yes," said David, wondering what she meant. He went in and said hello to Gruffen.

The young guard dragon was sitting in the small square window by the door. He had a sorry sort of look in his violet eyes. He flapped his wings to acknowledge

David's greeting then let them droop like a pair of wet socks.

"He's upset," said Lucy, "cos Gretel's in charge. She's guarding the den *and* Aunty Gwyneth's room. Gruffen's been made into front door monitor."

Hrrr-oo, went Gruffen and lowered his snout.

Just then, Aunty Gwyneth stepped out of 'her' room. She was dressed in her usual matching suit; today the colour was a bright lime-green. Her sharp eyes picked out David's. "Good. It's you. There is work to be done."

"Where's Mum?" asked Lucy.

"Here," said Liz, coming down the stairs. She looked a little tired, as if she hadn't slept well. "Hello, David. Are you all right?"

Aunty Gwyneth poked his shoulder. "Take a spade and remove that eyesore from the garden."

"What eyesore?"

"That ridiculous chunk of ice."

"It's still here? After all the rain we've had?"

"Destroy it," said Aunty Gwyneth, her eyes flashing violet. "And when you're done, prepare a light lunch. I will have my usual: six peeled mushrooms and half a lemon." She turned and disappeared into her room.

"Six peeled mushrooms," David muttered. "Are you sure she wasn't a badger in a previous life?"

181

"Don't be cheeky," said Liz, tapping his arm. "Just do as she says and we'll all be happy. She's right about that ice, it could do with clearing; it gets in the way when I'm putting out the washing. Don't worry about making lunch. I'm sure I can peel a few mushrooms."

"No, it's OK. I'm happy to help." David lowered his voice and patted his tummy. "You've got other things to think about."

"Are you *coming?*" Lucy shouted from deep within the kitchen.

"He'll be with you in a minute," Liz shouted back, and beckoned David further along the hall. "How are things at Henry's? Are you coping all right? How's…Gadzooks getting on?"

"He's having a moody," David replied. "Missing his windowsill, I think. He seems a bit restless. Out of sorts."

"Yes," Liz nodded, looking concerned. "All the special dragons are on their toes. I can't quite work out why."

"Elizabeth, it's time," Aunty Gwyneth's voice called.

"You go," said David. "I'll shift this ice."

But as he went to turn away, Liz pulled him back. "David, wait. I'm so preoccupied I nearly forgot. You had a telephone call – from Dilys Whutton. You know,

182

at the publishers? She'd like to see you at eleven tomorrow. I told her you'd ring if you couldn't make it. She sounds really nice. I think you should go."

"Oh, right—" David managed to say, before Lucy reappeared and yanked him down the hall as if she'd just captured a runaway dog.

A few moments later, standing by the window in David's room and watching him fetch a spade from the shed, Liz said to her 'aunt', "I'm really not sure about this, you know. I still say it was unwise, allowing David to see."

"A temporary diversion," Aunty Gwyneth replied. "Making the boy a part of our world has removed his need to poke and nose. He accepts what he sees as commonplace. Therefore, he will not make a nuisance of himself."

Liz sighed and tightened her lip. "I asked him about Gadzooks just now. He says the dragon's unhappy."

"That, my dear, was Gretel's doing."

Hrrr? went Gretel, looking round. She was hunkered on the floor by a table leg, grinding up seeds against a large piece of plaster, taken from the growing mess of rubble around her.

"Too much dill in the mix," said Aunty Gwyneth. "The writing dragon is active, but helpless; muted by the boy's muddled state of mind."

"What?" Liz turned away sharply from the window. "Is this what you meant by testing him? I don't want their relationship harmed. David's meeting a publisher tomorrow. He's going to need all the help he can get."

"The boy was a threat," Aunty Gwyneth hit back. "He smells of bears. *Powerful* bears. You expect me to tolerate that?"

"David's a storyteller," Liz said tautly. "Writing's in his auma. Take that from him and he'll have nothing left."

"Storytellers," Aunty Gwyneth scoffed. "Whistlers, wastrels and woebegones, all. The boy can scribe what twaddle he likes – that's exactly what it will be for now: gibberish."

"But his essay? He can't win his competition if he can't write properly. He won't be able to go to the Arctic."

"How sad," said Aunty Gwyneth, sounding anything but. "The bears will soon grow tired of him anyway – then move on as they always do. Now, enough prattle. We need to progress."

Liz looked in disgust at the bed. Not only was it stripped of its duvet and sheets, but the mattress had been torn in several places too. Plaster dust lay in every seam. Woodlice were scuttling in and out of the stuffing.

"Do we *have* to turn the room into a cave?" she tutted.

"It will aid you," Aunty Gwyneth replied. "You must dream back, to the first encounter. Take the egg. Hold it close to your body."

Liz lay down, cradling the bronze egg just above her waist. The embryo inside it wriggled and squirmed and swished its scaly dragon tail. "But I can dream back – with ease," she said. "I'm not even sure I need her potions." She rolled her head and looked at Gretel. The dragon was stripping an *Honesty* plant of all its pearl-coloured, papery shells. "Why are you using *Honesty* flowers? I don't remember them when Lucy was born."

Aunty Gwyneth raised her chin. "New developments occur all the time, my dear. The seeds have a soothing, aromatic quality. They will calm you during the transfer of auma. Hurry up," she snapped at Gretel.

The dragon gave out a disgruntled *hrrr*, scrunched up a nearby heap of shells and emptied the flat brown seeds into a bowl. They fizzed as they sank into the curious yellow liquid simmering and popping to her scorching breath.

"There is something else to show you today," said Aunty Gwyneth, a sly tone creeping into her voice. She turned to her suitcase and barked out the password. The case clicked opened and the scale rose smoothly into her hands.

Liz was immediately up on her elbows. "Great Gawain!" she gasped. "You brought that *here*? No wonder the dragons are all on edge." She raised her head to the ceiling. To the well-trained ear, a rumble of excited growls was beginning to pervade the upper reaches of the house.

"They would never dare touch it," Aunty Gwyneth said coldly. "I would turn them to vapour before they could snort." She teased her fingers through Liz's soft hair. "This kindling is very special, my dear. There has been nothing like it since Guinevere's time. It requires something from you: a curl of your hair."

"My hair?" said Liz, with a visible start. "Are you out of your mind? There's a chance he'll be born with fire."

"Every chance," the sibyl said darkly.

Liz pushed herself up. "No. This is wrong. What's going on, Gwilanna? What—?"

But in a flash, it was done. The sharpened end of the scale came down and a lock of Liz's thick red hair was severed. She let out a cry and fell back against the mattress, her bright green eyes turning instantly to violet and her lips parting with a gentle cry.

Gwilanna looked down her nose at her and smirked. "Dream it, my dear. Even the faintest contact with the dragon will bring him flying through the clouds of time. What a pity your reverie will not *last*." She snapped her fingers at Gretel. "Quickly!"

Grizzling and growling, Gretel dipped a green stalk into the bowl. She rolled it, then withdrew it fast from the mix. A droplet of glistening, pearl-coloured liquid hung, suspended, from the end of the stalk. Gretel swung it upright, into the light. She examined it with a hooded stare, then, with barely a twitch of her nostrils, cured it with a jet of warming fire. The droplet dried with a satisfying crackle, then bloomed into a beautiful four-petalled flower with a variegated pattern of green and violet. She flew it to the bed.

"Begin," said Aunty Gwyneth.

Gretel wafted the flower under Liz's nose.

"Now," said the sibyl, caressing the lock of hair in her fingers, "let us see if your *Honesty* has worked." She touched Liz's mouth with the tip of one finger and traced the lines of her wide, pink lips. "Speak," she commanded. "Tell the secret of your auma."

Liz rolled her head, first left, then right. Her mouth played out a bubble of dragonsong.

"Speak. I command you!"

The lips moved again. And this time something meaningful emerged. "Catch..." Liz breathed, and her

187

face was that of a joyous little girl.

"Catch?" sneered Gwilanna. "Catch what, girl? What?"

Liz clapped her hands around the egg and giggled. "Snow," she said. "Lizzie catch snow…"

Blazing ice

While the events in the house were unfolding, at the top of the garden, on the patch of wild ground where David had discovered Bonnington's treasure, Lucy was demonstrating her knowledge of hedgehogs. "As well as slugs and beetles and worms and moths and earwigs and spiders and snails, they eat these…" She pulled a small cluster of grapes from her pocket.

David smiled. "Tasty, after a crunchy beetle. Is Spikey actually using the hutch?"

"He's *in* it," beamed Lucy. "Fast asleep. You can't see him cos he's wrapped in leaves. That's his poo, though." She pointed to some rod-shaped droppings, near to the top of the short wooden ramp that led up to the raised hutch proper.

"Lovely," said David.

"They are," Lucy nodded. "If he was poorly they'd look like this." She opened her book at a diagram of various types of droppings. She pointed to a lime green puddle.

"Yeah, I get the picture," David said, squirming. He stood up and brushed down the front of his jeans. "Well, that's brilliant. You've done really well. I expect Spikey's very grateful to have a nice warm hedgehog hotel in the garden. I hope Bonnington's not bothering him."

Lucy shook her head. "Bonnington sits by the hutch at night, guarding."

David looked across the garden. The Pennykettles' big brown tabby cat was fussing about around an old stack of bricks. "Or he's nicking those grapes while Spikey's out foraging."

"He wouldn't do that; the dragons would be cross."

David looked her up and down. "What are you talking about?"

"I read it in here." She flourished her book. "White hedgehogs are close to the *Earth*."

"Well they would be, with legs as short as theirs."

Lucy scowled rather darkly at that. "You're stupid," she muttered, and turned away clutching the book to her chest.

With a shrug of indifference, David followed her down the garden, dragging his shovel across the lawn. He sank its blade into the ground beside the ice. "Shame we have to break this up. It's done really well to survive this long."

Lucy crouched down and stroked the surface, as if she was petting the head of the bear. "When will you do that story about Lorel?"

Lorel. No sooner was the word off Lucy's lip than the name was exploding through David's mind. Gasping, he pressed a hand to his head, struck by a tilting bout of dizziness.

"What's the matter?" asked Lucy, looking up.

"Don't know. Something touched me. Something... cold." Lorel. Lorel. Lorel. The name pulsed like a distant star: possible to see, impossible to reach.

"A ghost?"

David shivered and reached for the spade. He pulled it from the ground with a sucking squelch. "There's no such thing as ghosts. Stand back." He lifted the spade and prepared to strike. And it was then that something peculiar happened. He was looking down the shaft at the likely point of impact, when a low wind blew across the ice and its surface ignited in a pure white fire.

David staggered back with his mouth wide open, letting the spade fall out of his hands. And, as it did, a small miracle occurred – or so it seemed to Lucy, at least.

"Yes!" she whooped. A snowflake had just fluttered past her eyes.

In an instant she was gone, running to the house. She spurted through the kitchen and slammed open the door into David's room – right at the moment that her mother was uttering the word 'snow'.

Aunty Gwyneth whipped round like a snarling dog.

"Hhh!" gasped Lucy, falling back against the wall. The woman she knew as her sharp and bossy aunt looked more like an ancient, craggy old hag, with smoke-matted hair and teeth like snail shells and nails like pincers and eyes like wrinkled purple raisins.

And then, in a second, she was normal again. "Let that be a lesson!" she roared. "Never barge in when I am at work!"

Lucy cast a terrified glance at her mother. "What are you doing to Mum?" She ran to the foot of the bed, and her eyes grew as round as milk bottle tops when she saw the egg and its unborn contents.

"That is your brother," Aunty Gwyneth said quietly.

Lucy searched for words and found only these: "Mum, wake up!" She reached out to shake her mother's ankle but an unseen force pushed her back against the wall.

"Leave her," the sibyl hissed. A contraction of her fingers brought Lucy to her tiptoes, as if a hand had squeezed her like a toy. "Your mother is dreaming. Lost in the old world. She will wake when the transfer of auma is complete."

Lucy, struggling against the spell, found she was almost pasted to the wall. "I'm going to tell David. I know who you are! DA-VID! HELP!"

"Be quiet!" Aunty Gwyneth commanded. "Why is it that all of Guinevere's daughters come to inherit such crushing insolence? The boy *knows* who I am. He is in my grip. You are *all* in my grip. And you, most of all, will do my bidding or be locked in the attic – in a spider's web."

Lucy shuddered and her lower lip trembled. Spiders she didn't mind; spiders' webs she did.

"Now, speak plainly. What reason did you have for disturbing me?"

"I came to tell Mum it was snowing, that's all."

This remark seemed to hit Aunty Gwyneth like a hammer. She whipped around and stared through the uncurtained window. The sky was littered with pretty white flakes. "Impossible," she muttered. She flashed a quick glance at Elizabeth Pennykettle, frozen deep inside another time, then switched her angry gaze to David, who had sunk to his knees by the table of ice. "What's the matter with the boy? Answer me. Quickly!"

"Don't know," said Lucy, her eyes growing moist. "He said something touched him. Something cold."

Hrrr, went Gretel, who had flown to the windowsill to watch the snow.

Aunty Gwyneth answered her in dragontongue. "Yes, my dear. I sense it too. The Teller is here. He must be trying to restart his contact with the boy. But why?"

"I can hear you," said Lucy. "I know what you're saying."

"Festering nuisance, be gone," her aunt rapped. She clicked her fingers and Lucy was free to scamper away in search of David.

Meanwhile, Aunty Gwyneth walked to the window. She opened it a crack and caught the first bright snowflake dancing past. She smothered it deep within her fist. "How?" she muttered, as if by taking this one speck hostage she could come to understand the strange connection between the girl who had once caught the fire of Gawain and the drifting flecks of ice in the sky. But the answer to the mystery, as frail and delicate as the dot in her fist, eluded even her, and as the wind changed course and a pillar of flakes carried into her hair, she banged the pane shut and focused her attention on David once more. He was already being harangued by Lucy, and motioning with his hands that she should calm herself. "Of course," said Aunty Gwyneth, "the boy is the key."

Hrrr? went Gretel with a sweep of her tail.

"We have failed to ask ourselves a vital question."

The dragon tilted her head.

"Why him?" Aunty Gwyneth brooded darkly. "What

do the so-called guardians of the tear want with a useless storytelling lodger? We must find out."

Gretel immediately reached into her quiver.

"No, not with potions, by simple observation. The boy desires to travel north, does he not? Very well, we will aid his quest. We will encourage this alliance, not try to prevent it."

Hr-rrr? went Gretel, wiggling her snout.

"Of course I'm sure!" her keeper snapped. "The boy made a wish to know about the fire. Where better could he learn than the ice world of the Arctic? And when he travels there, we will follow. You, me and our newborn friend." Together, they glanced at the egg. "But first we have to know how our dear Elizabeth has managed to use *snow* to raise her auma."

Gretel flew to the foot of the bed. *Hrrr*, she growled.

"Yes, yes," said Aunty Gwyneth. "I know we cannot ask her; she is far away now. But we do have this..." she twirled the lock of hair "...and her daughter, and their creations."

This made even Gretel shudder. She, after all, had been made by Liz's hand. The rattle of her scales drew her mistress's attention.

"Not you," Aunty Gwyneth tutted. "You broke with the Pennykettles long ago."

Gretel lowered her head and blew what might have been a smoke ring of relief or the faintest puffle of disappointment.

"We need a new dragon," Aunty Gwyneth mused. "One of the simple-minded, talkative ones."

She cast her thought net about the house, and had her mind's eye not been focused in the den, she might have detected a tremor of terror from the shelf above the shirt rail in the wardrobe. But she did not. She took a pin-sharp breath and gave Gretel an order. "Bring me the wishing dragon," she said.

Aunty Gywneth tells a story

"Once upon a time, there was a dragon. A noble dragon, a magnificent dragon. A creature to whom all species of animal bowed their heads in reverence and fear. I think you know the beast I am speaking of, *wisher*. You are, after all, a descendant of his – in the very crudest terms, of course. You, related to the great Gawain! I wonder what he would think of you now...?"

Aunty Gwyneth turned and scowled.

G'reth gulped and swallowed a plug of smoke. Under normal circumstances, this would not have caused any problems for him. But the fact that he was hanging upside down, tail knotted round a thin wire coat hanger, which in turn was hooked around the light bulb holder swinging precariously left and right, had brought on a dreadful bout of coughing, which only added to his predicament – and his fear.

Aunty Gwyneth clicked her fingers.

Gretel, sitting on the corner of the wardrobe, opened her throat and released a jet of fire. There was a smell of burning and the green earth wire in the core of the light flex sizzled red-hot and duly snapped. The flex lurched, jerking G'reth another millimetre or two towards the mass of rubble littering the floorboards. Though his wings were bound (by Aunty Gwyneth's industrial-strength hair pins) he nevertheless managed to swing his head upwards. All that remained of the light flex now was a strand from the outer sheath of white and the light-blue neutral wire. With a whimpering *hrrr?* he looked towards Gretel. She blew a tart wisp of smoke and looked away.

"Of course, you will remember," Aunty Gwyneth continued, "that Gawain was the last of dragonkind. By that I mean *true* dragonkind. Elizabeth's pathetic little tenants do not count."

Hrrr? went Gretel.

"Be silent," said her keeper. "Find me a woodlouse."

Gretel saw one scuttling on the wall. Putting the spike of her tail underneath it, she flicked it into her mistress's hand.

The sibyl let it wander around her palm. "Let me ask you," she said, turning back to G'reth, "did you ever wonder just *how* Gawain came to be the only dragon left?"

Hrrrff, went G'reth shaking his head.

"Then I will tell you," she said, extending her finger towards his face and letting the louse scrabble loose on his snout. G'reth gulped and crossed his eyes. The louse jigged, then decided to explore an ear. G'reth immediately squirmed and bucked. The coat hanger bobbled ferociously on the socket. Suddenly, the floor seemed very large indeed.

With a crab-like pinch of her fingers, Aunty Gwyneth steadied the wire. "I wouldn't do that if I were you. If you fall, the shock will stiffen your clay. And if you're solid when you hit that sharp-looking brick..."

G'reth peered dizzily at the brick and gulped.

"Of course, this business could be over in a moment if you told me what you know about the power of snow?"

At this point, G'reth found an unexpected ally. *Hrr-rr!* barked Gretel, pulling her hooded eyes into a frown.

"*I beg your pardon?*" Aunty Gwyneth screeched, her voice so shrill it sent the woodlouse scurrying down G'reth's ear canal and onwards, deeper, into his throat. With a splutter he coughed it out; alive, but blackened. "Of course he *knows*. He is a wishing dragon. He is privy to the whispers of the universe itself. Do not dare to question me again. Burn the wire. Now!"

Gretel wiggled her snout and blew. The remaining pieces of sheathing dissolved, leaving just a shred of bare copper wire.

"Now, where were we?" Aunty Gwyneth asked calmly.

G'reth stared up at her with wild, wide eyes.

"Oh yes, the dragons' demise. A heart-breaking business, if ever there was. It always brings a modest *tear* to my eye. I do trust you're not the sensitive type? We wouldn't want to douse your *spark*, now would we?"

On the top of the wardrobe, Gretel shuddered. Douse the wisher's spark? Nothing could be worse for a dragon. Nothing.

"Let me ask you a question," Aunty Gwyneth snarled. "Do you know how long it took for a pair of dragons to breed their young?"

G'reth glanced at the wire above. To his louse-free (and very attentive) ears it seemed to be creaking. He shook his head.

"They could mate only once every ninety-six years. Imagine that? Barren for almost a century. When the planet was young, this mattered nothing. The dragons bred rarely, but freely, without threat. But in time, another species arrived on their world. A species that could reproduce in less than nine moons. A plague that learned to steal dragons' eggs, until no young dragons flew from their nests. This scourge forced the old dragons into the mountains, to the cold high places, to every untamed wilderness the world could offer. And yet, even here, the pestilence followed. Hunters came to flush them out. There was killing. There was burning. There were terrible tales. Dragons were accused of fearful atrocities. Men called them the serpents of evil. But a dragon's fire was never intended to kill. It was an instrument of life, not a tool of destruction.

"And so it came to be that, in time, only twelve old dragons remained. They met in council and came to a decision: they would fight no more. They would fly to the most inaccessible of places and there they would simply wait to die. Their fires would return in peace to the earth, and the earth would be left to decide for herself what should be done about the pestilence called man.

"Gawain came to an island in the north. A sparsely-populated place where he met the girl who would catch his tear when his frail life finally ebbed away. Did you know that his body turned instantly to stone when the fire tear landed in the girl's sweet hands?"

G'reth shook his head and snuffled gently.

"Oh yes, a most unfortunate end. Because his fire was not returned to the core, he could never rejoin the layer of clay from which the Earth Mother had first created his kind. So he is between worlds, even today. Set in stone on a mountain top. Oh dear me, your eyes are looking moist. I did warn you the story was moving, wisher. I do hope you're not going to *cry?*"

Hrr-oo, went G'reth, and took a snotty breath.

Aunty Gwyneth gave him a gentle push. As his body swung back and forth, the hook of the coat hanger clicked ominously around the smooth light socket. "To cry would not do at all," she said. "To shed what you laughingly call a fire tear would spell the end for you, oh yes. The tear would wriggle away through the boards and from there, straight into the earth, of course. You would be nothing before it reached the floor. So, if I were a clever wishing dragon, I would tell me everything you know. If you don't, I will tell you how grief-stricken Guinevere was when her beloved Gawain turned into a *boulder*. It is the saddest story a dragon can hear. Or I could simply have Gretel burn the wire and you will be smashed to pieces anyway."

Nnnphh, went G'reth, tightening his jaw.

"You have two minutes," Aunty Gwyneth snapped. She stood up smartly and turned to Gretel. "Guard him closely. I need to speak with the girl and the lodger." And prodding G'reth once more for spite, she left him swinging like a strung-up yo-yo.

Meanwhile, in the kitchen, David was still trying to calm Lucy down.

"But it's Gwilanna," she was saying.

"Yes, we've established that," he said, peeling carrots into the sink. "I'm not thrilled about it either, Luce. But at least she's here to help. You're going to have a brother. Aren't you pleased?"

"She's coming!" Lucy dived into a chair.

"Ah, good," said Aunty Gwyneth, breezing in. "Preparing a meal, I see."

"Shepherd's pie for me and Lucy," said David. "I've peeled you some mushrooms, of course." He pointed to the worktop where a generous bowl of raw field mushrooms had been set out with a drink of tart lemon juice.

Aunty Gwyneth took one and nibbled the cap. "Too rubbery," she complained. "But they will have to do." She sat down next to Lucy, who winced. "Stop wriggling, child. You're not a worm. You were at fault for bursting in. The delivery of a infant dragonchild is a delicate business. I was forced to adopt my normal presence in order to better protect your mother."

David dropped his hand on Lucy's shoulder, hushing her before she could start to babble. "I think we understand that now, Gw– Aunty Gwyneth."

Lucy tutted quietly and let out a sigh. "How long will Mum be asleep?"

"Until the full moon."

"Tomorrow evening," said David.

"Yes," said Aunty Gwyneth, giving nothing away. "Until then, I expect you to cook and clean and do whatever needs to be done." She rose to leave. "A heavy snowfall," she said, glancing out of the window. "Arctic conditions. Most unpleasant. I hope it doesn't force you to cancel with your publisher."

"Publisher?" Lucy looked at David.

"I'm going to talk to an editor, that's all."

"About *Snigger*?!"

"Snigger?" Aunty Gwyneth hacked up the word as though she had a touch of catarrh in her throat.

"He's a squirrel," said Lucy, "in David's book. He's doing another one soon – about bears."

"Is he?" Aunty Gwyneth said coldly. She took a small mushroom and ate it whole.

"He might be," said David, flicking a tap. A stream of cold water pattered into the sink. "Talking of bears, I didn't remove that ice by the way; it didn't seem worth it, as it was snowing."

"And it caught fire," Lucy beamed.

"It did what?" Aunty Gywneth stopped dead in her tracks.

"Ignore her," said David. "It was an optical illusion:

the sun, reflecting off the surface, I think."

"But you said—?"

"Be quiet." Aunty Gwyneth shushed Lucy at once. Narrowing her eyes, she took a long hard look through the window again. "Go outside and bring me a piece."

"Of the *ice*? What for?"

Aunty Gwyneth stared at him hard.

"OK, OK, I'm going," said David. And he hurried up the garden, leaving the kitchen tap still running and drying his hands on his jeans as he went.

Aunty Gwyneth turned to Lucy. "You saw this phenomenon?"

Lucy bit her lip.

"Oh, really, child! You must learn to pay attention." Aunty Gwyneth frowned and had another small mushroom. As she chewed it, she picked up the photograph of Liz, playing in the snow as a little girl. "Tell me, what do you know about snow?"

"It comes from the sky," Lucy answered faithfully.

Aunty Gwyneth was not impressed. "Don't be insolent, girl! I know where it comes from. Where was this photograph taken?"

"On holiday."

"Where?"

"In—" But Lucy's words were drowned out by the

clatter of the door and David stamping snow off his shoes.

Aunty Gwyneth threw the photo down. "Well?"

"It's gone."

"Don't speak riddles, boy. Gone where?"

"Dunno. Just...gone. Melted, I guess. The snow from the sky must have been warmer than—"

"Hhh! The sink!" Lucy squealed suddenly.

A tide of water was creeping over the edge. As the leading wave splattered to the kitchen floor, David leapt forward and twiddled the tap. "Drat, the plug must be in," he muttered. But all he dragged from the hole was a fistful of Brussels sprout and carrot peelings.

"Oh!" went Aunty Gwyneth and swept away. "I am not to be disturbed!" she barked, and disappeared into her room. As she slammed the door to, she snapped at Gretel: "Well, has he coughed? And I don't mean smoke."

Gretel shook her head. She had tried in vain, while her mistress was out, to reason with G'reth. If he told what he knew, he'd be freed, she'd said. But G'reth, pure as the falling snow, had said he knew nothing. He was just a wishing dragon: born to serve.

And now he was born to die.

"I am tired of this," Aunty Gwyneth said darkly. "Finish it. Burn the wire."

G'reth cried out in distress. Every scale on his

206

body fell flat with fear.

"Burn it!" Aunty Gwyneth shrieked.

Gretel huffed and puffed. Her claws made score marks on the wardrobe.

"Do as I say, or you're next," hissed her keeper.

And what choice did Gretel have after that? She made fire in the pit of her throat. *Hrrrrr!*

With a zing, the light flex broke and G'reth went hurtling towards the floor. Gretel covered her ears and turned. She was not, and never had been, a wicked dragon, and to see one of her kind smashed to splinters was more than her pretty violet eyes could take. But at the vital moment, when there should have been a horrible chinkling of clay, no such chinkling was heard. Gretel whipped around. G'reth was doing a rigid kind of bungee jump, his spiky little topknot tapping and scraping the bare wooden boards. Aunty Gwyneth had caught the wire.

"It's true. He knows nothing. Let him go." She dropped G'reth into the wastepaper basket and once again headed out of the room.

Gretel sighed with relief. Spreading her wings for flight, she prepared to go down to aid the wisher. But just as the air began to lift her, she became aware of a faint, faint sound – dragon scales, rattling underneath her feet. Alert now, she pottered to the wardrobe front. Using her back paws to cling to the cornice, she leaned over and managed to wedge the door open. It was dusty and gloomy inside the closet, but her sharp, superior vision was able to penetrate the dark with ease. What she saw, of course, was a listening dragon, its face buried deep in the cup of its paws, quaking in a corner behind a stack of sweaters. Gretel flexed her snout. She pulled back her head and stooped to think. A listening dragon? In her mistress's room? She swung herself upright and glanced at the suitcase. But it must have heard…? She shuddered and popped a wonky smoke ring, then looked thoughtfully around the room: at Liz, in slumber and completely unawares; at the dragon child, dancing in the glowing bronze egg; at G'reth, tortured and struggling in the basket; at the suitcase again; and finally at the snow drifting past the window. There were choices to be made here. Difficult choices. She took an orange rose from the back of her quiver, a flower her mistress knew nothing about, and one that Gretel had never thought to use. But glancing at G'reth again she knew it must be so. She glimpsed once more at the listening dragon. Then, silently, she closed the wardrobe door.

Something in the air

The following morning, David was ready, on the dot, at nine. Although his meeting at the publishers was not until eleven, the journey involved two changes of trains and he wanted to arrive in plenty of time. He showered and hurried downstairs. Henry had already left for work, and Gadzooks, as always, was enjoying the freedom of not having to pretend he was a lifeless object. He was sitting in the middle of the dining table, tapping his pencil against his snout and poring over something on his pad, when David crept up and peeped over his shoulder. "Planning a robbery, Zookie?"

Gadzooks immediately snatched up his papers. He shuffled them together and folded them away.

David threw him a searching look. "You're edgy this morning. What were you drawing? It looked like some sort of...escape route."

The telephone rang. *Hrrr!* went Gadzooks, and pointed to it.

"Yes, I can hear it," David said, and picked the receiver off its rest. "Hello. Bacon residence."

"At last! Where have you *been?*"

David frowned. He thought he knew that

voice. "Is that Zanna?"

"Of course it's Zanna! I've been trying to reach you for absolutely ages. What's up with your mobile?"

David pulled it from his pocket. "Nothing. It's fine. It isn't switched on."

"Oh, you don't say. *Quelle surprise.* Feeling heavy, is it? It should be, with all the messages I've been leaving!"

David tried to reason this out. "Did you want something, Zanna?"

There was a squawk of incredulity somewhere down the line. "How about your head on a stick? Are you *feeling* OK?"

David touched the aforementioned head. It was still on his shoulders and its temperature was normal. "Yes, thanks. Gotta run. I've got a train to catch."

"RAIN?!" she screamed.

But David had already hung up. Flashing a glance at his watch he said, "Better pop next door before I leave."

Hrrr, went Gadzooks, paddling his feet.

"You want to come?"

Hrrr!

David clicked his tongue. "You can't go on your windowsill, you know that, don't you?"

Hrr-ar! Gadzooks explained.

"The bin? You want to visit the bin?"

Hrr...ar! the dragon hurred a little slower.

"Oh, the *den*," said David, grinning stupidly. His grasp of dragontongue was still not great. "OK, come on." He tapped his shoulder.

Gadzooks was there in a flash.

As they made the short trip to the Pennykettles' house, David asked again, "By the way, what *were* you drawing just now?"

For once, Gadzooks wasn't paying attention. He was catching snowflakes in his paws, puzzling over their texture and shape. There was auma in the snow – as there was in all things – but it was fragile, fainter than a distant star. And it fizzled when the crystals turned to tears. He chewed the end of his pencil and pondered. He felt sure there was a real connection here, between the flaking ice and the fire of Gawain. It was, after all, the reason why G'reth had been horribly abused, and the motive for his business at number forty-two...

He was off the instant David opened the door. "Behave yourself," David shouted after him and carried on into the kitchen. Bonnington was sitting on the drainer, as usual, staring out into the snow-filled morning. Lucy was in her favourite seat, half-heartedly munching a piece of toast.

"Hi. Any news? Why the long face?"

"Gwilanna won't let me see Mum. She won't even let me look through the window. It's not fair. It's been ages. And the dragons don't like it either. They're whispering a lot and acting funny."

David sat down beside her and lifted the teapot. "Dragons are always acting funny. Try not to fret. By six tonight you'll have a bouncing baby brother, then we'll be back to normal again. You must be looking forward to it, surely? I know Gwilanna can be a bit strict, but it's important to maintain…security, I s'pose. I'm sure your mum's doing absolutely fine. If she was in hospital like a normal mum you wouldn't be able to see her *that* often, would you?" He poured a cup of tea. It looked stewed and cold.

"That's yesterday's," Lucy told him. "See what happens when Mum isn't here?"

Unfazed, David whistled down the hall. A young male dragon flew in at once, carrying a postcard in its mouth. He dropped it at David's place. David recognised the creature as the one he'd seen checking the plants for water. "Thank you. Where's Gruffen? I thought he was door monitor?"

The dragon wriggled its snout.

"Gwillan and Gruffen take turns," said Lucy. "Guarding the hall, I mean. Gwillan does lots of jobs for

212

Mum. He's a snuffler dragon. He dusts."

Without prompting, Gwillan bent his snout to a small patch of dust and 'snuffled' it into his wide, flared nostrils.

"Very impressive," David told him and pushed the cold tea under Gwillan's snout. "Warm that, will you?"

"That's not allowed!" Lucy protested, as Gwillan, with one snort, brought the tea back to the boil – but left it covered in a layer of dust. The snuffler gulped and his cheeks turned a very deep shade of green. He nudged the postcard closer to David then beat a warmish exit.

"Serves you right," said Lucy. "Who's your postcard from?"

David flipped it over. "Someone in Africa."

"Sophie! Let me see!"

"Ah, ah. My girlfriend, remember? It's personal. There might be intimate…thingies."

Before Lucy could issue her usual batch of insults, the telephone rang, drawing her away. Moments later she was back, looking even more disgruntled. "It's her."

"Who, Sophie?"

"No, the *other* one. She rang yesterday as well. I told her you were dead."

"*What?*"

"Can I read the card now?"

"No." David batted her arm with it. "And don't ever tell anyone I'm dead – unless I am."

"OK," she chirped, and whipped the card off him anyway.

Strangely, death was on Zanna's mind too. "Hang up and you're history," she threatened. "I want to know what's going on. First I get a cryptic text message from you, then you're giving me the big cold shoulder. Is your woman back on the scene or what?"

David, perplexed by both of these questions, thought it best to avoid all references to Sophie. "Text?" he queried.

"H-R-R-R," Zanna spelled.

"I didn't send that."

"Yes, you did. It came from your number. Stop messing me about. What's going on? Is everything OK? You promised you'd tell me about the egg."

At this, David's brain began to go swimmy. Egg? How could anyone outside the family know about the egg?

"What have they done to you?" Zanna pressed.

David bit his lip. It was times like this he wished Liz was awake. She was so much better at this game than him. "I've gotta go, sorry."

"David, don't you dare hang up! What have they done? Tell me or I'm going straight to Bergstrom."

Bergstrom. David remembered something about him. "Will you pass on a message for me?"

"Maybe." She sounded guarded now.

"Tell him...I didn't have time to write my essay."

He put the phone down and wandered back to the kitchen.

"Have you finished with her yet?" Lucy asked hopefully.

"You can't finish something you haven't started, Lucy."

Lucy wiggled her nose. It wasn't quite the answer she'd been hoping for, but it seemed to do. "Sophie sends her love." She pointed to a cluster of kisses on the card.

"Hmm," went David, glancing at the clock.

"I think she misses us."

David wasn't so sure. If anything, the card had been quite perfunctory. Not so much as a 'wish you were here'. He felt a tug of disappointment and buried it fast. "Going to the loo, then I'm off, OK?"

A-row, went Bonnington. He jumped down off the sink and started scratting in his litter tray.

"Yuk," went Lucy, and pinched her nose – though it wasn't clear which of them, cat or lodger, this gesture was intended for.

Upstairs, while David was performing his ablutions, he tried to rehearse what he wanted to say to Dilys Whutton. But every time he pictured the interview scene, his thoughts were swiftly derailed by a lot of busy *hurring* in the Dragons' Den next door. "What's going on in there, do you know?" He turned to the puffler dragon on the cistern. The puffler shrugged. It wasn't its business to know of 'goings-on'. It's duty was to puffle, which was just what it did, sending out a cloud of sweet-smelling jasmine as soon as David had pulled the chain. David washed his hands and went next door.

At the first creak of hinges the hurring stopped, then rose to the gentle background level that generally warmed the house so well. David peered around the shelves. Those dragons that weren't just lifeless lumps blinked or blew smoke rings or stretched their wings. His gaze came last to Liz's workbench. "Now, then. What are you lot up to?"

G'reth, Gadzooks and the guard dragon, Gruffen, all shuffled their feet and gave an innocent cough. Gadzooks put his notepad behind his back.

"You shouldn't be on there," David told them. "Guinevere mustn't be disturbed, you know." On the stand immediately behind the bench, Liz's special dragon was sleeping deeply. David looked to the opposite side where the dragon Liz had made in the image of Gawain was hunched in a corner, also fast asleep.

Suddenly, the peace was broken by a strident shout downstairs: Aunty Gwyneth calling for Gretel. All three dragons tensed their scales. "Stay out of trouble," David told them, and went to see what the fuss was about.

Aunty Gwyneth collared him in the hall. "Where is Gretel?"

"Dunno. Haven't seen her. Up the garden, collecting seeds, I s'pose. I'm going to the publishers. See you later."

Aunty Gwyneth stopped him with a talon-like grip. "There is an atmosphere in this house today. I hear whisperings. Murmurs of insurrection. I hope this is none of *your* doing?"

"Insurrection?" David looked puzzled.

"Rebellion," Aunty Gwyneth growled. Her eyes sharpened as if they could slice him in two.

David flapped a hand. "Oh, it's just the dragons. Lucy said they were acting funny. They're restless. Missing Liz, probably."

"Yes," said Aunty Gwyneth, "I suppose they are. Very well. You may go. You will return by three. Are there adequate mushrooms in the fridge?"

"I peeled a whole bagful late last night. Lucy, I'm going! See you later, OK?"

"Good luck!" she cried, running through from the kitchen.

"The boy does not need luck," said Aunty Gwyneth, picking a piece of fluff off his jacket, "merely the proper kind of...guidance."

This made David squirm. Guidance? What did the old crone mean by that? It wasn't like her to offer 'friendly' advice. Fearing she might try to peck him on the cheek, he grabbed his greatcoat and hurried away.

As soon as he was gone, Lucy asked politely, "Aunty Gwyneth, may I see Mum now, please?"

"You may not," was the harsh reply. "You will go into the garden and search for Gretel. There is an urgent task required of her."

"But it's snowing."

"Then wear a hat."

Lucy sighed and pulled on her boots. "I want to see my mum!" she shouted. But her words fell on hollow ears as usual.

Gretel, as it turned out, was closer at hand than anyone imagined. She was actually on the fridge top, near to the back where no one could see. In front of her stood the listening dragon, a glazed kind of look in its spectacled eyes. One flower – a mixture of buttercup and chives – had been enough to bring it under Gretel's control. Gretel, like her mistress, had sensed the growing unrest in the house and was cleverly fine-tuning the listener's ears, hoping to pinpoint the source of the revolt. She found it exactly where she thought she would: on the bench in the Dragons' Den. Three of them: G'reth, the silly little guard dragon, Gruffen, and the soppy-eyed writing dragon, Gadzooks, all tuning in to the dragon in the wardrobe, the one they were calling Grace. They were conspiring, plotting their revenge for the way G'reth had been made to suffer. Gretel blew a smoke ring in despair. Pennykettle dragons! Did they have nothing but soot for brains? They would all be quenched for this; tails used as disposable toothpicks. How could four incompetent pufflers hope to defeat her mistress, Gwilanna? She tuned in again, searching for details. The first snippet she picked up stiffened her scales. Hrrr-rrr-ar-raar. The password for the suitcase. Great Gawain! They were planning to steal the scale? How? None of them could carry such a weight, let alone get past… Wait. What was that? She tuned in again, carefully tweaking the listener's ears, trying to receive an accurate signal. The

hurrs faded in. The hurrs faded out. And then the
dragon Gadzooks broke through. Help would come.
G'reth was sure of it. Pff! went Gretel. Help? From
where?! The airwaves hummed again. And out of the
Dragons' Den came an answer. A word that made Gretel
curious and fearful in equal amounts.

What in clay's name was a *Spikey*, she wondered?

Hobnobbing with Dilys

The offices of Apple Tree Publishing were wedged between a builder's yard and a pub in a cramped and run-down area of London. It was hardly the castle of literary elegance that David Rain had imagined it to be. Redevelopment was everywhere. Half the road was chequered by scaffolding. Boards surrounded the knocked-out shop fronts. The smell of damp brick dust hung in the air. Black taxi cabs shuttled past, squirting slush onto the snow-packed pavements. And from every quarter there came a noise. Hammering, drilling, workmen shouting, music thumping out of the pub, the steady buzz of traffic, the rumble of a bus, the sucking whistle of an overhead plane. By the time David had found the right door (a giveaway, thanks to the window display of Apple Tree's award-winning TV character 'Kevin the Karaoke Kangaroo') he could barely make his voice heard over the intercom. Thankfully he did and the door clicked open. A pleasant young woman, wearing what appeared to be a pilot's headset, asked him his business. He brushed the snow off his shoulders and told her. *Mr Rain for Dilly*, she announced. She invited him to take a seat. Someone would be down to see him in a moment. *Dilly?* thought David. Seemed a bit irreverent for a senior editor. He shrugged. Perhaps it was a publishing thing. He plonked himself on a stylish futon and picked up a copy of *Kevin Goes To Texas*.

He was halfway through the classic, *Home on the Range*, when a woman appeared on the stairs to his left. She was tall and frighteningly slim; all arms and legs, like an alien visitor. She would have been several years older than Zanna, but not nearly as old as Liz. Her dark brown hair was short and chic. She was wearing a cream-coloured roll neck sweater, trapped at the hips by a low-slung belt which sat on top of a short suede skirt. She walked like a Siamese cat. David whistled inwardly and tried not to stare. He was checking out where the buffaloes grazed when the alien leg-stalks halted in front of him.

"David?" A delicate hand came out.

Dumbstruck, David shook it.

The alien apparition smiled. She had a generous mouth and sparkling eyes. High cheek bones. Perfect skin. "You're quite a bit younger than we imagined," she said, slightly over-pronouncing her words.

"Sorry," David muttered.

"No problem," she said. "Come and meet the clan." She turned and led him up the stairs. By the time they had climbed four winding flights, she seemed to have learned the best part of his background. "Geography? Isn't that a lot of maps and contours?"

"Mmm," went David, mapping the contours of her swinging hips.

They entered an open-plan office. Posters of book covers and children's characters leapt off every scrap of wall. The whole floor was divided up by orange partitions. In every space was a desk, a computer and at least one rack of children's books. "This is Editorial," the tour guide fluted, trailing a hand as they wandered past. "And over here is Design."

David smiled at everyone in turn. It wasn't difficult. All the computers were staffed by women. Young women, in T-shirts and jeans. They waved or said 'hi' and went back to their screens. The apparition stopped by a drinks machine. "Tea?"

"Thanks. One sugar, please. Excuse me, but don't any *men* work here?"

The hostess thought a moment. "Hmm. Robert, in Marketing. He's very useful for blowing up balloons at parties. Why?"

"Just wondered," David muttered. The prospect of being a children's author was beginning to appeal to him more and more. "What do you do? Are you Mrs Whutton's assistant?"

The 'assistant' smiled rather inwardly at this. "I make the tea – among other things," she said, handing him a scorching plastic cup. "Strictly speaking, it's 'Mizz', not 'Mrs'. I would accept 'Miss', but I always think it makes me sound a bit school marm-y. Just plain Dilys will do." She opened the door to a quiet office.

David went in, wishing that the floor would dissolve beneath his feet. "*You're* Dilys? I'm sorry. I thought you'd be..."

"Older?" she laughed. "I'll take that as a compliment – this time. Sit down. Help yourself to a biscuit."

David looked at the plate. Chocolate hobnobs. How could he resist?

Mizz Dilys Whutton sat down opposite. On the table in front of her lay David's manuscript. She stroked her fingers along its margins and pressed the pages neatly into register. "This is a lovely story, David. How did it come about?"

So David told her about his adventures with the squirrels, and how he'd written the story for Lucy's birthday.

Dilys Whutton cooed like a dove. "Ah, that's so *sweet*. You made half the girls here cry, you know."

"They've read it?"

"Oh, yes. Everyone has. Even Robert in Marketing. Anything we consider for publication is read by the whole office."

"But...you said in your letter you're not going to publish it."

Dilys steepled her fingers and tapped them together. "No, that's right. Let me tell you why. Every publisher has what they call a list, which kind of represents their general tastes. If we don't feel confident that a book will sit right on our list, we tend to let it go." She cast her eyes at *Snigger*. "I know that must be awfully disappointing for you, but there is a ray of hope. The reason I called you in today was to tell you how much I enjoyed your style. Your writing is full of innocence and charm, but it's also oddly captivating. If we could find a project that might interest us both, I'd like you to have another go."

"Oh," said David, and took another hobnob.

Dilys sat back and crossed her legs. "Are you working on anything else right now?"

"Well, erm..."

"Just an outline of something, perhaps?"

David looked at the window, at the patterns forming on the snow-flecked glass. This was his chance to make an impression. But what could he tell her when there *was* nothing else? Everything he'd tried to write just lately, including his essay, had come out sounding like gobbledygook. He sighed and focused his gaze on the snow. And as he did, something peculiar happened. From the light and angles and shapes and spaces he made out the face of a polar bear. In his mind he heard Lucy's happy voice chattering, 'He's going to do another book soon, about bears!' And before he knew it he was telling Dilys Whutton, "I have an idea for an Arctic story. It's going to be a sort of...saga, I think. It's set in a time when the ice was ruled by nine bears. One of them was a male called Ragnar."

Dilys broke a biscuit. "Go on," she whispered. "How does it start?"

"On an ice floe," David said, and suddenly the story started to come, as if all that had ever been required of him was to pluck it out of the surrounding air. Staring straight through the polar bear's eyes, into the grey city sky he said, "A mother bear is sitting with her female cub. They're looking across the Arctic ocean, at an island the bears call the Tooth of Ragnar. The mother is telling the cub its history. The island is a place of many legends, but it also marks a time of...terrible conflict."

"Between rival bears?"

David swept his head from side to side. "No. Bears

226

and men." The snow began to dot the windows again, and now, with every flake that settled, an image of the Arctic came along with it. A *village...an ancient tribal place... people wailing... hunger... drums...the wind, whistling ... darkness ... cold... a bear cub, lost and seeking shelter ... a man with a long bone in his hand, wielding it high above his head...* "No!" David let out a sudden gasp and a snow shower thumped against the office windows, almost punching a dent in the glass.

Dilys Whutton jumped and knocked her tea. She took a tissue from her sleeve and mopped the spill, then stood up and checked the window latch. "Sorry, these windows are very old. They get a bit spooky in weather like this. What made you cry out?"

"I saw a cub," said David, setting his gaze into the middle distance between himself and the corner of the office. "It wanders into an Inuit settlement where the people are starving and desperate for food."

Dilys bit her lip. "A cub? They killed it?"

"Yes." Here David paused and narrowed his eyes, as though his mind was having to reach far back in time. "Yes," he breathed again, "but it shouldn't have happened. In those days, bears were sacred to the Inuit. Hunting them was strictly forbidden."

"But if the people were starving?"

"No." David frowned and shook his head again. "This didn't have anything to do with need. Something turned them. Something bad. I'm not sure what. And the cub is no ordinary bear. He's Ragnar's only son. And when Ragnar finds out, he takes his bears and attacks the village. Bears from all parts of the ice join in. Not even the *Nanukapik*, their leader, can stop it. It's a terrible disaster. And it *shouldn't* have happened."

Dilys Whutton patted her chest. "Well, I'm breathless just thinking about it. An odyssey in the Arctic? We've never had that at Apple Tree before. This is very exciting, David. I want you to go away and write this, now. Send me six chapters and a synopsis of the rest. If I like it, I'll consider making an advance."

"Advance?"

"Money," said Dilys, with a twinkle in her eye. "I wish I could give you something now, but I'd really have to see how the story pans out. How long do you think it will take you to write six—?"

A knock at the door cut Dilys short. A young woman popped into the room. "Hi, Dilly. Sorry to interrupt. This just arrived by courier for you." She put a medium-sized, gift-wrapped box on the table, smiled briefly at David and left.

"Ooh," gushed Dilys. "Who's sent this?" She read the

card and frowned. "Hmm. No name. But I'm to open it at once, apparently. Do you mind? I love surprises."

"No," said David and took another hobnob. He watched idly as Dilys tore into the wrapping, but his mind was still focused hard on the bears. Where had that story come from? Was it true? Why did it feel so real? He turned his head to look again at the window, and in that moment Dilys Whutton exclaimed, "Oh, how sweet! Someone's sent me a dragon!"

"Dragon?" said David, smearing chocolate off his lip.

Dilys drew the sculpture out of its box. "How wonderful. It's got a bunch of flowers."

"*What?*" A shower of crumbs flew across the table.

"I wonder if they're scented," Dilys said, and put her nose to the dragon's posy.

"No!" cried David. "Dilys, don't—"

But Dilys had already sniffed. "Ooh," she went again, sitting back, looking dizzy. Her eyes crossed and she blinked a few times. She put the dragon down on the table. "Hmm, yes, I…hmm, would you excuse me a minute?"

"Certainly," said David, turning on the dragon the moment Dilys had stepped outside. "What in clay's name are *you* doing here?"

Furrff! went Gretel, very rudely indeed, as if to say

she'd rather be anywhere than here. Home: that was where she wanted to be, keeping an eye on the Pennykettle dragons. She picked up a bookmark of *Kevin the Karaoke Kangaroo* and launched it into David's tea.

"Pack it in," he hissed. "I asked you a question. Why has Gwilanna sent you here? What was in that flower you made Dilys sniff? This is an important meeting, Gretel. You're going to ruin everything if you—"

Suddenly, the door reopened. In a flash, Gretel reassumed her solid form. David flopped back in his chair and sighed. This was all going to go horribly wrong.

But Dilys sat down looking strangely chirpy. "I've just had a word with our publisher," she beamed. "I've told her I want to sign you up."

"*What?*"

"We're going to make you an offer, Mr Rain. *For Snigger – and* the polar bear book."

From the corner of his eye, David saw Gretel blowing pollen off her claws and polishing them smugly against her breast.

"It would have to be a standard contract, I'm afraid. You're an unknown, so we'd be taking a chance."

David raised his hands. "Hang on, this isn't right."

Gretel scowled at him darkly.

"Oh," said Dilys, looking disappointed. "Well, if you'd rather negotiate – through an agent, perhaps?"

Oh yeah, thought David. *Aunty Gwyneth: the agent from hell.*

Dilys shuffled in her chair and said, "We'd pay you a thousand on signature. Another thousand when you deliver the manuscripts; the rest on publication."

"A thousand?" David's mouth fell open.

"Pounds. It's not a bad offer, David. If you agree, I can have a contract drawn up by the end of next week."

A thousand pounds? The figure was making David giddy. He could go to the Arctic on that. *And* clear his overdraft at the bank.

"Go home and think it over," Dilys said, packing Gretel into her box. "Give me a call in a couple of days. It's been lovely to meet you. I'm so glad you came." She floated her hand and David shook it. "Lovely dragon as well." She slid the box across the table. "I'm glad you were able to do a bit of shopping. That will make a beautiful present for your aunt."

David smiled at her weakly. Gwilanna had thought this through very neatly. A potion for the contract and a potion to enable Gretel's return. He would have a few words to say to his 'aunt' as soon as he and his 'present' got home.

*

On the journey, he questioned Gretel again. As the train drew near to Scrubbley North station, the volume of passengers gradually thinned until he was finally alone in the carriage. He tapped on the lid of Gretel's box. The dragon forced her way out. She pottered to the window, looking fidgety and anxious.

"What you did up there wasn't clever," David told her. "It's not right, using potions to influence people. She's giving us money. That's fraud, you know."

Furrfff!

"And you can cut that out. Especially in here." David pointed at the 'No Smoking' sign.

Phoof! went Gretel, and covered it with ash.

David threw up his hands. "What *is* the matter with you lot today? First, Gadzooks is plotting something, and now you've got this ridiculous huff on. Did I ask you to come to London and—"

He stopped speaking, then, as if a plug had been pulled. There was a strange, uncomfortable feeling in his head, as if he were standing at the centre of a balloon and someone had let out all the air. Whatever had gripped him had also taken Gretel. She staggered backwards away from the window and started to reel like a circus clown. With a violent and noisy shake of her wings, she stumbled into the side of the box.

David grabbed her and held her steady. His vision was blurring now, and Gretel's figure was ghosting badly. But David could see her well enough, and what he did see chilled him right to the bone. The dragon's eyes were swimming with fear, their colour flickering violet, then green, then violet...then grey.

"Gretel, what's happening? Gretel? Gretel?!"

Too late. The dragon had no reply. She let out a screeching wail more grating than the train wheels braking on the tracks. She shook like a demon and her scales began to stiffen. And yet, with one courageous effort, she reached back into her quiver and drew out a flower. Her paw opened and she dropped it at her feet.

And that was how she stayed: stopped, like a clock. Something had drained the auma from her and left just a tired grey husk behind. All the colour that remained of the potions dragon was wrapped in the single orange rose, sliding back and forth on the plasticised table, rocking and rolling with the motion of the train.

David lifted it up to her nostrils. But in his heart, he knew she would not respond. For she had made no attempt to bring the flower to her snout, and that could only mean one thing: it was a cry for help, not a cure for ills.

The rose was meant for him.

David turns

Approximately ten minutes later, David burst into the Pennykettles' house and skidded to a halt outside his room. "Aunty Gwyneth! Are you there? There's something wrong with Gretel!" He looked down at the potions dragon, frozen solid in the open gift box, and ran a warm thumb along her snout. "Aunty Gwyneth, let me in!" He hammered the door. At last, it opened with a tired creak. "I was on the train," David spluttered, "and— Lucy? What are you doing there?" She was standing in the doorway with her head bent low, gentle snuffles rising out of her throat. With a sob, she left the door swinging open and flung herself down on the bed by her mum.

David edged his way in. What had once been his student lodgings was now little more than a ramshackle hovel. A cold, dark hovel at that. A candle, burning in a jam jar on his desk, was the only source of heat and light, apart from the egg in Liz's hands. It was glowing with a strong, amber-yellow luminescence, sending shadow pulses up the damaged walls. The dragon child inside it had grown considerably and was now curled double, almost breaching the shell. Liz, despite the devastation all around her, still appeared to be sleeping soundly.

And yet there was something horribly wrong. Lucy was in tears, and the house, which had always been so vibrant and warm, had been struck by the creeping odour of damp and a sinister strain of wanton neglect. David listened out. Not a hurr could be heard. Where on earth were the whuffler dragons? Why weren't they heating the place? He shook Lucy by the shoulder and asked her what was happening.

"It would be better if I answered that," said a voice, and Aunty Gwyneth drifted in. David stood back with a start. Her hair was down and rougher than rope; her face so very lined and ugly that it was possible to wonder how the bones could bear to support her skin. Her neat designer two-piece suit had gone through an odd metamorphosis of rips, until it resembled a piece of sacking. This was no longer Aunty Gwyneth. This was the ancient sibyl, Gwilanna. As she approached, she raised her hands. Resting upon them was a plastic box – a plastic box with a pale blue lid. "There has been an interesting development," she said. "Such a pity you missed it all."

"Go away! I hate you!" Lucy screamed. She sat up and threw a handful of dirt.

"Insolent wretch," Gwilanna sneered. She spat at the dirt and the crumbs turned into a posse of spiders. They came hurrying back in waves to the bed. Lucy screamed and drew up her feet. Gwilanna laughed and the spiders dissolved to dust.

"What's going on?" David demanded.

"She's killed all the dragons!" Lucy yelled. "Oh, Mum, wake up. Please wake up." She threw her arms around Liz's shoulders. But Liz's sleep was deeper than quicksand. No matter how firmly Lucy shook her, her eyes refused to open.

Gwilanna tilted the box to one side. From it came the sound of gently sloshing water. "There was a loss of power while you were out. I have yet to establish how it happened. I suspect it was sabotage, but that is by the by. When I came to investigate, I found the kitchen door open and the child in the garden, secreting this box and its contents in the snow."

"The snowball," said David, beginning to cotton on.

"I was trying to save it from melting!" yelled Lucy. "And she *stole* it! And now none of the dragons can move!"

David pulled Gretel out of the gift box. "Is that why she went like this?"

"Break her!" cried Lucy, lunging forward. "She's

236

evil. Break her! Do it now!"

"Calm down," snapped David, pushing her back. He turned to Gwilanna. "Are they all like this?"

"Oh, yes," she said, with a broken-toothed grin.

David gulped and thought of Gadzooks, remembering the vacant feeling on the train. "*Are* they dead?"

Gwilanna moved closer, searching David's face as if she had lost a few of the lice which crawled through the fraying twists of her hair. "No, they're suspended in a kind of...half-world, kept alive by virtue of the fact that Elizabeth, when she created them, gave them a little of her natural auma – as well as a crystal of...shall we call it *icefire?*"

"I hate you," said Lucy. "When Mum wakes up—"

"When your mother wakes up," Gwilanna cut in, snarling like a rabid dog, "she will tell me where this snowball came from or lose her precious dragons for good."

"She won't! She won't tell you *anything*! Ever!"

"Then I will pour the water away and leave her dragons as hollow as a drum!" Gwilanna made a rasping *hrrr* and the lid came flying off the box as if it had been lifted away in a storm.

Lucy squealed with fear.

"Stop!" cried David. "This is ridiculous. I thought we

were all on the same side, here?"

"You can't side with *her*," whined Lucy.

"Be silent," said Gwilanna. "Let the boy speak." She scraped David's cheek with the one of her nails. "Well, lodger? What have you to say?"

David pulled away in disgust. "I know what you're up to, Gwilanna. All that business with Gretel, in London. Making the publisher give me a contract. You want me to go to the Arctic, don't you? You want me to find the fire of Gawain."

"No!" cried Lucy.

"Shut up," snapped David. And now a cold light entered his eyes. The candle flickered. The floorboards creaked. The lodger turned his gaze on the plastic box. "What you have there is a speck, am I right? A droplet of a droplet of the dragon's tear?"

"Less than a cinder," Gwilanna said tiredly.

"What if I could get you the rest?"

"No!" Lucy shouted

"Stick your tongue!" Gwilanna roared.

And poor Lucy found her tongue shored up against her teeth. The hex only lasted a second or two, but it frightened her enough to shut her up for a fortnight. Sobbing heavily, she tried to run away. David held her back. "Sit down and behave." Lucy kicked him half-heartedly and swerved away. This was all too much. Her mother lost, her dragons gone, and the lodger who had written her birthday stories and saved the life of an injured squirrel…was he deserting her, too?

"These two can't tell you anything," he said, tilting his head towards Lucy and Liz. "Only the bears know the secret of the fire."

"Bears are charlatans, never to be trusted."

"Maybe not, but they seem to trust *me*. They want me to work for them; you knew that, I suppose? But *they* can't give me what I want."

"And what is that?" said Gwilanna, narrowing her gaze.

David looked down and stroked Gretel's wings. "I saw what she did in London. If it's really that easy to get me a contract, it won't be difficult arranging a bestselling book. I'm not like you people; I didn't hatch from an egg or find a way of living that was way beyond my expiry date. I'm normal, and that's how I'm going to stay, unless you give me something more. Help me achieve success with the books and I'll lead you straight to the fire tear. But I'll need Gadzooks restored. The bears work through him. He's my contact with them. The other dragons can go to the clay."

From the top of the bed, Lucy made a sound like a

wounded dog. Tears came pouring down her cheeks.

Gwilanna, however, was not easily convinced. "You? A storytelling nincompoop? Why should I put my trust in you when it was *your* dragon which led a revolt to try to steal the contents of my case?"

"She's got the scale!" cried Lucy. "She brought it with her."

David ignored her and looked at the sibyl. "Revolt? What are you talking about?"

Gwilanna snatched Grace up from the desk. "*This* was hiding in the wardrobe. While I was out of the room with the girl, the others used her to speak the password. But I returned, unexpectedly, and battle was done. They had a guard: the dragon called Gruffen. It tried to burn me with a prick of fire ... and only succeeded in melting the snowball. Amusing, don't you think? Their heist ruined by their very own auma. Every dragon froze where it stood. I found your scribbler on the windowsill. It had opened the window in order that the stupid wishing dragon could attempt to fly the scale away."

David sighed and sank down onto the bed. So that was why Gadzooks had been drawing an escape route. "Where are they – Gadzooks, Gruffen and the wisher?"

"I cast them aside, amongst the rubble in the corner."

David didn't even look. "And Grace? Why have you kept her back?"

"I was intending to crumble her to dust, for amusement. She may be in a void, but she can still know discomfort. She was the informant. She needs to be punished. They *all* need to be punished. But why don't I let you have this pleasure? If you wish me to trust you...break her ears."

"No! She's Sophie's dragon!" squealed Lucy.

"Take her!" rapped Gwilanna.

And David did. Pressing his thumbs against the paper-thin ears he calmly met Gwilanna's gaze. "Cross me and we're enemies for ever," he said.

"No!" shrieked Lucy.

But her squeal of protestation could not disguise the sharp *click click* of clay. By the time her voice had faded into silence, the listening dragon could hear no more.

The secret of the rose

"Well, well," said Gwilanna. "How the worm turns."

"I hate you!" Lucy screamed at David. "I wish you'd never come! I never wanted a lodger! And I don't want a stupid brother, either!" And before anyone could stop her, she had snatched up a lump of ceiling plaster and brought it crashing towards the egg. But it was she, not the egg, which came off worst. A shower of sparks lit up the room as the plaster turned red and started to fizz. Lucy gave out a yowl of pain, but the tears which followed were really more to do with her torment than her burns. She flung herself down in a pitiful heap, sobbing so heavily the bed began to shake.

"Idiot child," Gwilanna sneered. "Did you think I would leave the egg unguarded?"

"She'll learn," said David, chewing his lip. He rolled Grace onto a spare bit of mattress and dropped the broken ears in a hollow beside her; they clinked forlornly against her scales. "What do you intend to do about the dragons? Won't you need Gretel? Can she be revived?"

"That we will discover, shortly," said Gwilanna. "I have placed a small quantity of icefire water inside a drawstring pouch in the garden. It should be frozen—wait! What was that?"

David turned his head. Like Gwilanna, he had heard something rattling in the kitchen. "Sounds like Bonnington using his cat flap."

The sibyl ground her teeth. "That dim-witted furball. Next time I find it under this bed I will turn it into a pair of slippers. Come. Bring the girl. I don't trust her to be left alone with the egg."

David yanked Lucy onto her feet and dragged her after him into the kitchen. Gwilanna pulled the back door open. "The pouch is by the potting shed. Bring it, boy. Hurry."

Hugging his upper arms for warmth, David hurried outside and crunched across the patio. Since his return from London, the weather had slumped to the lowest rungs of the meteorological ladder. The wind was scooping the marrow from his bones and every snowflake that managed to flick his cheeks stung like the crack of a tiny whip. He arrived at the shed, but the pouch was not in sight. He fiddled in the drifts around the base of the plant pots. Nothing there either. This was ridiculous. Where was the wretched thing? The wind laughed and picked at his brain. He searched twice more, then reported to Gwilanna.

"*Not there?*" Her voice was like the screech of a circular saw.

"Look for yourself. It's not a trick."

Gwilanna put the ice water on the drainer. "Keep her away from that. If she moves towards it, snap her ears, too." She swept out into the snow.

The moment she had gone, David and Lucy began a frantic babble. This was all very well, for both of them had a great deal to say. But they quarrelled in such a competitive fashion that neither was able to deliver their point or really be aware of what the other was saying. So it was no surprise that both of them failed to see Bonnington slinking out from under the table. The big tabby cat, unfairly described as a dim-wit and a slouch, was not displaying those attributes now. His ears were pricked, his bearing agile and his shining copper eyes like points of steel. He moved to the centre of the kitchen floor and lifted his hunter's gaze to the drainer. With a silent bound, he was on it.

Lucy, it was, who first caught sight of him. "Hhh!" she gasped, pointing a finger.

"This rose," said David, not looking at first, so desperate was he to show her Gretel's flower. "Just listen to me, Lucy. Just…what? What is it?" The panic in her eyes made him turn his head.

Bonnington was lapping the water from the box.

"Bonnington, NO!"

Over the next few seconds it seemed as if a circus troupe had invaded. Gwilanna stormed in, purple with rage, almost breaking the door off its hinges; David was haring towards the sink, kicking cat litter into every quarter; Bonnington was scrabbling his way off the drainer, then running, ears flat, tail down, for his life. And the box? One moment it was safe in David's hands, the next it was somehow flipping through the air and landing with a clatter in the kitchen sink.

Lucy's fists came up to her mouth.

Even Gwilanna looked moderately shocked. "The auma," she whispered and snatched up the box. It was empty. The last drops gurgled in the sink. "You festering fool!" She turned on David and hurled the box sideways across the room. Lucy yelped as it smacked into a pinboard behind her and bounced back, almost catching her head.

"It was the cat. I was trying to—"

Gwilanna seized him by the throat. "My pouch is missing. What do you know of it?"

"Nothing, I swear."

She tightened her grip.

"Uthin'! H'nest! Lemme go."

Gwilanna snarled and pushed him against the fridge. It rocked and the listening dragon fell over. There was a crunch as the frame of its spectacles broke. "Bring me that cat," Gwilanna growled.

"You leave Bonnington alone!" cried Lucy.

"No. Let her be," David croaked, stepping in before Gwilanna could react. "I'll find the pouch. The cat's probably carried it up the garden. He steals things and hides them away sometimes."

Gwilanna's eyes began to swirl like soup. Suddenly, her nose began to jump and twitch. "There is something not right about you," she hissed. "I smell a potion on you. Show me your hands."

David tried in vain to resist, but how could he oppose the power of a sibyl? His trembling fingers began to uncurl. The orange rose rolled over his palm. "Gretel dropped it on the train," he gulped. "I meant to leave it in the gift box. I don't know what it's for."

Gwilanna snatched it off him. She twisted the flower into one wet nostril, squeezed the stalk and took a gruesome sniff. Her eyes shone violet and boiled with rage. "Treachery," she hissed. "Camomile and peach. Gretel has turned you back."

"What?" said Lucy. "He *can't* be back. A proper David wouldn't be as nasty as him. He broke Grace's ears."

"All for nothing," the sibyl smirked. "It was a useless sacrifice, a futile attempt to infiltrate my plans and make me believe he was my *ally*. The boy has been playing tricks, my dear. We should have known all along that he was merely trying to secure my trust so that he might upset this hatching. He is fouled by bears and will not change. He would steal the scale at the drop of a claw – and take your brother away from you."

"Don't listen to her," David said to Lucy. "That egg she's hatching is not your brother."

Gwilanna narrowed her gaze.

"Oh yes," said David, squaring up. "Gretel turned me back all right. She was made by a Pennykettle – or had you forgotten? She had enough basic goodness in her to realise her mistress was up to no good, and so she passed your secrets to me. Your mum did want another child, Lucy, and put enough of her auma into that egg without ever thinking it might be quickened. Then Zanna happened by, and everything fell very neatly into place. Your 'aunt' here recognised the perfect conditions to kindle the baby *she'd* always wanted. Except it's not a baby, is it, Gwilanna? It's never going to lose its dragon features; it'll lose its human ones instead."

Lucy's mouth fell open in astonishment. "Mum's making a *real* dragon?"

Gwilanna ignored her and spat at David: "You cretinous, interfering dunce. I should turn your bones to ash for this, but I still might have a use for you yet."

"Forget it. I'll never help you," said David. "Stop the kindling and wake Liz now. Let the dragon go back to the clay. It's doomed, like the others you've tried to rear. Without the auma of the icefire, it can't survive."

"Oh, but it can," Gwilanna said, coldly. "Elizabeth is no ordinary host. She has been touched by the ice for years. She, like the red-haired girl who spawned her, has the true dragon's fire within. And what is within, can also be without."

"What does she mean?" Lucy asked David anxiously.

"Find that pouch," Gwilanna snapped. She pointed backwards at the clock on the wall. Its hands, as though possessed of a whirlwind, whipped round and stopped at four forty-seven. "You have until then, the first phase of the hatching. If the snow is not mine by the time the moon rises, the girl's mother will join her dragons."

"How?" bleated Lucy. "What does she *mean?*"

Using his hands like a pair of book ends, David moved Lucy towards the hall. "Get your coat," he said quietly, eyeballing Gwilanna. "We're going out, into the garden."

"But—?"

"Lucy, don't argue." David pushed her away.

Streaming with tears, Lucy went to fetch her coat.

"A wise decision," Gwilanna said smugly.

David looked back at her with all the loathing his heart could muster. "If any harm comes to Liz I'll—"

"You'll what?" sneered the sibyl, staring down at him. "Who are you to meddle in the ways of dragons? If you want to aid Elizabeth, find that pouch."

Surprisingly, however, David didn't even try. On the doorstep, he abandoned the search and told Lucy they would go to Mr Bacon's instead. The snow was falling star upon star, bringing a cold grey fog down with it. No one could possibly see through that.

But the lodger was wrong. There *was* one creature with eyes capable of piercing such a mist. He was hiding in a plant pot behind the shed, confused and afraid, and wondering why the universe had brought him here. Somehow he had survived the loss of auma and escaped from the terrifying sibyl, Gwilanna (sneaking out cleverly through Bonnington's cat flap). As far as he knew, he was the *only* survivor. And that troubled him, deep to his spark. But he must go on. He must not shed his tear. He was a wishing dragon, born to serve. He had a duty to his naming master, the David, and the greater needs of the Mother Earth.

And so he brought his dish-like paws together and let

the universe guide him once more. This time it responded with an eddy of wind that tugged his gaze to the centre of the garden. Through the flurries he saw…great Gawain! A bear! It rose up out of the snow as if it had merely been sleeping flat. Startled, G'reth glanced quickly at the house. If the sibyl saw this, what further terrors might she unleash? But the bear, expert at hiding himself, merely tilted his black-tipped snout in a manner that suggested G'reth should follow. The wishing dragon flicked his tail. He let his spark glow bright a moment and melted the excess snow from his wings. In doing so, he leapt with fright at his stupidity. What was he thinking? Warming his scales so close to the pouch! With remarkable dexterity for one with paws as large as his, he pulled back the drawstrings and peeked inside. A nugget of frozen water winked back. He pulled the drawstrings tight and hurred with relief (upwards into the sky this time). A low growl reminded him the bear was waiting. G'reth hurred and flipped the pouch over his shoulder. Spreading his toes so his feet would skate the snow, he started on the next phase of his journey. This time, he would not have to travel far. Just to the box at the top of the garden…

…where the pink-eyed hedgehog, Spikey, would be waiting.

The calm before the storm

David and Lucy, meanwhile, were ready to depart for Mr Bacon's house. Lucy was not at all happy about this. She wanted to know, not unreasonably perhaps, why they were walking out on her mum, and what David planned to do about finding the pouch, having thrown the remaining icefire down the sink? To be fair, Gwilanna's ultimatum *was* at the forefront of David's mind, and as they stepped out into the gathering storm, he promised Lucy faithfully he would stop Gwilanna, rescue Liz and restore all the dragons back to full flight. What he omitted to say was how. When, by return of breath, Lucy barked that question at him, a pit of despair opened up in his chest; for the truth was, he didn't know what to do. The one shred of hope he was clinging to now were Bergstrom's instructions to watch and wait. Bergstrom: what had become of *him?*

As it happened, someone else was watching and waiting. Just within reach of Henry's door, a brittle voice said, "Hello, remember me?" and Zanna appeared in front of them. She was shivering inside an ankle-length coat, that she wore wrapped over her like a cape. Snow flakes had gathered in the trim around the hood, giving her the look of a faerie ice queen. 'Icy' perfectly described her mood, as Lucy was about to discover.

"What's *she* doing here?"

"You'd better ask him that," Zanna growled back, causing Lucy to shrink away.

"Zanna, ease off," David said. "I know I've been ignoring you. I can explain."

Zanna raised a pencil-thin eyebrow. She folded her arms and took another pace forward, putting her scarlet lips near to his. "It had better be very, *very* good."

And there they stood for a moment, transfixed; she searching for the trust she had lost; he idly wondering if he ought to kiss her.

It was Lucy who eventually forced them apart. "I'm cold," she whined, tugging David's arm.

He blew a snowflake off his nose and fiddled for his keys. Seconds later they were in the house, warmed by the glow of Henry's fire.

"Right, let's hear it," Zanna said, perching on the leading edge of the sofa.

David threw off his coat and flopped down in the recliner. Blow the rules; he'd had a hard day. He told Zanna everything, explaining how Gwilanna had turned his mind and how Gretel had managed to turn him back, the polar bear story that had come out at the publishers, and all that was going on next door. At the end of it, Zanna sat back, dazed.

"Gwilanna's raising a proper dragon? But how could I quicken an egg like that?"

"I have a theory, but I don't think you'll like it." David waited a second, then looked her in the eye. "I think you're a sibyl, like her. You just don't know it, yet."

"Told you she was a witch," sniffed Lucy.

"Not a witch, a prophetess," David jumped in. "A wise woman. A seer. Being a sibyl doesn't make you bad. In the legend of Gawain, Guinevere went to Gwilanna for help. In the beginning, she trusted her."

"Yeah, and look where it got her," said Zanna.

"All the same, I think you've got dormant powers. When I sniffed Gretel's rose, I sensed that Gwilanna is wary of you. I'm not sure how we can use that yet, but when we find the pouch, we should see what effect the icefire has on you."

Lucy Pennykettle sat bolt upright. "That's for the dragons. *She's* not having it!"

"I didn't say I wanted it," Zanna said coolly, exchanging bad-tempered glances with her. "But I do want to help your mum and your dragons, and whatever is in that egg." She turned again to David. "What are you planning to do?"

David glanced at his watch. "We've got about an hour

before the moon rises. If we can't find the pouch by then, we'll have to take her on somehow."

"Take her on? This is Gwilanna you're talking about. You can't just march in, all guns blazing."

"OK, some sort of diversion, then? Maybe we can stall her with a piece of snow that isn't the real icefire?"

"For a nanosecond, maybe," Zanna said doubtfully. "It might help if we knew some more about this snowball. How did your mum first come by it, Lucy?"

With a nudge from David, Lucy said reluctantly, "She went to Norway when she was little."

"Norway?" David tipped forward in his chair.

"She was playing in the snow and she lost her hat. It blew off in the wind and tumbled down a hill. This man found it and brought it back. When he gave it to Mum, there was a snowball in it. He told Mum the snowball was very special. He said it would never melt in her hands. So she put it in a box and brought it home. She'll be mad when she finds out what you did."

"It wasn't me, it was Bonnington, OK?"

"Bonnington?" Zanna looked up, puzzled.

"He drank some of the icefire water," said David.

"And David knocked the rest down the sink," Lucy jabbered.

"I didn't. I—"

"Shush," Zanna said, flapping them quiet. "Bonnington drank a dragon's fire? What's that going to do to him?"

David and Lucy gave a synchronised shrug.

Zanna went back to the incident with the snowball. "This man, has your mum ever talked about him? About what he looked like? She must have said something?"

"She said he was tall…and had eyes like a bear."

"Bergstrom," said David, without a second thought. He flopped back and slapped the arm of his chair.

"The polar bear man?" Lucy asked straight away. "The one who asked you about the dragons?"

"Must be," Zanna said quietly to David.

Lucy was on her feet in a flash. "Phone him!" she insisted, almost pulling David's arm from its socket. "Find him! He'll come! He'll come and help Mum!"

David, however, refused to be harried. If it was true and Bergstrom *had* given Liz the snowball, what was the motivation behind it? It could not have been something he did by rote with all of Guinevere's female line, or Gwilanna herself would never have been curious about the strength of Liz's auma. Why had Liz been singled out?

"Come on-nn," begged Lucy, rifling through David's pockets for his mobile.

He moved her aside and spoke to Zanna. "Did you go

to him, like you said you would?"

"Twice, but his room was locked both times. When I couldn't find him, I came round here."

"Ring him!" Lucy badgered.

"Try," said David, giving Zanna the nod. He leapt from the chair and hurried to the door.

"Where are you going?"

"Upstairs. Won't be long."

"But?"

"Do it,' said Lucy, and plonked the phone in Zanna's lap.

Zanna called the college. Dr Bergstrom, they said, was not answering his extension, and no one in the geography department seemed to know where he might be found. Zanna moved the telephone onto the sofa. "Sorry, no good."

Lucy flopped down and beat her fists against her thighs. "But we've *got* to help Mum."

"We will," said Zanna, squeezing her shoulder. "This man – Dr Bergstrom – I don't believe he'll let your mum be hurt. He's a good man, Lucy. He knows about Gwilanna. He'll stop her, even if we don't manage it. I think there's something odd going on here that none of us understands too well. It's all connected with David's wish and the way that…the universe is dealing with it. I know you're scared. I'm scared, too. But we won't let

Gwilanna win, I promise. Hey, you know about the Earth Mother, don't you?"

Lucy looked at her sideways and nodded.

Zanna pulled out a chain from under her top. Dangling off its end was a silver pendant, made in the shape of a circular labyrinth. She unclipped it and gave it to Lucy to hold. "That's an Earth Mother symbol, used by the Hopi Indian tribe. I know you think I'm, well, a bit strange, but I'm going to say a prayer on it. I believe that the Earth, and all the creatures upon it, are connected together in a universal spirit. In ancient times, people used to think that spirit was bound by the fire of dragons. If you and I can reach it, we might not need Dr Bergstrom at all. Do you want to try? We need to focus on something close to the soil."

"Like a hedgehog?" Lucy wiped her face clean.

"Yes – oh, that's right, David told me you'd seen one in the garden. I like hedgehogs. It's white, isn't it?"

Lucy looked at the far conservatory windows. Wide fringes of untouched snow were dressing the sills like Christmas trimmings. "Yes."

Zanna came round and knelt in front of her, taking Lucy's hands in hers. "In the old days, people used to believe that the Earth Mother often took the form of a hedgehog."

"I know," said Lucy. "It's in my book." She had tried to tell David this, that time she'd shown him Spikey's hutch, but all he'd done was joke about it.

But it was clear that Zanna didn't think that way. She chewed idly on her hair for a moment, then she too was looking through the windows, as if the resolution to all their problems might be out there, hibernating. "Where's David got to?" she wondered aloud.

"Bathroom, probably," Lucy said. "I'm not going to look."

But even if she had, she would not have found David in the bathroom. At that moment, he was inside Henry's study, pursuing a spiritual quest of his own.

The room was still and silent and grey, drawing what little light it could from the spreading cushions of white outside. The slanted almond-shaped eyes of the bear looked out from the shadows of the chimney wall. David moved to the side of the room. "I know you're here, Dr Bergstrom," he whispered, letting the very tips of his fingers glide smoothly over the photographs and books. "I know what it is you've done. You knew when you gifted Liz the fire that one day a chance like this would come – a chance to seize the scale from Gwilanna's clutches. But Liz is in trouble, now. She's lying on a bed in Gwilanna's 'cave', in danger of never waking up.

You've got to help me save her. For Lucy's sake, if nothing else. I've watched and I've waited. Now it's your turn. Show me what I need to see." And he looked into the mesmerising eyes of the bear.

A window juddered in tune to the wind. Under floor level, the pipework dinked. An odour that might have been the reek of fish oil seemed to leech out of the leather-bound books. Shadows rolled across the chimney wall. And it could have been the darkness playing tricks, or a crease or a fold in the surface of the print, but on the head of the bear a mark appeared: three uneven jagged lines, torn into the flesh by a blow of some kind.

A cold unlike any cold he'd ever known, brought the student lodger to an utter standstill. He was looking at the cub struck dead by a bone. The son of Ragnar, grown to adulthood, slain but somehow alive again, a blaze of white fire burning in its scars.

The ice bear opened its monumental jaws, drawing the oxygen out of the room. David fell sideways against the desk, one hand clutching against his chest. But though his breaths were hard to find, images began to fill his brain like a flock of birds landing *en masse* in his head. Gadzooks, struggling in vain to reach him; the dragon-child biting at the shell of the egg; Bonnington, under Gwilanna's bed, sparks of violet in his staring copper eyes; G'reth, alive, at the door of the hutch; the hand of a clock ticking ever onward; the strange etchings on an Inuit talisman, changing their positions as the universe turned...

...and over and above and pervading all this, water bonding back to ice, the molecules speeding hither and thither as if they had memorised their unique positions and all that was hindering their revival was time. Water, freezing in a kitchen sink, plugged by, of all things, mushroom peelings.

And then, suddenly, a door slammed to. A sound that in retrospect could have been the bang of a starting pistol. For from that moment on, the world began to race.

Henry Bacon was home from work.

"Suzanna?" he queried, as she hurried to the hall to intercept him.

"Hello, Mr Bacon. I've, erm, come to revise some college work with David."

Henry brought forth an approving grunt and made his way past her, into the lounge. He stopped abruptly when he caught sight of Lucy, perching on his favourite chair.

Before either girl or Henry could speak, David came thumping down the stairs. "Zanna, gotta talk to you. In the kitchen. Now."

"Stop," said Henry, clapping a hand to his lodger's shoulder. "Rule seventeen, boy. No parties, trysts or similar functions. What's going on?"

"Power's out next door. Lucy's here to keep warm."

Lucy obligingly rubbed her arms.

"No power?" said Henry, looking confused.

"Temporary problem with the fuses," said David, and yanked Zanna into the kitchen.

"That was pretty dumb," she hissed, "letting Henry know there's a problem next door."

"Never mind Henry. This is important. I've just had a kind of...'revelation' upstairs. I know where the pouch is: G'reth's taken it to Spikey's hutch."

"How? I thought the dragons were all out of action?"

"*Liz's* dragons, yes. But Lucy made G'reth, not her mum. She didn't put any of the icefire into him. So he wasn't affected when the snowball melted."

Zanna turned to the window. "And he's gone to the hedgehog? That's weird because—"

"Boy, where are you?" Henry Bacon burst in, cutting Zanna off dead. "Get your key. No time to lose."

"Key? What are you talking about?"

Henry hoisted up a bright green tool box. "Bacon's patent electrical repair kit."

"He wants to go next door!" cried Lucy, rushing in.

David shook his head. "No, that's not possible."

"Nonsense. Can't leave Mrs P without light. Ah, light: good point: torch." And he turned and strode briskly out of the kitchen.

Lucy started to hop like a rabbit. "Mr Bacon mustn't see the egg."

"She's right," said Zanna. "Gwilanna will fry him. Good work, Rain. You wanted a diversion, you just got a corker. Now what?"

David ran a hand through his mop of brown hair. "There's a gap in the fence at the top of the garden. Take Lucy and find that pouch. Bring it back here and

262

keep it safe. Lucy, Zanna will explain, OK?"

"What about you?" Zanna asked, looking worried. "What are you going to do?"

The front door opened and Henry boomed, "Come on, boy! Haven't got all day!"

David took a deep breath and gritted his teeth. "I'm going to save Henry's bacon."

The snow was falling like cut-glass splinters as David charged out into the crescent. Mr Bacon had already crossed the drives and was bending down outside number forty-two, calling out for Liz through the flap of the letterbox. To David's horror, the door swept open.

Gwilanna appeared on the step, in a dark blue Aunty Gwyneth suit. "Who are you? And what do you want?"

David skidded in at pace, almost knocking Henry over. "This is Henry from next door, Aunty Gwyneth. He wants to check the fuses, but I've already told him that—"

"Oh, get out of the way," barked Henry. Bustling David aside, he touched his torch politely to his temple. "Henry Bacon, at your service, Madam. Have your lights working in a jiffy, no charge. Is Mrs P about?"

'Aunty Gwyneth' looked him sharply up and down. "Elizabeth is resting."

"Not to be disturbed. We understand," said David. "No problem. We'll ring an electrician in the morning. Come on, Henry."

"Wait." Aunty Gwyneth looked Henry in the eye. "I will grant you five minutes to investigate the fault. I want a full report. Do not be surprised by anything you see." She left the door hanging and marched into the kitchen.

Henry swept inside before David could stop him, heading for the cupboard underneath the stairs. "Been trying to catch a glimpse of the aunt for days, boy. Fine-looking woman. Frosty, but firm. Like a filly who knows her own mind. Is she attached?"

"Forget it, Henry, she's out of your league. Just check the fuses. Then go home."

Henry dipped inside the cupboard, his torch beam dancing like a laser in the darkness. Within seconds, his head struck the ceiling with a bump. "Doh! There's one of those models in here. Sitting on the fuse box, gargoyle pose. What's it—? Good grief! Your wires are like over-cooked sausages. Surprised you haven't blown every circuit in Scrubbley. How in blazes have they got like that?"

David glanced in. Gwillan was standing 'frozen' on the fuse box. 'In blazes' was probably an apt description of how he'd left the lighting circuits. If Henry reported that to Gwilanna, the young snuffler would be severely punished. What to do?

As if the universe had recognised his quandary, suddenly things began to stir. An overwhelming cold invaded the house, just as if a ghost had risen from the cellar and spread its death chill into every corner. The lampshade in the hall began to swing back and forth. The stairs creaked. The ceilings rumbled. The leaves on the cheese plant rustled and curled. Then, from deep within David's room, there came the most awesome crash of glass.

Gwilanna was at his shoulder in an instant. "What was that?"

David couldn't answer. The intense cold seemed to have frozen his senses. Or turned them again in an odd sort of way. A change was occurring, deep within his psyche, as if something was trying to contact him. He could feel the unmistakable presence of—

"Bears," murmured Gwilanna, as a howling wind ripped through the hall, flapping doors as if they were bed sheets.

From deep beneath the stairs Henry Bacon shouted,

"Felt a bang, boy. All right up top?"

David slid along the stairwell. He closed the cupboard quickly and dropped the catch. No matter how much Henry Bacon liked bears, he couldn't be involved in this.

'This' was a mini-blizzard in his room. The window, thrown wide and almost off its hinges, had shed its glass in jags across the floor. Snow was whipping into every corner, sticking to the walls, to the furniture, to Liz. For the first time in days, David saw a flicker of movement in her eyelids. She was going to wake. The dragon baby, too. It was scratching at the shell as though desperate to touch the weak glow of moonlight that was wrapping the garden in a silver-grey sheen.

Suddenly, a figure fluttered onto the sill.

It was G'reth – and in his wide, dished paws was the pouch.

In the garden, meanwhile, Zanna and Lucy had reached the hutch. Lucy immediately hunkered down and swept a thick layer of snow off the ramp. She peered inside. "They're not here," she reported.

"Um?" asked Zanna, her teeth chattering like typewriter keys and her attention more on the house than on Lucy. Was that a crash of glass she'd just heard?

"G'reth and Spikey. They're not here."

266

Shivering wildly, Zanna bent to look. The hutch was nothing but a mess of leaves. So much for David's 'revelations'. Anxiously, she checked her watch. Thirteen minutes. That was all they had. She dropped a hand on Lucy's shoulder. "I want you to go back to Henry's. Now."

"Why? What for? We haven't got the pouch."

"Something's wrong. I heard a crash from the house. David might be in trouble. I'm going to check it out."

"Me, too. I'm coming."

"No!" Zanna turned and raised her hands. "It might be dangerous, Lucy. Please. Go back."

The wind switched and Lucy had to close her eyes. When she opened them again, Zanna's slim black shape had been swallowed by the storm.

"But what about your prayer?" Lucy ran a step forward, holding up the silver Earth Mother necklace. The chain loosened and the pendant dangled free. Snowflakes immediately gathered around it, forming a glowing lantern of ice. "Zanna," Lucy whispered. "Zanna, look at this." And then a voice uttered her name on the wind. A voice that spoke in very deep dragontongue. With a start, Lucy looked back over her shoulder.

Sitting in the snow was a large white bear.

"You?" croaked Gwilanna. "What spell is this?"

Hrrr! went G'reth and showed her the pouch.

"I have eyes. I can see it. Bring it to me. Now."

The wishing dragon spread his wings and flew. He soared high into the air and circled twice. At the start of the third, he let the pouch go. It landed on the floor at Gwilanna's back.

"Idiot," she snarled, scrabbling for it.

G'reth paid no attention to the slur and dived down straight away to the desk, landing silently by the flickering candle. At the same time, David caught a movement near the bed. Bonnington: low down, ready to spring, his once copper eyes like violet buttons.

Gwilanna found the pouch and fiddled with the drawstrings. Her reaction to the contents surprised even David: there was shock in the old hag's eyes. "A tooth?!" she screamed. "Is that meant to be funny?!" She hurled the tooth viciously across the room. It pinged off David's computer screen and ricocheted into the rubble somewhere.

G'reth sucked at the candle and the flame went out.

"Traitor! The dark cannot hide you!" screamed the sibyl. She lifted a hand to release a spell, only to find her fingers freezing as a gale force wind drove in from the garden, bringing with it a wall of snow.

David made his choice and made it quickly. Whatever the significance of this tooth, and whatever G'reth and Bonnington were up to, he was going to be part of it. He took Gwilanna down with a rugby tackle that would not have won any prizes in the sport, but did enough to distract her attention from G'reth. The wishing dragon zizzed to the suitcase. In one quick breath he had spoken the password and the contents of the case were beginning to rise. Enter Bonnington, the much-maligned cat. In two sure-footed bounds, his lithe brown figure was over the debris and the scale of Gawain was in his jaws. Every strand of his fur, each filament of whisker, bristled with an ancient spasm of fire. But protected from within by the ice he'd lapped, he made it to the window and crouched there, ready. Ears flattened, he leapt for the sill. But the scale, heavy and awkward to carry, caught against the lip and he was thrown backwards in a twisting fall. Instinctively, he flipped and spread his paws, only to feel three shards of glass piercing the soft pink tissues of his pads. With a yowl, he let the scale drop. And by then his chance of glory had gone.

For by now, Gwilanna had overcome David. The moment he had brought her crashing to the floor she had squirmed away, uttering a dreadful hex. The boards beneath the lodger had quickly given way, sending him crashing to the soil below – a fall of a couple of feet, no more, but the rubble that followed him through the hole, sucked in by a vortex of Gwilanna's hate, had piled in on top, encasing his body and squeezing the air fully out of his lungs. One pitiful hand had poked through the mound, twitched just once then fallen flat. Gwilanna, shrieking with spiteful laughter, had given one condescending click of her fingers and the boards had swiftly repaired themselves. It was over, just like that: the hole was covered, and the lodger was gone.

From Gwilanna's mouth, then, flew a blaze of sparks. Every snowflake thawed in an instant and the blizzard cleared with a deafening splash, the deluge knocking G'reth from the air. The dragon had been flying to Bonnington's assistance when the sudden change of atmosphere had stopped his wings and brought him plummeting hopelessly down, into the raffia wastepaper basket. The impact had turned the basket over, spilling him, winded, under the desk. And there he had lain for several seconds, blowing a series of defective smoke rings and praying that his tail was still intact. But once again, the universe had treated him kindly, for while the accident had brought him no nearer to Bonnington, it had helped him rediscover the fragment of tooth, given to him in the den of the Spikey. It was lying between two pieces of brick. G'reth reached out and closed a paw round it. There was auma in the fang. Powerful auma. But what could a wishing dragon do with it? He righted himself and peeked about. Gwilanna was closing in on Bonnington.

"You soft-brained, fish-stinking hair-ball," she hissed, her matted hair dripping and her sacking drenched. "I will chop you into pieces and put you in a can of your favourite meat." She rolled a finger. The scale leapt up like an antique tiddlywink and came down like a brand new axe. Bleeding and limping, but wits intact, Bonnington dodged it just in time, saving his tail by the width of a flea. He hissed and spat as any cat would, but the tiny burps of fire which left his throat only made Gwilanna crackle with anger. "You dare to fight *me* with fire, cat? I will fry you whole from the inside out."

"Try it and the dragon dies," said a voice.

Gwilanna whisked around.

Zanna was standing beside the bed with her hand poised over the dragon's egg.

Lucy had never seen a bear before. Ordinarily she knew she ought to be afraid. The creature, even sitting, was nearly twice her height. Its power was plain to see. But the bear had spoken kindly to her, using the ancient language of dragons. How could she fear a being like that?

"Are you Lorel?" she asked, using the tongue.

A sharp wind played around the ice bear's ears, making its white hairs ripple gently. "Sometimes," it said.

"Why are you here?"

The bear lifted its snout and blew through its nose. Warm air filled the space between them. Lucy fancied she could see a host of sparks as the cloud settled sweetly over the hutch. Fanned by the breeze, it wafted through the mesh. "Look. Inside box," said the bear.

Lucy bit her lip and hunkered down. Nestling amongst the abandoned leaves was the tiniest snowball she had ever seen. It glistened and the ice lantern pulsed in her hands. "May I take it?" she asked, taking it anyway.

"Yes," said a new and gentler voice. "In your hands, it will never melt."

Lucy turned. Behind her now, in place of the bear, was the shimmering outline of a beautiful woman. She was tall and fair-skinned with flowing red hair, and her eyes were a pale, translucent pink. She seemed to be wearing a dress of white, but when Lucy looked closely she realised the 'clothing' was really snow, mixing and gathering into ever-moving folds. "Are you... Guinevere?" she asked.

The woman smiled. "Sometimes," she said. Flowing forward, she took the lantern back and placed another small gift in Lucy's hands. It was a pure white hedgehog spine. "Thank you for the shelter and the food you gave. Now you must bring me one last offering. Close your eyes, child. Let the fire guide you."

Lucy let her gaze fall onto her palms. A hedgehog spine in one, the icefire in the other. She rolled her fingers into fists.

Then she closed her eyes.

"You've got three seconds," Zanna said. "Tell me where David is or I send the dragon back to the clay. You know I can do it. I quickened this egg. I can petrify it, too." She lowered her hand until the bright amber glow was breaking against her wavering palm. The dragon baby opened its salivating jaws. So thin was the membrane surrounding it now that its quiet *hrrrs* for freedom continually pricked the air.

"My dear, I'm quite impressed," said Gwilanna.

"Cut the garbage, witch. Where's David? Talk."

"Under the floorboards. Buried. Gone. The boy is no use to anyone now."

Zanna's eyes darted about the floor. "You're lying."

"Use your powers, girl. A true sibyl can reach out into the underworld – in more senses than you imagine. Dream it. Let your mind cross over. Dream you can see his cold, stiff corpse. His bones crumbling to wind-blown ash. His life-blood seeping into the dirt."

"Stop it!" Zanna shouted, as the images began to feed into her mind. A tear broke loose, cutting a strait through her neat mascara. "It's a lie! He's not dead. I know it's a trick!" And she pressed her hand even closer to the egg. This, alas, would be her undoing. The baby, impatient to escape his gloop, *graarked* and pushed up eagerly to meet her. The touch made Zanna leap in fright. In that instant, Gwilanna swept forward and seized her.

She took her by the wrist and twisted her down to a kneeling position. "Ridiculous, love-struck, sentimental girl. I will crush you like the frail black butterfly you are. You are the one who is playing tricks, hoping to distract me while the idiot cat…" Gwilanna flung out a hand and the scale flew again, almost slicing Bonnington's ear tips "…tries to take what is rightfully mine." She squeezed Zanna's arm until the vessels bulged. Her pin-sharp nails raked the young girl's flesh. Warm blood burst from three sharp cuts. Gwilanna wiggled her nose and sniffed. "Yes, you have the makings of a powerful sibyl. In another time, I could have taught you much. But harm this dragon? Your sickening sanctimonious charity would never permit you any such *wickedness*, even if you did possess the will."

"*Nnnph*, try this for will," rasped Zanna, and brought a brick-end down on the old hag's foot.

Gwilanna shrieked in pain and threw her rival against the wall. "For that, you will suffer, worse than the boy!"

"I'm not afraid of you!"

"No," said the sibyl, "but you are afraid of *this*…"

Zanna screamed and put her hands to the crown of her head. Lightning! Her thought waves were turning to lightning bolts. She cried out and rolled into a foetal position, fists pressed hard against her ears.

Gwilanna gave out a contemptuous snort. This was far too easy. The boy, the girl, and the cat, defeated (she kicked a clod of plaster at Bonnington's head and he drop-tailed under a chair for safety) and all that the bears could muster was a blizzard. A blizzard, against the power of the ancients! Pathetic, blubber-chewing, plumped-up oafs. When her work in this house was done she would drive every one of them off their ice. She moved triumphantly towards the egg. A column of moonlight played into the room, lighting the bed like an operating table. The dragon baby made a graarking sound and its front paws reached for the everlasting auma of the natural world. "Yes, your time has come," Gwilanna whispered, and from a fold of her sacking she withdrew what would be the dragon's first meal: the lock of red hair she had cut from Elizabeth Pennykettle's head. She held it up to the eyes of the moon. So pretty. So very pretty. What a pity this particular daughter of Guinevere should have to be emptied of her precious *sap*. She let a strand of hair float down like a seed. It kissed the egg and a bubble appeared in the fragile crust. It broke, with more of a squelch than a crack. The dragon's left nostril filled the rift. It sucked at the air and its claws tore keenly at the site of the rupture. Within seconds, its snout was poking clear.

"Come, my pet," Gwilanna leered, rubbing the hair like pirate gold, teasing a spoor across the dragon's nose. "Find the scent. Just one bite and— ow!" Impertinence! The little monster had nipped her! "The hair!" she snapped. "Eat the hair, you *grike!*"

The dragon clicked its teeth.

"Of course, the scale. It must be served upon the scale."

And she turned towards the window in search of it – in time to see Bonnington on the sill. He had the scale in his jaws, ready to flee.

Gwilanna's rage was instant. What was it about this purring dolt? Did it *want* to become a pair of *mules*? How could it dare to try again?

The answer, had she been aware of it, was easy. What the sibyl had failed to remember was the primary function of the dragon, G'reth. The universe had been quite clear on this: G'reth's task (phase two, wish quotient three) was to aid the return of the scale to its source – that source being the last true dragon, Gawain. Only when this need of the Earth was served could the critical part of his wish be granted: the disclosure of the secret of the dragon's tear. A fall into a basket of ripped-up paper was never going to stop him completing his mission. So, while Gwilanna had been distracted, he had crept out of hiding and pitched up finally in the corner by the window. There, to his woe, he had come upon the husks of his brave companions: the guard dragon, Gruffen, and the David's faithful servant, Gadzooks.

They looked in a terrible state, Gadzooks especially,

who had frozen trying to write a message. This niggled G'reth to a frenzy of smoke rings. He desired with all his spark to aid these dragons (and in turn the stricken David), but knew he must keep to his fated path. That had led him to the wounded Bonnington. Closer he'd crept, under the chair where the cat had taken refuge. With a delicate *hrrr*, he'd warmed the cat's tail. Bonnington had sprung round hissing at first, and only an expeditious dip of his head had saved G'reth's snout from a savage mauling. Cat and dragon faced each other. Communication would not be easy. Bonnington had minimal dragontongue and G'reth had even less felinespeak. A flurry of signing had followed. If the cat were to take another route – onto the bricks behind the chair, and from there, onto the chair back itself – the leap to the sill was not that great.

And so this simple plan was enacted. While the argument between the sibyls raged on, Bonnington had cleaned the last few stings of glass from his paws, then gone for the scale while G'reth had stood guard. What dreadful, dreadful luck it had been to see Gwilanna turn round at the very last second…

Hrrr-rr-rrr! cried G'reth as loudly as he could. In dragontongue he'd shouted 'Down here, whale-breath!' Not the best of slurs, but it had done the trick.

Gwilanna's gaze had shifted away from Bonnington and the cat was gone in a furry flash – G'reth too, diving under the chair as the sibyl's black tongue lashed out like a whip, catching his wing and slicing off a minor stabilising sprig. Now he was afraid. Very afraid. This time the sibyl's rage would be ruthless. She wouldn't rest until his fire was quenched. The lash came again, with a spray of sour spittle that drilled small burn holes into his scales. In the name of Gawain, he must think quickly. The tooth. He still had the piece of Ragnar's tooth. Surely he could use its auma *somehow?*

The tongue came again, arriving with such explosive force that he was catapulted backwards into a nest of wallpaper; one of many scattered loosely about the floor. Quickly, he tunnelled through it, using the overlapping strips as cover, emerging on the opposite side of the chair, nose to tail with the dragon, Gadzooks. And that was when the idea came. It was difficult and desperate and it might not work, but it was all he could think to do. The tongue flashed again, lassoing his torso. He winced and clamped his feet to a gas pipe. Just a few seconds. That was all he needed. He stretched towards Gadzooks, wedging the tooth between his pencil and pad. Gwilanna tugged. The copper pipe buckled. G'reth let one leg go. It was burning with pain, but that was not the reason he needed the release. As the angle of his body had changed, it had brought him snout to snout with the writing dragon. He closed the gap between their nostrils…and blew.

A millisecond later he was in Gwilanna's hands. "Wretched interfering puffler!" she screamed. "I will peel your scales and—" She turned him over and examined him closely. Frozen. Like the others. How could that be? How had he suddenly lost his auma? And what…what was that noise?

She threw G'reth away (he sank into the folds of the long-discarded curtains) and turned her gaze to the quivering ceiling. There was a rumble in the Dragons' Den. Auma, great waves of it, was returning to the house. She flashed a glance at Liz. After nearly two days in the world of the ancients, the daughter of Guinevere opened her eyes. Her dry mouth breathed one short word, "Lucy…"

"Eat the hair!" Gwilanna screamed, and dived for the egg. It was empty, wasted like a worn-out football, the baby it had quietly nurtured, flown. One four-clawed print in the glob of amber goo on Liz's tummy was the only evidence of any kind of hatchling.

"No!" yelled Gwilanna, in a voice that could have

brought the whole house down...or the floorboards ripping up...

With a thunderous crack of wood, a fist appeared from below floor level. Clenched within it was what looked, at first, to be a kind of dagger. It was not a dagger. It was a polar bear's tooth, curved and yellowed, grown to the size of an adult fang. Gwilanna backed away from it, fear in her throat. Even Gadzooks took a flutter to the wardrobe. It was he who had brought about David's revival. Woken by the transfer of auma from G'reth, he had taken in everything that dragon had known and applied his unique brand of dragonfire to it. While Gwilanna had been puzzling over the switch, Gadzooks had flown to where David was concealed and squinted carefully between the boards. A hand was all he'd been able to see; but a hand was all he'd needed. Through a knot in the planking he'd released the tooth. It had bounced and settled in David's palm. Like a fly trap, the fingers had closed around it. A remarkable change then began to take place. The tooth had grown from a fragment to a fang and the rubble over David had slowly stirred.

Kerrowww! The floor erupted. David emerged, detritus pouring off his head and shoulders. He looked terrifying, slightly ghoulish even, his brown hair dressed in choking dust; spiders' webs, long blackened with age, clinging to every lobe and contour; his cheeks a mess of cuts and grazes; his mouth spitting pellets of sand and lime. He rose into a room that was now very different from the one he had left. The auma was overwhelming. Not only had the dragons come back to full strength, but something was melding their sparks together into a single purging fire. There was no escape for the sibyl, Gwilanna. She writhed in terror as the force consumed her and drove her back against the fireplace wall, her arms splayed wide like a pinned-up moth, white fires raging in the orbs of her eyes.

This ordeal was enough for any evil to bear, but the nightmare was only half done for the crone. Now David seized her, pressing the tooth hard up to her throat. He looked into her eyes and knew, despite the burning, she could see and understand. His body shook with a silent anger, mirroring the fury in his voice. "In the Inuit village of Savalik, in a time before I can even imagine, you caused the death of a polar bear cub. This is his father's tooth." He touched the point to the skin of her neck. "You turned The People against the bears, beginning a conflict that lasts to this day, all because you wanted the fire of Gawain. Your greed destroyed their world. Guinevere was right to keep the tear from you; Lorel was right to protect her secret. Would it be so wrong for me to end your pathetic existence, *sibyl?*"

"Yes," said a voice. "Let her go."

Panting, David tightened his grip. "I can feel the auma of the ice bear, Ragnar. He says she deserves to die."

"David, it's over. Let her go." Elizabeth Pennykettle laid a hand on his arm. "Use that and the line of Guinevere ends here."

Gwilanna gave out a rasping croak. "They need me, lodger. Make your choice…"

David had one last push. "Come near me and my dragons again and I'll leave your blood on this tooth, I swear." And he pulled back angrily, leaving Gwilanna spluttering for breath.

Lucy hurried in then, carrying the icefire in her hands. She started slightly when she saw Gwilanna, but one tilt of the ice towards the sibyl made her reel like a frightened crow.

"That's enough now," Liz said quietly, crossing her arms over Lucy's shoulders and hugging her tightly into her body.

Lucy stared hard at her one-time 'aunt'. "Go away," she said, in a voice so small yet so full of menace that Gwilanna, the sibyl, could only obey.

Reverting into her suited clothes, she moved warily towards the door. Defeated, yet still as cantankerous as ever, she scowled at the shell of the suitcase and hissed, "Thieves. You don't know what you've done. This is the beginning, not the end, *Elizabeth*. Come!" she barked at the watching Gretel.

But now there came another blow for the crone. Gretel spread her wings – then lowered them again. She looked at Gadzooks, who had flown to the bed to comfort Grace, then at Gruffen perching on the wardrobe top. (G'reth, oddly, was nowhere to be seen.) Pennykettle dragons: foolhardy, but brave. A strong sniff of dandelion would not go amiss with most of them. This house could use a good potions dragon. She curled her claws and refused to move.

Fury blazed across Gwilanna's face. "You will be sorry for this," she ranted. And with one last glower at them all, she was gone.

By now, David had Zanna on her feet, examining the gashes in her arm. "It's nothing, they're only scratches," she was saying, wincing as he wrapped a hankie around them. "Honest, I'll be OK." She kissed him gently and turned to Liz. "Thank goodness, you're safe. Where's…?"

"The baby," said David. "Where's the baby?"

He dropped to his knees and squinted anxiously under the bed. Although the light was poor, the gloom could not have hidden the shape of a dragon.

"What about the window?" Lucy gasped. "Mum—?"

"Sssh," said Liz, kneeling down by the stricken Grace. She touched the edge of the broken ears and a tear escaped her violet eyes. "Grace will know. She can't hear, but she can receive impressions." She stroked the dragon lovingly, nodding her head to show she understood what the listener knew. "The baby fled, scared away by Gwilanna. G'reth has gone after him, to protect and guide."

"Guide?" Zanna whispered. "Where's he taking him?"

Hrrr! went Gretel, working it out.

And even David could translate this. "The bear man," he muttered, and his heart began to race. "G'reth's taking him to Dr Bergstrom."

"My car," said Zanna. "We can be at Rutherford House in minutes. It'll seat all four of us. Come on, let's go." But as she made the first move towards the door, something quite peculiar happened. Gretel took off and sped across the room, landing with a thump on Zanna's shoulder. Zanna squeaked in shock and jerked to attention. "Hhh! What's happening?"

Hrrr, went Gretel, paddling her feet. Zanna turned to look at her and squeaked again.

"Can you see her?" gasped Lucy, breaking free of her mum.

Zanna gulped and gave a slow, slow nod.

"More than just a shimmering blur?" asked David (which was all a normal person ever saw of dragons moving – and then only if they were incredibly lucky).

Zanna nodded again. "She's scratching her ear with the tip of her tail."

Hrrr, went Gretel, flicking a blob of ear wax across the room. She took a waft of Zanna's fine black hair and teased it out between her strong front claws.

"How can that be?" David asked Liz.

"I'm not sure," she replied, "but we don't have time to dwell on it now. She wants to bond with you, Zanna. Will you accept her?"

"But Mum, she's a sibyl," Lucy put in. "And Gretel is...y'know."

"I know," said Liz, looking into Zanna's eyes. "But Gwilanna didn't deserve her. It's time she was allowed to do some good in the world."

Suddenly, the lights flickered on in the hall.

"Oh heck, that's Henry," David muttered. "I forgot all about him; he's in the understairs cupboard, mending the fuses. What's he going to say when he sees this mess?"

"You leave Henry to us," said Liz. "Lucy and I will stay behind, here. You go on – but be careful, all of you. Gwilanna may be tracking the dragon baby, too."

David took the polar bear's tooth from his pocket. "Don't worry, I still have this."

"There won't be any need for that," said Zanna, making David lower his hand. "The baby's welfare is all we want to think about. I do accept Gretel," she said to Liz. "I hope I'll always be worthy of her." And she stepped into the hall, pulling David after her, lifting the latch on the cupboard as they went.

*

With Zanna driving as fast as she dared, they reached the common in under ten minutes. Rutherford House rose out of the snow like a decoration topping a Christmas cake. Zanna swung the car round the empty car park and used her lights to illuminate the entrance. The ivy-covered columns, laden with snow, glistened in a pool of halogen blue. "What do you think?" she asked, just as Gretel gave out an excited *hrrr*! and pressed her paws and snout to the windscreen.

"There," said David, pointing to the column just left of the entrance. Clinging to the ivy was the small green figure of the dragon, G'reth.

David opened his door and quickly got out, calling to G'reth as he moved towards the house. G'reth, hearing him, changed his position, causing a sprinkle of snowflakes to fall. Out of the flurry there came a figure. It was Bergstrom. He had the dragon baby in his hands.

"Is he safe?" cried Zanna, forging through the snow.

Graaark, went the dragon, throwing its small, ridged head into the air.

"He's tired and a little confused," said Bergstrom, allowing Zanna to hold the infant. "G'reth has taken him beyond this plane in order to bring him here more quickly. Who is this?"

Gretel, riding on Zanna's shoulder, leaned away from Bergstrom's stare.

"Her name's Gretel," answered David, taking her down. "She was Gwilanna's dragon. Now she's with us."

Bergstrom studied her carefully a moment, then relaxed his gaze and beckoned them in. He led them down the corridors, into his room.

Still cradling the baby, Zanna made for an armchair in a darkened corner. "You're beautiful," she whispered, pampering the creature with gentle flicks and strokes of her fingers. "I'm going to give you a name: Grockle."

"Grockle?" David curled his lip.

"Listen," she said, tickling the dragon under his jaws. *Grraark...graark...grr-ockle,* he coughed.

Zanna beamed with delight at this. But amusing though it was to hear the dragon 'speak', the sound it was making didn't seem natural. It reminded David of sandpaper rasping hard against wood. He turned to Dr Bergstrom and asked, "Why is he making that grating noise?"

Bergstrom, looking on, answered bleakly, "He's trying to find his fire."

Graark! went Grockle, louder than before. David and the Pennykettle dragons jumped. But not a single whiff of smoke left the baby's snout. He rocked back and forth in Zanna's hands, blinked his amber eyes and settled. *Graark*, he said, more quietly now. It was almost a question; a sad little whimper that Zanna interpreted without the need for dragontongue. "He doesn't have any, does he?" She touched Grockle's belly. It was cold, like stone. "He's been born without fire."

"But he's a dragon," said David. "He must have fire."

Dr Bergstrom shook his head. "A dragon is a servant of the Mother Earth, David. It's not possible to produce a spark in them without the ability to call upon her fire. Elizabeth Pennykettle has that ability. Gwilanna, for all her powers, does not."

David crouched down and touched Grockle's scales. They felt leathery and dull, unpleasantly clammy. "Then why bother trying? What was she hoping to achieve with him?"

"And what's going to happen to him?" Zanna added quickly, anxiety breaking through her confusion.

On the desk, G'reth tightened his jaws and gulped.

"Grockle is a kind of half-creature," said Bergstrom. "If Gwilanna had successfully drained the auma from Elizabeth Pennykettle's body into his, he would have grown to be a powerful beast; a fiend under her control."

"No," said Zanna, not wanting to hear this. She drew back, holding Grockle to her breast. His soft black tongue, no wider than a strip of tagliatelle, licked at the makeshift bandage on her arm.

"Even then he would have been a shell, no more. To complete the task, she would have needed fire."

"That's why she's after the tear," said David, suddenly working everything out. "She was going to use Grockle to intimidate the bears and make them give up Gawain's fire."

"But why?" asked Zanna, calming Grockle down as he graarked and stretched his bronze-coloured wings. He nipped at the hankie. She peeled it off. "What good would it do her to have a pet dragon?"

"To answer that," said Bergstrom, turning away, "you have to know something of Gwilanna's history. In Guinevere's time, she was the wisest, most powerful sibyl on Earth. She had a reputation as a healer of ills, through the use of herbs and flower remedies."

Gretel lifted an eye ridge and sniffed.

"Even though she was reclusive and kept her own counsel, Gwilanna was held in the highest regard by those who came to seek her advice. But there was always one issue that rankled the sibyl and set her apart from the elders of her tribe. She clashed so heatedly over this matter that in time she was cast out and almost put to death. The nature of the dispute might surprise you: she condemned them for their growing persecution of dragons."

"*What?*" David gave a snort of contempt.

"It may be hard for you to grasp, but Gwilanna, like Guinevere, believed that the old world was better ruled by dragons than by men."

"I'm with her on that one," said Zanna. "I think Grockle's hungry. Can I feed him something?"

Bergstrom spoke in dragontongue to Gretel, telling her to seek out fresh green leaves.

Gretel zipped off towards a tall *dracaena* in a Japanese planter appropriately decorated with sleeping dragons.

David scratched his head, coughing away plaster dust as it fell. "So Lucy was right. The Earth *was* ruled by dragons once?"

"In the age before mankind, yes," said Bergstrom. "It was men who hunted them to near-extinction, until only twelve of the creatures survived. Those twelve, mighty and courageous as they were, opted not to pursue the fight and died in isolation in their chosen resting places around the globe. Gawain, as you know, came to the island which the bears now call the Tooth of Ragnar. Gwilanna was enraged by this turn of events, for it left no place for her kind in the world. So, mad or misguided, whichever you prefer, she desired to strike back and take the one thing no human – or sibyl – had ever possessed, the tear of a dying dragon."

David took a moment to think this through. "There's something I've never understood about that: if Gwilanna wanted the tear so badly, why did she send Guinevere for it? Why not simply catch it herself?"

"Afraid, if you ask me," Zanna interjected, encouraging Grockle to perch on her arm. The dragon tilted his head and peered at her cuts. He grockled inquisitively and sniffed at the slow-congealing plasma. Zanna allowed him to lick the wounds clean, then raised his chin with the tip of her finger. His teeth, like a row of clean white bunting, stood out fiercely in his lower jaw. Fire or no fire, he could rip and tear. Who in their right mind would dare to beleaguer a dying dragon?

"She's right," Bergstrom confirmed. "By the end of his life, Gawain had little trust of man; he would have turned any sibyl to dust in a breath. So Gwilanna sought another, safer route and found it in the shape of the virtuous Guinevere. When Guinevere came in search of advice, asking how she might save the dragon's essence, Gwilanna seized her chance. Here was an unexpected gift – a girl willing to risk her life just to be with the dragon at his death. So she traded information about the tear for the seemingly worthless donation of a scale. What had she to lose? If the foolish girl died, what was it to her? She had gained a dragon's scale, a rare prize in itself. But if the girl succeeded, then the tear was in her grasp. As you know, Guinevere succeeded in her quest, but nothing worked out the way either had imagined."

David looked up hopefully. "Do you know what happened – to Guinevere, I mean? I overheard Liz telling Lucy once that she was drowned trying to hide the tear. Is it true?"

Bergstrom rolled his gaze to one side. He watched Gretel passing broken leaves to Zanna, who in turn offered them in pieces to Grockle. The little dragon clicked his teeth and exchanged them in his craw for tiny burps of air.

"It's warm in here," Bergstrom said suddenly. "Why don't you and I go for a walk?" There was a flicker of movement in his left hand. He was fingering the Inuit talisman, making the hand-carved figures dance.

David glanced across at Zanna and realised that time, or the plane of existence they knew as reality, had somehow shifted. She and Gretel and the dragon called Grockle were in a small bubble of their own for the moment. He stood up cautiously. G'reth immediately flew to his shoulder, only to be told by Bergstrom to stay.

Hrr-rr? the wishing dragon beseeched him.

"Your work is done," the bear man said. And he placed his thumbs into the wide dished paws until the dragon's eyes grew dizzy with awe. G'reth fluttered like a blown seed back to the desk and sank down puffing a wisp of smoke. Bergstrom took a jacket off the back of a chair. "Wear gloves, David. It's cold out there."

"Where exactly are we going?"

Bergstrom levelled his blue-eyed gaze. "Onto the ice," he said.

The fire that melts no ice

"Ice?" David queried, as their shoes broke the edges of the snow on the common.

Bergstrom punched the ends of his gloves together. He put his face to the sky and let his blond hair trail against his upturned collar. "We'll go this way," he said, with a lilt of Norwegian, and began to cut a path across the widest, bleakest part of the grounds. They were well above sea level here, and the yellow pips of lamplight on the far horizon seemed to roll away with every crunching step. It was cold, and another grey fog had fallen, freezing the uppermost deposits of snow and giving it the texture of cereal flakes. As he walked, David scuffed the grass underfoot and thought, idly, of tundra and caribou. He was wondering if this was what the north would be like, when Bergstrom spoke again.

"So, will I see you in Chamberlain, David?"

David bit his lip and looked the other way. This was a loaded question, he thought. He hadn't written the essay or shown any sign of doing so. Was Bergstrom trying to test his allegiance? "I have the money. And I think I've proved that dragons exist."

"Then you'll come?"

"Yes."

"Good. Then it's settled." Bergstrom smiled and held out a hand. David shook it and they walked on in silence for a while.

But many questions were stacking up in David's mind, and as they passed a small coppice of hawthorns he asked: "What's going to happen to Grockle? Are you taking him to Chamberlain too?"

Bergstrom put his head back and listened to the wind. "You need not be concerned about Grockle. Why don't we talk about the fire tear? You must have wondered many times how bears came to be the guardians of it?"

Doubling his step to match the larger man's stride, David admitted, "Yes. Once or twice." It wasn't meant to be a casual remark, but Bergstrom threw back his head and laughed, lobbing the repeats of his deep-throated hoots twenty or thirty yards across the common.

Slightly unnerved, David turned and trudged backwards for several paces. The fog had all but eclipsed the house and still they were drawing further away. "Are we going far? I'm worried about Zanna on her own in there. Liz warned us to watch for Gwilanna."

Bergstrom turned his head to the east. "Zanna is in no danger," he said.

David chased the look and for a heart-stopping moment, thought he saw the curve of an animal's back. A bear, perhaps? Were they being tracked? He rubbed his eyes and they swam with motes, but the only shapes he could piece together were trees.

"How much has Elizabeth told you, David?"

"About Gawain?"

"Yes."

"No more than I told you in our tutorial – except that the tear was hidden by Guinevere, not taken inside her as I first thought."

Bergstrom nodded, warm air chuting out of his nostrils. "You put out a wish to the universe."

David winced and touched a glove to the centre of his forehead. "I'm sorry. It's caused a lot of trouble, I know."

"It has also made many good things possible. Even as we speak, the scale of Gawain is passing through worlds to the Tooth of Ragnar. In a short while, the dragon will be complete again. His spirit will rise from the ancient stone and the earth will breathe a little easier for it. This way, I think."

David veered away to his right, stumbling after Bergstrom like a small child in its father's wake. "I don't understand what you mean by that."

"You will, when you know the secret of the tear."

"You're going to tell me?" David held back, panting.

Bergstrom came to a halt and turned. From his eyes came that customary, domineering glare. But he was lifting his gaze beyond David as he said, "That is not for me alone to decide."

On impulse, David twisted around – and the sight he saw before him would change his life for ever.

There were nine of them, on pillars of ice, arranged in a gentle quarter moon, with the bear at the centre on the largest pillar. He was perfect in every way. From pointed ear tips to ice-frayed pads, not a hair was out of place. And though his snout was high and his bearing proud, there was no real air of conceit about him. His dark brown eyes were so serene that any dread David felt was quickly put aside in favour of wonderment, reverence and awe. Was this the animal they called Nanukapik? The bear tilted its head, as if David's thoughts had been carried on the wind, creating the breeze which now blew crystals around its feet, rippling the fur by its great, hooked claws. David nodded. The bear nodded back, then swivelled its head to the bear at its left. This one was younger and slimmer than the others. David knew in an instant it had to be Lorel. The bear trod its paws and sat up a little straighter, as if it felt the need to prove that it was *fierce* and not just a simple-minded Teller of Ways. Then the Nanukapik turned the other way. The bear on his right side narrowed its eyes. Its snout was covered with fighting scars, and even from a distance David could see the hardened weals on its neck and shoulders where the skin had been permanently torn in combat, showing up the thick black blubber below. But it wasn't the scars or the blemishes of war that froze the breath in David's lungs. The ice bear snarled and rolled its lip, and though its teeth were broken and bloodied, only the upper canine was missing. That rested in David's pocket.

"Ragnar," he whispered, and took out the tooth, offering it back on his shaking glove.

The ice bear switched its gaze to Bergstrom.

"The tooth is a gift to you, David. A symbol of everything these nine bears lived for. It will protect you against the likes of Gwilanna and guide you through the journeys ahead. But beware, like any blade, it cuts both ways. Speak any knowledge of the fire in its presence and the spirit of Ragnar will be at your shoulder. This is the price you pay for the wisdom Lorel is about to give you. Listen, now, to the Teller of Ways. He will speak to you in dragontongue and dreams."

Lorel leapt down off his pillar. The bear, though slim, was a powerful predator and David instinctively dropped back a pace. But Lorel did no more than come around in front of him and sit on his haunches like a cream-coloured cat. He widened his eyes and parted his jaws. David gasped and staggered back slightly as an image of the aged dragon, Gawain, ripped across his visual cortex. The beast was lying on a mountain top with the pale moon rising to a crescent at his shoulder. Slowly, he closed his spangled eye and a single tear ran loose on his snout, glistening at its centre with a violet flame. A pair of hands reached out to catch it. They belonged to a beautiful red-haired girl.

But from that moment on, everything shook. Guinevere screamed as the fire spread outwards along her arms. She opened her hands and the tear fell again. And whether it was providence or prior calculation, the essence of the dragon dripped into the lumen of a hollowed-out bone and never did escape into the Mother Earth. Instantly, thunder broke. It could have been an act of planetary wrath or a terrible ritual of dragon death, but the Earth tilted and the heavens split and the last true dragon began to set. It started at the very tip of his tail, with a grinding tone so sickly dire that the air all around seemed to moan with grief. Gawain was turning by pieces to stone; becoming one with the mountain top and not the clay from which he was born. As the last of his rutted green scales turned to grey, the mountain cracked with a mournful wail and began to slide into the cold, dark ocean. Guinevere ran for her life, carrying the vessel close to her breast. She ran for the place called the Bridge of Souls, that bony strip of land which connected the island to the ancient continent. On the final descent, where the ground levelled out, she was met by the sibyl, Gwilanna.

"No," said David, shaking his head, for he could picture the greed in Gwilanna's eyes and knew she had not come to offer assistance.

The husky voice of Lorel entered his mind. "Dream," he said in broken dragontongue. "Look again. Sibyl is not alone."

At Gwilanna's side stood a mesmerized child. Her hair was long and thick and wild. Gwilanna stroked it with the back of her fingers. "My dear, you have done well," she said.

"Stone," wailed Guinevere, lurching forward, her red hair following the tracks of her tears. "You tricked me! How can he ever be at rest?"

"Give me the tear," the sibyl crowed. "I will see to it that dragonkind is not forgotten."

Guinevere looked at the frightened girl. Was this the daughter Gwilanna had promised? Raised from clay and hair and scale? She shook her head.

"We had a trade!" screamed the sibyl, as the Bridge of Souls heaved into the air, bent upwards by the ruinous collapse of the island. "A child from the fire! The child for the tear!"

"They've got to run," breathed David, grinding his teeth. On the ocean, a tidal wave was growing. If the jaws of the earth did not take Guinevere, the waters of the world would sweep her away.

Lorel, the Teller, spoke once more. "See. Beyond." He squinted into the middle-distance.

In the space behind Gwilanna, a bear was loping along the bridge. His ragged and partially wetted fur was a rich brown colour and his eyes seemed to sparkle out of his head. Amid the thunderous detonations of rocks in water, his approach had gone unnoticed by the sibyl.

"He is Thoran," said Lorel, gruff but clear. "She, red hair, saved him once. Took metal from his side. Gave berries. Healed." He growled and showed his canine teeth.

With a swipe so fast that David almost missed it, Thoran hooked his claws into the sibyl's sackcloth and hurled her far out into the ocean. He immediately beckoned Guinevere to come. She ran to the child first and quickly hoisted her onto her hip.

"We go," said the bear, and turned to the mainland, only to see the far side of the link go crumbling into the rising water. In its wake, the great wave hit, breaking against the peak of the island and throwing wild plumes of foam across the bridge.

"I carry. Take one. Come back," said Thoran, and he hit the water with a mighty splash.

"Her first," Guinevere shouted and carried the child to a flat, safe rock from which she might be placed onto Thoran's back. As the bear trod water, positioning himself, Guinevere knelt in front of her 'daughter'. "You are Gwendolen," she whispered, cupping the child's face. "Remember that your father was the dragon, Gawain." And she placed the girl's fingers into the vessel, so she might know her father's auma. The child cried out and cleaved to her mother, but the bear was always calling them away. More waves! Big rocks! No time! We *go!* For there was danger everywhere, danger in the *air*. And how could they be certain that the sibyl was dead?

The truth became plain on the second run. With Gwendolen safely transported to land and Guinevere herself now riding on his back, Thoran was almost at the end of his rescue when he looked up and saw Gwilanna on the shoreline. She was drenched from head to toe, holding Gwendolen by the hair.

"Urr!" growled Thoran, paddling harder.

Guinevere, suddenly aware of the danger, looked up and screamed, "No, let her go!"

"She is mine," said the sibyl, with an angry sneer. "If I cannot have the tear, then no one will." And with a laugh that could itself have shattered rocks, she commanded the waves to turn and roll, driving Thoran and Guinevere out to sea, as far as any sunset could possibly reach.

David felt himself numbed with fear. "Then it's true. She *was* drowned. She didn't survive."

"Nnn," the Teller rumbled. "Thoran strong."

"But the ocean. All that expanse of water? Even a bear…?"

"Strong," the Teller insisted. "Thoran swim, to centre of stars."

David shook his head. "I don't understand."

"North," the bear grunted.

"Where? To the Arctic? To the ice cap? *Where?*"

Lorel gave one flick of his snout. "You dream it. Now. Centre of stars."

So David closed his eyes and let the images come. Nightfall. Moonlight on a peaceful ocean. Guinevere, exhausted, on Thoran's back. The great brown bear was paddling still, but fighting to keep his head above water. His chest and shoulders ached with cold. He could no longer feel his claws retracting. "Swim no more," he managed to say, expelling more water than air from his lungs.

Guinevere, delirious with hunger and thirst, laid her lips against Thoran's ear and began to hum a sweet lullaby to him. It was the song she had used to calm Gawain in his last few days of torment on Earth. As she sang, the wind rippled across the ocean, weaving a mist upon the surface of the water. From the centre of the veil, a figure appeared.

"Gaia," said David, taking a breath.

"Umm," grunted Lorel. "She-mother. Earth."

A voice floated down from the woman's mouth, gently wafting Guinevere's hair. "Child, your work is done," she said. "The dragon is forever in your heart. Now you must return the fire to me. Give it, child, back to the earth."

Guinevere moved her thoughts to the vessel. Her fingers, frozen by cold and time, could barely unlock themselves from its shape. Thoran dipped his shoulder and the ocean lapped. It's cold bite touched the girl awake. Water all around her. Stars above. She tugged at the vessel and its ties snapped easily away from her neck. She opened it up to the northern sky. Great arcs of colour patterned the heavens, but Guinevere only had eyes for the tear. "Forgive me," she whispered, "for taking this from you." And stroking one hand over Thoran's head, with the other hand she spilled the tear into the ocean.

Water to water.

Fire to...

"Oh my God," cried David, reeling back. His legs weakened and he dropped to his knees in shock. For as the fire tear joined the meniscus of the ocean, so its surface began to thicken and freeze, until a plate of blue-white glaucous ice had formed as far as the eye could see. And though he could never hope to understand how, David felt his mind become one with the ice, as though he shared every interlocking droplet of water and could glimpse, for the briefest moment of time, all that the water ever knew or ever was.

And there was more.

As Guinevere rolled off Thoran's back, the bear put his claws into this miracle of nature, to satisfy himself it was real beyond dreams. And he too became part of the change. Every hair on his body paled from brown, until he was one shade darker than white. It suited him well, this new cream pelt. Indebted, he rose on his stiff hind legs and roared and roared at the northern sky. The ocean was his to walk; the reign of the great white bear had begun.

David, shaking, threw off his gloves and scooped up two large hunks of snow. "The ice," he tremored, squeezing it into his aching fists. "The ice cap. All of it. The ice is the fire."

Bergstrom came to crouch beside him. "And the fire is the ice," he said, igniting it.

Tears emptied from David's eyes. "Who *are* you? What do you *want* from me?"

Bergstrom waved a hand and the snow ceased to burn. "Since Thoran's time, the world has changed a great deal, David. Some of those changes have not been good. The ice is melting. Climates are shifting. The earth is in a state of violent unrest. I need people who can help me to reverse those changes. You, Zanna, Elizabeth and Lucy, even Gwilanna in her way, have played a part. Returning the scale to the Tooth of Ragnar will mean Gawain's body can go to the clay. This will bring stability – for a short time. But the ice, and the bears who dwell upon it, remain in the deepest peril. You can help me to save them."

David gave an incredulous laugh and let the snow tumble out of his hands. "How?"

"By doing what you do best. I want you to write – about the Arctic."

"Write?"

"Remember what I told you when we first met? About stories?"

Well-chewed bones. David nodded, remembering.

"Creativity is the auma of the universe, David. A good story, written with heart and feeling, can touch many people and raise their awareness of global issues. It was no accident that Gadzooks came into being. I owe a great debt to Elizabeth Pennykettle. She has used the icefire wisely. We should even thank our crone, Gwilanna. When she used her influence on the publishers, she helped us more than she really knew."

David thought back to Dilys Whutton's offer. It seemed strangely ironic that Gwilanna should be paying to fund his research into a novel that might help to save the bears she so disliked. "I told them I'd write a saga," he said. "I don't even know where I'm going to start."

Bergstrom patted his shoulder and they stood. "Tonight, when you return to the Crescent, go to the room of photographs. Let the tooth guide you towards a book. What you find there will help you begin. Good luck, David. When we meet again, it will be in Chamberlain. Now you must go. Suzanna needs you."

"Zanna? Why, what's wrong?"

On Bergstrom's shoulder, a wraith-like shape appeared.

"Grockle?" breathed David, and suddenly Zanna was screaming for him.

"David! Where are you? *David! David!*"

"Zanna?" he yelled back, swinging round.

She came through the mist and thudded violently into his arms. Her face was awash and messed by tears. "Grockle," she clamoured.

"What is it? What's wrong?"

A mountain of grief poured out of her eyes. "He turned to stone."

David stood back, gathering his thoughts. A dragon without fire. Gawain. *Stone.*

"Dr Bergstrom!" he cried out and swung back again. "Dr Bergstrom! Wait! Come back! Where are you?" And he chased across the common where Bergstrom had been. But all he found were tracks in the shifting snow. A single trail of five-clawed prints, dusted by the wind drifting in from the north.

At home, Lucy and Zanna cried enough tears to fill up a fountain. David, his gaze never far from the floor, explained as much as he could to Liz. She bravely accepted all that had happened and tried to explain that Grockle wasn't dead, merely in a place where he could fly in peace, free from the dark suspicions of a world so fearful and misunderstanding of dragons. This was of little comfort to Gretel, who had tried, from the very first hardening of scales, to use every flower available to her. She was close to shedding her fire tear that night. Only the warmth of G'reth saved her.

As for David, he returned to Henry Bacon's later, carrying such a pulsing mix of emotions that sleep seemed like an impossible venture. So he went to the study instead, to the room of photographs as Bergstrom had called it. In his pocket, in his hand, the enamelled tooth of an ancient bear guided his eyes across the spines of books, until they settled on a single name that seemed to stand out above all others: Lono. He slid it off the shelf. A large-format book with full colour plates. It fell open at the first of them. The picture was faded and cracked with age, its once-white borders yellowed to the shade of a polar bear's pelt. There were polar bears in the picture. Two of them. One large, one small, sitting on the ice with their backs to the camera. David felt a tear prick the corner of his eye as his gaze travelled down and he read the caption.

A mother and her female cub relax on pack ice in early

spring. *A second cub is just out of frame to their right. The island in the background, a favoured nesting place for buntings and skuas, goes by the name of the Tooth of Ragnar.*

Tidying up

Over the next few days, the mood in the house was sombre and still. Nobody said very much about Grockle and everyone wanted to drift away into their private space to reflect: Zanna returned to her college work, Lucy went back to school, and Liz disappeared to the Dragons' Den to make repairs to those dragons injured in the skirmish with Gwilanna.

It was left to David and Mr Bacon to get on with the business of tidying up. Mr Bacon, as usual, didn't hang about. At eight-thirty sharp on the morning following Gwilanna's departure – having first rearranged his day off from the library – he marched David round to number forty-two and told Liz what was going to happen. "Ordered a skip last night," he said. "Operation tidy up, under way promptly. Wheelbarrow shuttling from room to drive. Rubble cleared in a jiff."

"No," she said.

Mr Bacon jumped.

"No wheelbarrows in my hall."

Henry pursed his lips. "Understood, Mrs P. Brush and bucket. Manual carriage it is, then, boy."

Unimpressed by the thought of hours of hard labour,

David made his own suggestion: "Can't we just sweep it under the floor?" He nodded at the hole he'd smashed in the boards.

Henry made a curt remark about carpets (and the sweeping of problems under them) then went home and found two buckets. He hooked the larger one over David's arm and told him to start anywhere he liked.

It took all day and more. They dumped the mattress, the curtains and the broken boards, too. The latter were replaced with fresh-smelling timbers, which Mr Bacon sawed to size and hammered neatly across the joists. There was a moment of panic when Bonnington decided to explore the hole and was nearly boarded up for all eternity. He was swiftly ejected and work continued. To no one's surprise, Mr Bacon was a hero of do-it-yourself jobs. Not only did he reglaze the broken window and fix plaster boards onto the damaged walls, he also rewired the light flex and holder and warned David not to hang his clothes on it in future – or whatever stupid prank he'd obviously been doing to tear the cabling apart in the first place.

By the close of the weekend, the structural work was done. David was shattered and slept like a lion. But at breakfast on Monday, Mr Bacon shook him awake once more and told him that a steam stripper, a blow torch and two sharp scrapers were waiting in the hall and he expected good use to be made of them.

The steam stripper proved a complete disaster. Within minutes, the room was filled with a muggy grey cloud that made the windows stream and had Gadzooks peeling sodden sheets of paper off his pad. The blow torch was even worse. The first time David lit it, it virtually exploded. He called in Gwillan when Liz wasn't looking. With the dragon's help, the paintwork was all burned off by lunch.

Later that afternoon, Zanna returned. On the surface, she seemed her usual self, chatting amiably to Liz (and Gretel) in the kitchen and admiring Mr Bacon's handiwork. But David sensed a quiet despondency about her, as if she wasn't quite sure she belonged anymore – in the house, or even near him perhaps. When she rolled up her sleeves and grabbed a scraper, cheerily saying that she ought to do her bit, David found himself strangely on edge, and their conversation soon began to mirror his disquiet.

"Got some news from college this morning."

David, reacquainting himself with the mysteries of the steam stripper, waved away the mist and asked her what.

"I won Bergstrom's essay competition."

On the windowsill, Gadzooks stopped doodling. G'reth, who'd been meditating on the falling snow, shook himself awake and turned to listen.

"Seems like Zanna's theory that Loch Ness could support a whole family of mini-monsters won the great doctor's approval. Hey."

"Hey," repeated David, smiling, but sounding just a little bit shell-shocked. "You'll be going to the Arctic, then?"

"I don't know. Haven't made my mind up yet."

"Well, what is there to think about? You just won the geographical trip of a lifetime."

"I'm not sure it would be appropriate," she said, jabbing at an obstinate swatch of paper.

David looked across at the dragons. Both of them shook their heads and shrugged.

"I'm not very happy with Bergstrom, David."

"Oh," he grunted, laying the steam stripper against the wall. "You're still upset about Grockle, then?"

"Of course I'm still upset about Grockle! Bergstrom should have warned me what was going to happen. He knew, and yet he let me..." She finished her sentence with another angry stab at the wall.

"Here, try this," David said, moving across with his plate of steam. "It's much easier if you soften it first."

"I'm all right," she grumbled, jutting out an elbow. She switched the tool to her opposite hand, revealing the graze where Gwilanna had scratched her.

David gave it a protracted look. "That's taking its time to heal. It's still weeping. Don't you think you should bandage it?"

"I did. It doesn't help. It'll scab when it's ready. Besides, it doesn't hurt."

David tilted his head and stared at it again.

"*What?*" she said, irritated by his puzzled expression.

"Don't know. It reminds me of something, that's all. Remember before the fight with Gwilanna I went upstairs into Henry's study?"

"Yeah. So?"

"I saw a mark appear in the polar bear print. In the middle of its forehead, here." He traced a mark with his fingertips. "Three cuts, very similar to those, made when Ragnar's cub was hit by a bone."

Zanna turned full on to him now. Dressed in leggings and a plain black T-shirt, with minimal make-up and her hair knotted back, she looked far less daunting than she normally did, but David still felt his mouth going dry as she cocked her head to her shoulder and said, "Rain, the hag just dug in and gouged. She wasn't being particularly artistic at the time. Besides, you said an Inuit hunter killed the cub."

"Yeah. Gwilanna was behind it, though."

"Oh, so now I'm cursed by the mark of the sibyl?"

"No, I never said that. It's just... Oh, forget it. I'm sorry I mentioned it."

But Zanna wasn't going to let it drop. "This is about me and Gretel, isn't it?"

"*What?* What's Gretel got to do with it?"

"I didn't ask to be able to see her, David. When Lucy used the icefire, it changed us all. You were filled with the auma of Ragnar, Gwilanna got her evil fingers scorched and I got a free pass through to dragon world. In some people's eyes, that makes me a witch."

"Zan-na…"

"Shut up. I'm making a point. You've never been able to get your stuffy, blinkered brain round my 'fashion sense' as you condescendingly like to refer to it. And now it turns out that I am, in fact, sibyl girl, you're just fondly congratulating yourself on how smart you think you were." She jerked her arm upwards and nearly scraped the stubble off David's chin. "I don't care what you think I am. Gretel is my special dragon now, and we are going to work in Grockle's memory. And we don't have to go to the Arctic to prove it!"

"Zanna, listen…"

"No, David. I don't want to know!" And her scraper hit the boards with a painful clatter and she ran out, leaving the room door shuddering.

The hand that came to steady it belonged to Lucy. "What's the matter with Zanna?"

"It's none of your business."

"She was crying. What have you done to her?"

"Nothing. Go away."

"She was talking about Grockle."

"Lucy, if you know what's good for you, beat it."

Lucy, as always, stood her ground. "Sometimes, I wish you'd stayed under the floorboards."

"Yeah, well. Right now, I wish I had."

Hrr-oo, went G'reth and covered his ears. So many unhappy wishes. He was glad that no one was using their thumbs.

"You're still mad at me," Lucy went on, "because I was right all the time about Spikey and because you didn't trust Gadzooks enough."

On the windowsill, Gadzooks gave his scales a rattle and kept his head decidedly low. He was staying well out of this.

David sighed and let his forehead rest against the wall. "What do you want, Lucy?"

"Mum's in the kitchen. She wants to see you."

"What about?"

"What you did to Grace."

David closed his eyes and wished the world would go away. "Tell her I'll be there in a minute," he muttered. But when he turned round, Lucy had already gone.

"Tea's brewed," said Liz, without looking up. She was at the table when he walked in, carefully painting a dragon's ears. A hollow feeling rebounded in his chest when he saw that the dragon in care was Grace. Liz jiggled her brush in a jar of spirits then wiped it quickly against her smock. "What was all that with Zanna just now?"

"Oh, nothing. She's still upset about him." David nodded at the fruit bowl where the small stone figure of Grockle was curled up in perfect, petrified sleep.

"Well, that's understandable," Liz said quietly. "She quickened him. She's bound to feel it deeply."

David glanced across the kitchen and caught sight of Gretel, sitting on the worktop, pulling vegetables apart. It troubled him to see her pick up a mushroom. She saw him watching and tossed it aside. "Is there nothing you can do for him?"

"Sit still," Liz whispered to Grace, drawing a neat green line along her snout. Gwillan, who was sitting on

320

the butter dish beside her, opened his throat and warmed the paint dry. "Even if I could bring Grockle back, I'm not really sure I'd want to, David. This world was never right for a dragon like him. In her heart, Zanna knows it. She just needs time to come to terms with it, that's all. Be patient. She'll be back. How's the decorating going?"

"Just the chimney wall to do. Lucy said you wanted me."

"Hmm. I thought you'd like to know that Grace is mended." Liz turned her around.

Remarkable. Grace looked better than ever. A wave of raw, deep-seated relief slackened every muscle in David's shoulders. "Can she hear OK?"

The dragon rolled her eyes like a couple of pear drops. David smiled and took that as a 'yes'. He reached out to knuckle the edge of one shell. To his disappointment, Grace leaned away with her ears bent back.

"Hush," said Liz, hurring the word and sending Grace into a gentle sleep. "She's a little insecure right now. When you break the ears of a listening dragon, you take far more than their hearing, I'm afraid. She's another who's going to need time. Deep down, she understands why you did it."

"I'm not sure I do," David muttered. "Part of me

thinks I snapped her ears because I was still upset about Sophie."

Liz raised a sympathetic eyebrow. "Well, that's the trouble with decorating, isn't it? Leaves you too much time to think."

David grunted and reached for the tea pot. He squeezed the handle but released it again. "I'm sorry, Liz, for all the trouble I've caused. Grockle, Gwilanna, the room, you."

A-row? went Bonnington, as if someone ought to put him on the list. He was sitting on the drainer, idly watching a pair of blue tits digging peanuts out of a hanging feeder. He lifted his paw and, not for the first time, seemed confused to see it strapped in a bandage.

"If I hadn't made that wish—"

"David." Liz stopped him with a green-eyed look. "It's not your fault. It was meant to be."

David half-threw up his hands. "Now you're starting to sound like Zanna. Why are you letting me off so easily? You always warned me not to poke about in the den and...well, look what happened."

Liz closed her case of paints, untied her smock and draped it across the back of a chair. "Sit down. I want to tell you something."

David dragged out a chair and sat.

"Has it never occurred to you why I took the risk of bringing a lodger into this house?"

The lodger thought about it briefly, then shook his head.

"I didn't meet Dr Bergstrom in Norway."

"What? But Lucy said—"

"I told Lucy I saw a man because it was easier for her at the time. But I didn't see a man; I saw a polar bear. When he gave me the snowball he told me there was powerful auma in it, and that one day, no matter how I chose to use it, it would guide me to someone for whom his kind would have great need. I used the snow to make dragons, as you know, among them the one you named Gadzooks. The moment you told me he'd found the name Lorel, I knew that the waiting was over. Don't be sorry, David. Everything you wished for had to be. The only misfortune was losing Grockle."

Gretel shuddered and Liz called softly to her. But as the dragon got set to fly, the front door banged and a few seconds later Zanna walked in, carrying a couple of tubs of emulsion. "Went to get paint," she said a little sheepishly. "*Harvest Moon*. Special offer. Yuk."

"That's my girl," laughed Liz. "Sit down. Have a cup of tea."

Zanna shook her head. "Thanks, but if it's OK with

you, I'd like to have a word with David first."

"Erm, sure," he muttered, getting signals from Liz. He followed Zanna gingerly into his room, pushing the door just to as he entered.

Head down, still holding the paint, she said, "Look, I'm sorry I lost my rag. I'm upset about Grockle and angry with Bergstrom, but it wasn't right, taking it out on you. Please say we can still be mates." She looked up, searching for signs of forgiveness. "I did bring horrible paint for your room – and plasters for my arm – and sweets, I got sweets; liquorice, your favourite. I'll finish your section of wall if you like?"

David smiled as though it was hurting him deeply. He looked her slowly up and down. A fragile paint maid, all in black. "Put the tubs down," he whispered. Her dark eyes searched his face for a reason. A moment went, but he didn't give an answer. Instead, his hand came up to her face, and raising her chin with the crook of his finger, he kissed her gently on the lips.

The paint tubs thudded to the bare wooden floor. Somewhere in the background, the doorbell rang. But David and Zanna, lost in their embrace, took no notice of the squeals of surprise which came winging down the hall a few seconds later. Only when Lucy came crashing in, demanding that David should come right away, did annoyance and embarrassment force them apart.

It was David this time who lost his rag. "What have I told you about bursting in like that?!"

"But, but, but..." Lucy could barely keep her feet on the ground.

"If it's a squirrel or a hedgehog, you picked the wrong time."

"It's not a hedgehog," said a gentle voice, and a tall slim figure brushed into the room.

The world began to swim in David's head.

The caller was his girlfriend, Sophie.

Departures

It was like some kind of autumnal time warp. Out came the best plates, the cakes, the biscuits, and everyone was ushered into the kitchen to listen to Sophie's homecoming news – everyone except Suzanna Martindale. Despite Liz's best attempts to make her stay, and David's stutteringly awkward introductions, she smiled, made suitably polite excuses and left before Sophie had removed her coat. Sophie, watching patiently from the wings, asked no questions and made no remarks. When the front door closed she put her arms around David and drew him into a gentle hug. "I missed you," she whispered, and pecked him on the cheek. He told her the same, without the peck. He could still taste Zanna's lipstick on his mouth.

Looking tanned and healthy, with her copper-blonde hair bleached even further by the African sun, Sophie chattered, non-stop, for an hour. She brought out photographs: elephants, zebras, hippos, water holes, stunning scenes of the African bush, the wildlife park, the hut she had slept in where the beetles were as long as the tea cups were high and she hadn't dared to go barefoot for at least a week, sunsets, sunrises, cloud-covered mountains, the people she worked with, the jeep they got around in, and last but not least, the only one of her – in a pair of shorts and a khaki shirt, feeding leaves to a baby elephant that she had personally helped to rescue.

"They're lovely," said Liz.

"I want to go," said Lucy.

"Why are you back so soon?" said David. The question had been on his lips from the start.

"Later," she said to him, rubbing his hand. "Anyway, come on, that's tons about me. What's the Pennykettle clan been up to? Is this a new line?" She pointed at Grockle, and everything went quiet.

"He's a one-off," Liz said, smiling gamely. "Grace has missed you. David, can you pass her?"

David took her off the worktop and handed her to Sophie.

"Hello, Grace," she whispered. "You look radiant. Did you hear me sending my love to you, from Africa?"

"Excuse me, I'm going upstairs for a second." David could take no more. He stood up, pushing back his chair so hard that Bonnington jumped and landed in his water bowl, soaking his bandage and making Liz tut. David muttered an apology and hurried away.

He did go up the stairs, but not very far. Halfway, he

turned and sat down on the step, staring into space for what seemed like an age before lowering his head into the cradle of his hands. Gwillan, snuffling dust higher up on the landing, fluttered down to ask if he might be of help. David asked him to go and find Gretel. But before the little dragon could move away, Sophie appeared at the foot of the stairs. She didn't seem surprised to see him there.

"Is this a private moment or can anyone join in?"

David put Gwillan on the box window shelf. "Oh, hi, I don't mean to seem rude. I've been decorating all day. Feeling a bit tired."

"It's OK," she said quietly. "No offence taken. Maybe all you need is a breath of fresh air?" She was reaching for his greatcoat before he could refuse. "I like walking in the snow. Let's go out."

"So, what *have* you been up to?" she asked, looping his arm as they ambled down the crescent.

David looked up at the snow-laden roofs, at the wind dislodging crystals from the icicles hanging off the amber streetlights, at the moon, very big and very round and very present. At the stars. At the centre of the northern stars. "Oh, you know, college; the usual stuff."

That made her laugh, as much as any far-flung tale

about dragons. "Nothing's ever 'usual' with you, David. What about your stories? Written anything new?"

The free hand in his pocket touched the tooth. What would he give, to tell what he knew? And what would it mean to her if he did? "I've started one – about polar bears."

"I didn't know you knew about polar bears?"

"I don't, not much. But in eight days time I'm going to the Arctic...to do some research."

She stopped walking and pulled him round. "My God, you're serious." She shook herself, stunned. The bobble on her knitted hat swung across her shoulders.

"Geography field trip – to Chamberlain, in Canada. I'm paying for it from the proceeds for *Snigger*."

Now her eyebrows arched and her mouth fell open. "You sold *Snigger*?"

"I got a two-book deal with a publisher, yes."

"David, that's *fantastic*. Wow. I don't know what to say." A car sluiced past, throwing slush onto the pavement, making them dodge and walk again.

"I was going to write – or call you," he said. "I didn't think you'd mind – about the Arctic, I mean, as you were s'posed to be away in Africa. Why *are* you home?"

They turned a corner, brushing chunks of snow off an overhanging holly. Sophie ringed his arm and the space between them narrowed. "Well, this sort of pales in comparison to your achievements, but I have to say it all the same. The post I was offered is below my potential – according to the director of the wildlife program. They want me to take on something new, in one of their big reserves in Kenya. It's a three year post, with a degree attached. If I take it, I won't be coming home much."

David nodded in time with his steps. "Hmm. Sounds good."

"Yes," she said, softening the word with a quiet sigh. "In career terms it is, very good." They went two more paces, then she stopped him again. "That girl tonight, the one in your room—"

"She's just a friend from college. She's—"

"David, it's OK. It's not an attack. If she's someone special, I'm pleased for you." Sophie paused and rubbed a mitten under one eye. A tear dallied on the edge of her lashes. "I came round here tonight to tell you that...I'm releasing you from any obligation to me."

"Sophie—?"

"No, listen to me. Please. I practised on the plane, don't spoil it for me." She did her best to laugh and lightly thumped his chest. "I'm very fond of you, you know I am – but for now, it has to be over between us. I wanted to tell you this in person so you wouldn't feel binned or dumped from a distance. I'm really pleased about your writing. You're so lovely and caring; you deserve success. I'll buy all your books, I promise, every one. I just won't be around to see them being written. Hold me and say you don't hate me. Please."

"I don't hate you," he whispered, and pulled her in close, until her head was on his shoulder and her tears were on his neck. They stayed like this until a snow shower fell. Then he walked her home.

That night, when he told the story to Liz, she was almost in tears herself. "Oh dear. This is all so terribly romantic. I'm pleased she had the courage to tell you to your face. She's a good girl, Sophie. Very thoughtful. Very kind. I'm glad she took Grace this time as well. That will keep a bond of sorts between you. You'll always be friends. Always. She loves you. And, if nothing else, I suppose it uncomplicates the other matter."

David looked up over his drinking chocolate.

"I can't bear to see those paint scrapers side by side, abandoned."

"It's not funny," David muttered, trying to keep a straight face.

Liz dropped the kitchen blind and locked the back door. "If you think you're hurt, imagine what Zanna must be going through now. If you want my advice, you'll ring her – tonight."

"Tonight? It's half past twelve."

"So? You're a student. Act like one."

He tried four times, including once the next morning. Her answer phone spoke back every time. He sent e-mail. That was dead as well. At lunch, he abandoned his scrapers and stripper and went into college, searching for her. In the coffee bar he found her best friend, Liddy. "Gone home," she trilled, with a look that suggested that David had not only bought the ticket, but driven the train as well. Even so, he blagged Zanna's home number from her (and sneaked the address while Liddy wasn't looking).

"You're history, Rain. She won't talk. Zanna's strong."

"Will you give her a message, then?"

Liddy rolled a cheese and onion crisp around her mouth.

"Tell her Gretel misses her."

Liddy clicked her tongue. "And who's that from, Hansel or the gingerbread man?"

"Funn-ee," said David, and rose to leave. "Just tell

her to call me, OK? What's she doing about the field trip, do you know?"

Liddy popped another crisp and waved bye-bye.

In the office, David checked the list of applicants. His name was there, approved by Bergstrom. By the name S. Martindale was an ugly blank.

The next morning, he went to Gretel in the den. She was sitting over Grockle as she often did, dropping flower petals over his petrified body, as if she was hoping they would break his spell.

"I know you can reach her," David said in dragontongue. "Gadzooks and G'reth...they always come to me. I just want her to know I wasn't two-timing her."

Hrrff, went Gretel, turning her back. She blew a smoke ring and spiked it once with her tail.

"Right," said David. "In that case, there's only one thing for it..."

He went to G'reth. "I want to make a wish."

The wishing dragon reeled back, crunkling his snout.

Hrr? went Gadzooks, knitting his ridges.

"It's not like the other one," David assured them. "It's about Zanna and me."

The two dragons exchanged a wary glance.

"Come on," said David. "I've got to find her."

"Not through wishing, you don't," said Liz. She came

in, looking extremely stern. In her hands was a wide brown envelope. She slapped it against his chest. "This just came by special delivery. It's from Apple Tree Publishing. It feels as if it might be a contract or something. I suggest you sit down and read it, thoroughly, and forget about making dubious wishes. Remember: if they're not beneficial, they'll turn."

"But—?"

"Kitchen or Henry's. Take your pick. Go."

He picked Henry's, but he didn't read the contract, fully. Twelve pages of yellow bond gobbledygook. The second page promised him money on signature. The last had a dotted line for just that purpose. He picked up a pen...and put it down again. His signature could wait. Zanna couldn't.

He went to the address he'd stolen from Liddy.

An hour on the train had left him plenty of time to practise his speech, but when he got there, a neat little cottage in Surrey, her sister answered the door. She looked older than Zanna by a couple of years. She wore tight blue jeans and a roll neck sweater. She was pretty – in a green-eyed, savage kind of way. 'Savage' just about described her mood.

"Oh, dragon boy. I've heard about you. Straying a bit far from Scrubbley, aren't you?"

"Is she in? I'd like to talk to her." They were on the step and it was freezing cold.

The sister put a tan leather coat round her shoulders. "Nope. Gone to see her ex, I think."

"Ex?"

The sister made kissy-kissy sounds. "Oh dear, that didn't go down well, did it?"

David changed his sour face for something more manly. "I don't care who she's with—"

"Ahh, brave soldier."

"—I just want to give her a message, that's all."

The sister checked her watch. "Fifty-three seconds. Then I'm going out. So you'd better make it quick. Unless you'd like to sit on the step and freeze? She could be quite some time. She was always very fond of her ex, as I recall. Thirty-eight seconds."

David paused for thought.

"Thirty-five."

"Tell her, whatever she thinks of me, the trip to Chamberlain is too good to miss. She won the competition fair and square. She should go. Bergstrom wants her there. I know, I can feel it in the tooth."

"In your *teeth*?"

"Tooth. Singular. Just tell her."

"Tooth, right. Nineteen seconds."

335

"And tell her…Sophie's out of the picture."

The sister took a sharp breath.

"OK, scrub that. Tell her Gretel misses her…and so do I."

This time, the sister softened her stance. "That it?" she asked quietly.

David looked away. The seconds ticked down. "Say…I finished the wall, but I used her scraper."

"Oh good, I can see the attraction of that!"

"Just tell her," David said despondently, and he turned and walked away without another word.

Halfway down the path, she called out to him: "Hey, lover boy!"

David stopped and let his shoulders droop.

"I'll do my best, OK? She's touchy. Takes time. Don't hold your breath."

I won't, thought David and went to catch his train.

It was a good job he didn't – hold his breath. As the days went by and the time for his departure to Chamberlain drew close, there was still no contact at all from Zanna. David immersed himself in his room – papering, painting (he drew an arrowed heart on the wall with his roller), and singing along, badly and loudly, to the radio.

"He's in love," Liz explained to Lucy one night. "This

is what happens when someone spurns you."

"Well, I wish he'd be in love in tune," Lucy grumbled, a sentiment shared by David's dragons, who were both seen stuffing cotton wool into their ears.

But still Zanna didn't come back.

In the evenings, David spent a lot of time at Henry's, reading what he could about the Arctic. Mr Bacon, not surprisingly, was terribly enthusiastic (and secretly very proud) about his lodger's field trip, supplying text after text from his personal library, and even showing David parched old letters, hand-written by his grandfather, from a tent pitched on pack ice off the coast of Svalbard. They grew a lot closer in those last few days, so much so that on the night before David was set to leave, he chose to show Henry the polar bear tooth, saying it was a gift from his tutor, Dr Bergstrom, who he thought might be 'related' to the man in the photograph with Henry's grandfather. Henry held the tooth and a wisp of emotion passed across his face. He felt strangely aware of the old man, he said. David patted his shoulder and took the tooth back.

"Rule forty-one, boy," Henry said stiffly.

David looked confused. He knew the rules now, and there were only forty.

Henry wiped a handkerchief under his nose. "'Look after yourself'," he said.

In the morning, Lucy couldn't stop snuffling.

"It's only six weeks," David said, hugging her.

"The house won't seem the same with you gone," said Liz. She folded a tea towel and left it on the drainer.

David smiled and shook his head gently. "I am coming back. Don't rent the room out. Promise me, now – or you won't get your presents."

"Presents?" Lucy perked up at once.

"Yep. I got you going away presents. Let's put my luggage in the car, then you can have them."

"Erm, no, we're not taking you to the airport," said Liz. "I couldn't face a goodbye there. We've arranged a taxi. Should be here any minute."

"So I'll have my present now," beamed Lucy.

David laughed and made them sit at the table. Gretel, who'd been perching quietly on a stool, plaiting hairs from Bonnington's tail, flew over to watch. "Well, it's not much, but it's meaningful, I think." David opened his jacket and pulled out a sheet of printed text. He gave it to Lucy. "There; it's the start of my polar bear book."

Lucy scanned it quickly and handed it back. "Read it," she begged.

"I can't, not now. What if the taxi turns up?"

"Don't worry, the taxi will wait," said Liz. "Go on, read it. I'd like to hear it too."

"And the dragons," said Lucy, springing up on her chair.

Hrr! went the listener on the fridge.

"Transmitting," said Liz. "We're all ears, David."

"All right," he said and laid the script out. "It's going to be an Arctic saga. Lorel will be in it. And so will Ragnar. But it starts with a mother bear, talking to her cub. They're sitting on an ice floe, looking across the ocean at Gawain's island. This is how it goes: *'Over there is an island the bears call the Tooth of Ragnar,' Lono said to her daughter, Svenia, as they settled together at the edge of a lead.*

"A lazy second passed. Svenia watched as the stiffening breeze swelled the waters of the cold, black ocean. Yawning noisily, she lifted her head and squinted across the creaking ice. The island her mother spoke of was away to their right, a hard and permanent giant on a fragmentary plate of white. It shimmered moodily under the pale Arctic sun and cast a blunted shadow that was long and unending. Splashes of snow marked its innermost contours. Birds circled and returned like flying chips of stone. Beyond it, dimmed by distance, lay a thin smear of land.

"'Islands,' said the cub with a disparaging grunt, 'they're

all the same, islands.' And raising a bloodstained paw to her mouth, she began to niggle at the shreds of blubber that had lodged between her claws from an early morning feed.

"Lono raised her wise old head and stared absently at the high-pointed rock. 'There was a time,' she said, 'when the ice was ruled by nine bears, and one of these was a bear called Ragnar.'

"There was an odd blend of vagueness and secrecy in these words, enough to cause Svenia to interrupt her grooming and give the Tooth of Ragnar another protracted glance. It really did look just like a tooth, a dark and jagged canine, tipped with snow. At its peak, it was snarled and slightly hooked, and not unlike the two island-shaped protrusions that hung down prominently from a bear's upper jaw. But that was as far as the imagery would stretch. Any cub could see it was nothing but the usual crag and stone. She was about to turn away when her mother spoke again.

"'He was a fighting bear. He sat to the right of the Nanukapik, Aluna. You remember what Nanukapik means?'

"'Great bear,' said Svenia, dibbling her fighting paw in the ocean. The waters moved with a satisfying ripple. 'Can I go and see where Jorn is now?' Slowly, she rose into a begging

340

position, scanning the ice on the far side of Lono for any sign of her truant brother. As usual, he was nowhere to be seen.

"'Greatest bear,' Lono corrected her.

"'Hmm,' the cub grunted, still raised, still looking. A fast-moving black-speckled cloud had caught her eye and was threatening to topple her if she lowered her concentration. The cloud quickly resolved into a small flock of buntings. The fold of their wings against the crisp edge of morning cut loud into the silence that suddenly surrounded the two female bears. Lono glanced up and followed the birds' flight path. For a few seconds they described a perfect diagonal between herself and the Tooth of Ragnar. They careened and dipped into the north face of the rock and were swallowed up by distance and the backdrop of stone.

"'You are a daughter of his line,' said Lono.

"Svenia's forepaws thumped onto the ice. 'My father? You're going to tell about my father?' There was shock and surprise now in her voice. 'But you always said you wouldn't. You said a bear never needed to know about that.'

"'Aluna was not your father,' said Lono. 'He was your ancestor.'

"The young bear wrinkled her snout. Ancestor? She, a daughter of some ancient, groggy bear? 'You mean he's old; dead even?'

341

"'Many seasons ago,' Lono replied. She stretched her neck to let the wind cool her throat, then looked across at the Tooth once more. 'But here his spirit is always alive…'"

"Gosh," said Liz, "that's jolly exciting. And quite a bit different from *Snigger*, too. Where did you get those lovely names?"

"Oh, the usual source. Plus one from Henry's books. Anyway, what do you think?"

"I like it," said Lucy. "When will you do the rest?"

"Ah," went David, with a twinkle in his eye. He pulled the contract from Apple Tree out of his jacket and turned to the final page. "When I sign here, I'll have to write the rest."

"Sign," Lucy urged him.

But Liz raised a hand. "Wait. Have you read through this properly?"

"Sort of. It's just…legalities and stuff."

"Exactly. You ought to know what you're signing. Perhaps Henry could check it for you?"

"It's all right," said David. "It's just boring blurb. Don't spoil my big moment. Pen, someone?"

Lucy grabbed one off the worktop and handed it over.

"*Signed…David…Rain,*" David muttered, scratching his name on the line marked 'author'.

Immediately, the doorbell rang.

"Me!" cried Lucy, and shot down the hall. As she unlatched the door, a wind tunnel formed between the hall and kitchen, sucking cold air from the open kitchen window. The pages of the contract fluttered wildly. Gretel jumped back staring at it.

"What was that?" said Liz, listening intently to the dragon noises circulating round the house. She glanced at Gretel. The potions dragon blinked.

David covered the contract and reached for the tooth. "It's nothing. Just the wind. And the dragons do seem a bit hyper this morning. I opened that window at breakfast time because Gwillan was hurring so much he was steaming it up."

"Yes, they've been 'fluenced'," Liz muttered quietly. "They're sad, as well, to see you go. We don't want any fire tears shedding."

"Quite," said David. "I'd better get going. Will you do me a favour and post this today?" He pushed the contract across the table. "At least then, when I come back from the trip, I can pay you back all the money I've borrowed."

Lucy hurried in. "The taxi-driver's here."

David hoiked up his case and carried it to the door. A large black car had backed onto the drive. Its boot was already open. To David's surprise, another suitcase was taking up half one side. He peered at the label… *Martindale, S.*

"Zanna!" he yelled, and she stepped into the open. She was plainly dressed in blue denim jeans and a grey college sweatshirt. Her bangles and gothic make-up had gone. Her hair was tied back in a long, thin braid.

"Wow, you look amazing," said David.

"No, Rain, I just look different," she sighed.

He dropped his case and hugged her tightly, so tightly that Lucy was heard to say, 'Mum, he's going to break her in a minute'.

Zanna didn't seem to mind. Resting her forehead on his, she breathed, "When you've done saving the world, do you think there might be a small place in it for me?"

"Always," he said, and kissed her three times, on her forehead, her nose and finally on her mouth.

Everyone was hugging each other after that.

When it came to David's turn to throw his arms around Liz, he took the opportunity to speak a quiet word. "I didn't forget your present by the way. It's not much, just a message – from a bear called Thoran. He wants you to know that Guinevere didn't drown."

Her hands clutched at the back of his jacket. "Thank

you," she whispered and kissed his cheek. "Promise me you'll be careful up there."

He drew back, nodding. There were tears in her eyes. "Look after the dragons, won't you?" he said. He kissed his fingertips and waved towards the house. From the upstairs windows, dozens of small green paws waved back. He put away his case and closed the boot. "North?"

"You bet," said Zanna.

And they were gone, in the briefest screech of tyres.

Hand in hand, Liz and Lucy walked back to the house.

"What shall we do now?" Lucy asked.

"I need to post David's contract for him." Liz picked it up off the kitchen table. For a moment she stood there reading a chunk, then she began to quickly flick through it. At the final page, she stopped and stared. "Lucy, you know that pen, the one David used to sign his name. Does it leak?"

Lucy drew a few lines with it, on her hand. "A bit, yes."

"As much as that?" Liz turned the page around.

From the lower curves of David's signature, three long trails of ink had formed.

Lucy tilted her head... and shuddered. "They look like Zanna's scratch."

The heart of the house stopped beating for a moment.

"Where's Gretel?" said Liz, looking towards the worktop.

But Gretel wasn't there. She was in the Dragons' Den, hurring a lullaby and standing over Grockle. In her paws was a lock of Liz's red hair.

Other Red Apples to get your teeth into

Something's after Jiggy McCue!
Something big and angry and invisible.
Something which hisses and flaps and stabs
his bum and generally tries to make
his life a misery. Where did it come from?

Jiggy calls in The Three Musketeers – One for
all and all for lunch! – and they set out to send
the poltergoose back where it belongs.

Shortlisted for the Blue Peter Book Award

More Orchard Red Apples

❑ The Fire Within	*Chris d'Lacey*	1 84121 533 3
❑ The Salt Pirates of Skegness	*Chris d'Lacey*	1 84121 539 2
❑ The Poltergoose	*Michael Lawrence*	1 86039 836 7
❑ The Killer Underpants	*Michael Lawrence*	1 84121 713 1
❑ The Toilet of Doom	*Michael Lawrence*	1 84121 752 2
❑ Maggot Pie	*Michael Lawrence*	1 84121 756 5
❑ Do Not Read This Book	*Pat Moon*	1 84121 435 3
❑ Do Not Read Any Further	*Pat Moon*	1 84121 456 6
❑ How to Eat Fried Worms	*Pat Moon*	1 84362 206 8
❑ How to Get Fabulously Rich	*Thomas Rockwell*	1 84362 207 6
❑ How to Fight a Girl	*Thomas Rockwell*	1 84362 208 4

All books priced at £4.99

Orchard Red Apples are available from all good bookshops,
or can be ordered direct from the publisher:
Orchard Books, PO BOX 29, Douglas IM99 1BQ
Credit card orders please telephone 01624 836000 or fax 01624 837033
or visit our Internet site: www.wattspub.co.uk
or e-mail: bookshop@enterprise.net for details.

To order please quote title, author and ISBN
and your full name and address.
Cheques and postal orders should be made payable to 'Bookpost plc.'
Postage and packing is FREE within the UK
(overseas customers should add £1.00 per book).

Prices and availability are subject to change.

1 84121 533 3   £4.99

David soon discovers the dragons
when he moves in with Liz and Lucy.
The pottery models fill up every
spare space in the house!

Only when David is given his own
special dragon does he begin
to unlock their mysterious
secrets, and to discover
the fire within.

1 84121 539 2   £4.99

Jason's Aunt Hester is a grouchy old stick.
But a witch? Surely not?
But then, why is there a whole crew of pirates
held prisoner in her cellar...?

Aided by Scuttle, the saltiest, smelliest seadog ever,
Jason sets out to solve the mystery and defeat
the evil Skegglewitch.

'I be laughing so much I be a-toppling overboard'
Pirate Times